Praise for Mimi Barbour

TOGETHER AGAIN

"An entertaining, finely crafted story of two very different people thrown together by magic but destined to become soul mates."
~ Reviewed by Jacqui Nelson

"Wow love this Book. Keeps you on your toes...recommend to you all"
~ Reviewed by Marie E. Price

"The author really draws the reader into the story and gets them hooked from square one."
~ Reviewed by Evelyn

"Time travel Magic - I found it funny, endearing, full of imagination."
~ Reviewed by Jerrie

Also Author of:

Vegas Series
— Action–Packed Thrillers! —

Vegas Series – Complete Boxed Set
Partners – (Book 1)
Roll the Dice (Book 2)
Vegas Shuffle (Book 3)
High Stakes Gamble (Book 4)
Spin the Wheel (Book 5)
Let it Ride (Book 6)

The Vicarage Bench Series
— Spirit Travel at its Best! —

Vicarage Bench Anthology – (Books 1-3)
She's Me – (Book 1)
He's Her – (Book 2)
We're One – (Book 3)
Together Again – (Book 4)
Together for Christmas – (Book 5)

Angels with Attitude Series
— Angels Playing Cupid! —

The Angels with Attitudes Series – (Books 1-3)
My Cheeky Angel – (Book 1)
His Devious Angel – (Book 2)
Loveable Christmas Angel – (Book 3)

Elvis Series
She's Not You
Love Me Tender (Book 2 Released in Summer 2014)

Undercover FBI Series
Special Agent Francesca (Book 1 released in April 2014)

Other Titles
The Surrogate's Secret
Mimi's Mix (Box Set)
'Tis the Season (Box Set)
Hearts, Flowers & Romance (Box Set)
Christmas Runaway

TOGETHER
AGAIN

The Vicarage Bench Series
Book Four

MIMI BARBOUR

This is a work of fiction. Names, characters, places, and incidents are either
the product of the author's imagination or are used fictitiously, and any
resemblance to actual persons living or dead, business establishments, events,
or locales, is entirely coincidental.

TOGETHER AGAIN
The Vicarage Bench Series – Book Four

Copyright 2013 by Mimi Barbour

Print ISBN: 978-09878167-2-6

Contact Information: mimibarbour66@gmail.com

Cover Art by Steven Novak
Edited by Nan Swanson

To my wonderful editor, Nan Swanson. Without her hard work, support, and faith in the Vicarage Bench series— and especially this fourth story, Together Again—I would still be a sad, unpublished author praying for "the break."

Chapter One

Bury, England, 1968

Dani ran up the steps of the ivy-covered house and then hesitated, her courage wilting. Seconds passed while her hand hovered above a brass knocker decorated by the devil's grinning face.

How appropriate, she thought, the handle of doom. *Stop it! You know you'll find hope here, or at least some help.* She pulled her trembling fingers back to rub her forehead. *If only my conscience would stop nagging.* Agitated nerves shot streaks of nausea throughout her stomach, and the thought of what lay ahead made her take a step backwards.

I can't stand out here all day. I need Uncle Robert's support. He's the only one who can guide me through this—this disaster.

Resolved once more, the teen stretched forward, lifted the golden lever and banged it down with force. Her beloved uncle appeared, swung open the door and stood behind the screen. His puzzled expression dissipated quickly replaced by an enormous smile of welcome for the girl making the racket. He had no chance to speak, because as soon as she spied him, the control Daniell Howard had been maintaining broke.

"Uncle Robert, can we talk? I need help, and I didn't know where else to turn."

Robert Andrews, Bury's Doctor of Psychology, flaunted the adoration he felt for his niece every time they were together. She'd always known she could count on his cooperation. Their eyes met, and she saw at once that he'd caught on to her desperation.

The smiling man pushed open the screen door and, in his most gentle tone, said, "Dani! Of course, dear girl, come in, and we'll enjoy the sunshine while we visit in the garden."

He stroked her rebellious red curls, hugging her to him, before giving her a little push toward his favourite retreat. "I'm working out there, going over some notes. Make yourself comfy, and I'll bring along a tray with refreshments, including some of Mrs. Dorn's homemade biscuits with jam and cream."

The slender girl nodded, patted the hand squeezing her shoulder and headed in the direction his finger pointed. As she approached the entrance to the enclosure, the sun's filtered rays could be seen beyond the open doorway. Framed by greenery and hanging purple blossoms of wisteria, the glorious sight beckoned her to his sheltered paradise.

Various handwritten notes were scattered across a round wooden table, weathered to grey that sat in the centre of the paved courtyard. Along with an ashtray, holding her uncle's cold pipe and a smudged glass half-filled with milk sat an empty plate with a generous sprinkle of sandwich crumbs. Those bits of bread tempted the sedge warbler perched high in a nearby bush, who noisily expressed his frustration over the lure of the unreachable tidbits.

Dani paced the area. She enjoyed the array of foliage aromas bombarding her and, wanting to get closer, subsided onto her uncle's favourite seat. It was a perfect reproduction of the bench that for many years had sat in front of the town's old vicarage. Behind this seat grew an exact replica of the magnificent rose bush in the vicarage garden. Not at all surprising, since her uncle had propagated his bush from that same one. The flowers were an incredible anomaly; in each of the two places three different colours of roses apparently grew from one set of roots.

The white blooms glowed with an inner radiance that gave them an abnormal depth like one sees in newly fallen snow.

The pink, a hothouse shade, wove around the other two and appeared too vibrant for words.

And the red hue, her favourite, held her mesmerized until, involuntarily, her fingers reached to stroke the velvety softness. *How incredibly beautiful!* She sighed when she noticed her hand shaking.

Anxiety returned, and so did the sickness in the pit of her stomach. Hugging herself for a few seconds, she rocked back and forth. *How could I have been such a fool?* The question raged at her, along with the knowledge that, as soon as she confessed, there would be no taking it back. *Well, there's no taking back what I've done, either, and now I have to figure out what to do about it.* Unable to relax, she began to wander the small area. *God, I hate feeling so out of control.*

On her third trip around the small patio, she passed too close to the table and accidentally knocked a pile of papers and a notebook to the floor. They scattered from one end of the terrace to the other. As she slowly gathered them, trying to put them back into order, her eye caught a name familiar to her.

Apparently, Lucy McGillicuddy, whom she knew as the pleasant town librarian as well as a close friend of the family, was also one of her uncle's patients.

Uncle Robert's profession as a psychiatrist tended to be the focus for many animated discussions that stirred derision and scepticism from most of their relatives. But not Dani. She thought it a very interesting occupation and both respected and loved her uncle for his progressive thinking.

Her eyes caught the words "time travel." Avidly, she began to read her uncle's squiggly, handwritten notes pertaining to the paranormal activities he'd researched. I shouldn't be reading these, she thought, but also accepted that no red-blooded teenager with any curiosity whatsoever could have ignored the magnet of those words any more than she could.

According to the doctor's observations, the rose bushes behind the bench in front of the vicarage held an unexplained power. And Lucy had experienced the plant's enchantment first hand.

"Wow!" Dani skimmed her uncle's comments, becoming totally engrossed in the story. She muttered in a voice filled with wonder. "Lucy's body was invaded by another spirit? A girl called Jenna McBride, a super model from the future? Cool!"

Her uncle's career as a reputable scientist meant that he dealt with proven facts, not questionable fiction. Therefore, she believed in his deductions and studied his prognosis carefully. She soon garnered all the pertinent facts of the case, thanks to the speed-reading she'd taught herself.

When spirit travelling and invading another's body no deterioration or any lasting afflictions occurred at all to either the physical landlord or the spiritual tenant, whose own body would remain in a coma throughout the duration.

Absorbing the contents of the papers while restoring them to the table took only a few moments, but devising a plan happened almost instantly.

Not hearing anyone approaching from inside the house, Dani deemed it safe to try out a little experiment with the bush nestled behind the bench in her uncle's garden. If the magic worked the same as it did with the mother plant, her problems wouldn't go away. But she needn't deal with them right this instant, either. Procrastination worked for her at the best of times and this, quite possibly, had to be the worst.

Dani took her small scissors from the crammed schoolbag she'd flung on the ground near the table. Snipping off a gorgeous red rose, she placed herself on the bench and pricked her finger.

Chapter Two

Bury, England, 1978 (ten years later)

Troy Brennan heaved an exhausted sigh as he settled on a convenient bench situated near the picturesque gardens. When he'd started this adventure, he'd never expected to end up in front of an old vicarage in Bury, England. A quaint little town, to be sure, but it didn't rank in his top-ten list of places to see before he died. However, as a reporter, he'd been to some hellholes in the past, following what he called "hot leads," so he really shouldn't complain.

The flight from Chicago had been tedious and uncomfortable and he already missed the big city's amenities. He preferred screeching traffic, hordes of people, and a range of nightclubs and good restaurants. His mood soured. This little burg offered none of the above. The Cozy Inn, a place he'd passed by earlier, had "old-fashioned" screaming from every balconied window and whitewashed wall—but at least they'd advertised affordable rates. Something to check out later.

As a freelance reporter, he didn't have a big paper backing him to cover the expenses for this little expedition. The money had to come from his personal dwindling resources. His fault, he supposed, for not being on top of things. Considering he had a fortune sitting in his inheritance account back home, it seemed ironic that at this moment he was almost broke.

His grandfather, a newspaper tycoon from the thirties, had bequeathed him his riches, but Troy had little use for that money. He'd lived for several years following one story after another—no home, no roots, and until recently, no intention to have either.

He subsisted on what he earned, banked the excess, and normally didn't have a worry in the world. But this time things were different. Who even thought about running to a bank while in hot pursuit of a story? Normally, he kept a cash reserve of a few hundred dollars hidden in his wallet, but he'd dipped in over the last few days and hadn't got around to replacing it.

His check book, which he rarely carried around now that he had access to plastic, sat in his desk drawer at home, absolutely worthless to him there. And paying off the balance on his charge card hadn't entered his mind lately, either. Once he acquired the story he'd come for, it would be worth all the extra expense, but until then he'd have to be careful.

As far as he knew, no other reporter milling around Chicago's luxury hotel the day before had seen the famous author sneak off to the airport. His uncanny luck had held.

He'd glimpsed a young woman entering by the employee's side door. Her cheap, red plastic raincoat and matching headscarf caught his attention—that, and the fact that attractive women unfailingly caught his eye. Her sexy allure was no exception, plus long-legged blondes were his preference. This girl had decent gams, firm and nicely rounded, ending in silver-tipped stiletto heels.

Strange thing about those pretty legs! When the coat reappeared, the gorgeous legs weren't quite so long, and the plain black heels weren't nearly as high. The few seconds it took his brain to compute had given her a head start, but again his luck held as he flagged a taxi. In seconds, he told the driver to "Follow that cab." Troy had never imagined having to say those hokey words. He flinched as the driver did the uplifted eyebrow thing in the rear-view mirror. Troy shrugged, hands held out in supplication.

By pursuing the car closely, Troy found it didn't take a skilled detective to conclude that his quarry was headed towards the airport. What did take skill was getting a seat on the same plane. He managed it by duping the ticket-lady into giving him the same itinerary as the woman she'd just served.

"Hey, go figure," he said, pointing to the raincoat-clad figure now walking toward the boarding area. "She's going to the exact place I am. You can go ahead and make out my ticket like hers."

"It's not really so strange, sir. We only have two flights a day to England, and lots of people fly through London to Manchester." Her perfunctory smile didn't warrant his full-face response; relief prompted his pleased reaction.

For him, flirting came easily, but this time he hadn't intended any tomfoolery. It took some doing to slide himself out from under the uniformed woman's clutches. With her phone number written on the ticket flap, and his maxed-out Visa card burning his hand, he made his way to where he could keep his eyes on the notorious subject of his next blockbuster exposé. One that, with any luck whatsoever, could win him his own by-line with the *Chicago Sun-Times*.

Troy and the small woman in the red plastic coat were separated by four rows on the plane. She sat on the opposite side, aisle seat. By using his most charming manner on the chubby lady ticketed in the aisle seat in his row, he was able to switch to keep his subject in plain view. He turned around periodically, pretending an interest in the lavatory light, then made numerous visits, keeping tabs on her behaviour throughout the long night.

To watch without her knowing wasn't an easy task, but he'd perfected his undercover surveillance technique years before. Her aura of melancholy made him wonder at her behaviour. She only pretended to sleep. Politeness to everyone she met seemed to come naturally, but her introspective attitude was a warning in itself—"Back off and leave me the hell alone."

Troy still couldn't understand why he hadn't moved in on her. As a rule, in his trade, he'd be forced to ignore her kinds of signals. How else could he manage to obtain the powerful stories he'd gotten over the course of his distinguished career?

He knew his name stirred interest in the Chicago newspaper circles, interest he'd worked hard to inspire. He prided himself on getting features no one else managed to get.

So what was it about this broad that had him pussyfooting around—giving her breaks, treating her differently? Like now, for instance. After trailing her for hours, he found himself on a bench watching her from afar while she meandered alone.

He guessed her brave act appealed to his sensitive side and, instead of approaching to hound her about her story, he sat and stared, held back by the beautiful picture of serenity she now presented.

She'd removed her scarf and shaken her head to free her mass of blonde curls. They bounced every which way, a springy jumble of beauty framing her heart-shaped face. The wind took control and played havoc until, apparently tired of eating the strands, she swept the works behind her ears and collected it into a ponytail.

As if she heard silent music, she seemed to float from place to place rather than walking like a mortal. She wandered through the vicarage grounds and around a

natural pond surrounded by variegated green plants. Some
flaunted colourful flowers and others highlighted berries.

Rather than approach, to manoeuvre his way into her
confidence, he waited. The bench's position allowed him a
full view of her every move. For now, he felt content to give
her space.

Just then a grey-striped kitten jumped onto the bench
near him and began to wash itself. Surprised, Troy watched
as the feline's tongue licked in sensitive areas. The animal
paid him scant attention, and, once satisfied its body and
paws were clean, his furry companion crouched to survey
his surroundings. In a flash, the silly puss decided to swipe
at a magnificent red rose that hung over the back of the
seat, the breeze fluttering its luscious petals over the pointed
ears.

The thorns looked deadly, and since Troy had a thing
about protecting small creatures, he snagged the branch to
push it backwards, out of harm's way. A wickedly sharp
barb pricked him, and reflex had him pulling his hand away,
making things worse. It pierced deeper, until drops of blood
emerged. He swore and extricated himself, then whipped
his hand up to his mouth, scaring away the tabby.

As he sucked at the wound, he felt a strangeness enter
him, like a low vibration of electric shock. It reminded him
of a few occasions in congested traffic when he'd avoided a
looming accident by a split-second decision. The resulting
fear had made swallowing difficult and blinking impossible.
Panicky nerve endings began rioting in his stomach, and
sweat poured from his trembling body. He bent over, head
between his knees, hoping to gain some relief. Could there
have been poison in the spine that pricked him?

A loud humming slowly diminished, and then faded
completely as seconds ticked away. A voice, clearly heard,
brought him upright in an instant.

"What happened?" A young girl spoke.

Troy peered all around and saw no one. "Excuse me?" His voice sounded loud in the solitude of his surroundings. He turned in every direction, not understanding how words could be so distinct when there was no one in sight.

"It worked. Oh, my God! It really worked. I'm—ah—visiting your body. This is way too cool."

"Are you suggesting I'm possessed? Seriously?" His voice lowered and a droll note entered. "That I have—"

"Yes I am, and don't talk out loud. People will think you're bonkers," the female whispered.

Plainly an unbeliever, Troy stood up, wobbled, and made his way around to the back of the bench to check behind the rose bushes. Then he circled to the other side, looking for the speaker so he could prove this weirdness a hoax. There wasn't a soul in sight. He sat back down. It was either that or fall down.

"My spirit is inside you. We're soul-roomies for a while." The girlish voice had a surprising huskiness that stopped it from being totally annoying.

The answer hit him all at once. He scrutinized the top branches of nearby trees for his hidden pretender, but there weren't any close enough for her trick to work.

Of course! There must be a device attached to the bench. Her voice had to be coming through some kind of electronic gadget. After another careful search, however, he found nothing.

"Listen, you, whoever you are. Cut it out. I'm tired and in no mood to play along. Show yourself from wherever you're hiding, explain how you've managed this setup, and the laugh will be on me."

Two churchgoers, passing by on the winding path, stared at him, then hurried towards the vicarage. They glanced back before turning the final corner, and he heard their nervous giggles.

"See! I told you not to talk out loud. We can converse with our thoughts. Try it. It's easy."

By accepting her advice, he would be acknowledging the validity of her words, something he refused to do until he'd looked into every other avenue. After all, he was a reporter, a researcher—a whackjob, if this turned out to be true.

"You're not nuts. I promise. It's the roses. There's some abnormal spell stuff inside them. When you jabbed your finger the magic must have gone into your bloodstream and mine at the same time."

Okay, he'd try it her way and prove her wrong.

"You weren't here pricking your finger. There's only me and the darn cat I tried to save—the ungrateful little pest took off."

Good God! She was right. He could converse with her even more comfortably from the inside. The acid in his stomach spilled over, and he felt the burning sensations spread. He'd better pay attention to this ghostly presence, because she seemed to know what had happened, and he hadn't a clue.

"My uncle propagated roses from this same bush, planted it in his personal garden, and I pricked my finger there, on his plant. It's the fact that we did it at the same time of day, you see, that's important. Or at least I think that's how the magic works."

On the one hand, accepting he heard her words from inside his head rather than through his ears scared the hell out of him. But on the other hand, he didn't want to be arrested and hauled off for talking out loud without anyone else in sight. They'd think him either high or nuts, and neither option appealed.

"So how do we undo the spell?"

"We can't, or at least not for some time. You're a Yank, right? I can tell by your accent."

"I don't have an accent, you do, and I'm an American, from Chicago."

"Shi-caw-gow! Right! No accent. How come you're here in Bury? Are you on vacation?"

"No, I'm a reporter following a story, and quit taking this situation so damn lightly. What the hell—ah—heck is going on? How did you come to be inside me or wherever the hel—heck you are?"

"You do swear a lot. I don't mind. I'm almost seventeen. It's not as if I haven't heard it before."

"You're how old?" He yelled—out loud. Real loud!

"Shhhh! See, those old guys are looking this way funny-like. If you act too batty, they'll call the coppers, and then we'll be in a fine fix, won't we?"

"Look, I want you to leave me alone now. I'm too tired to figure out what's going on here, so do me a favour and be a good kid. Come out from wherever you're hiding, and I'll buy you an ice cream or something."

"I'm sorry to be a bother, but I'm here for some time. As far as I can tell, the spell takes a while to wear off. It's the gospel truth! You can hear me from inside. Admit it. We're talking, right? I know it and you know it."

"Quit telling me what I know. If you are inside me, or whatever 'wooo-wooo' you're on about, then where's the rest of you—your body? If you're so smart, tell me that." He jabbed the air with a forefinger to make his point, a natural hand waver and face maker when he talked. Or maybe it only happened when something displeased him; fortunately, no one was watching him at the moment.

"A bit touchy, you foreigners. I was in my uncle's garden, I pricked my finger on a rose thorn, and—crikey, here I am inside of you. My body is probably in a coma, lying across his bench, waiting for poor Uncle Robert and the tea tray he went to organize."

Troy's head sank down again into his waiting hands. He massaged his fingers through thick waves and rubbed, as if he could extinguish the events of the last few minutes. This phenomenon was just too much for a guy who hadn't gotten any sleep the night before.

He emptied his mind, completely shutting down, but a second or two before everything went silent, he heard her giggling childishly and chanting, *"yesss... yesss...."*

Chapter Three

Here we go, Dani, my love. A nice cuppa for me, and a mug of coffee brewed for you, since you refuse to recognize the proper traditional drink. And, you'll be happy to note, Mrs. Dorn baked the same biscuits you devoured the last time you were here to vis..."

Dr. Andrews came to a dead stop by the wooden table. The tray clanked down, rattling the cups and saucers, breaking some of the china. Liquid spilled, flowing in all directions until it reached the table edge where it dripped to the ground in a modest waterfall.

The biscuits tumbled and bounced eventually rolling over and landing in all directions on the cobblestone walkway—food for the noisy but patient warblers to feast on later.

"Bless my soul, not again!" Dr. Andrews ran to the girl's limp body, folded like an envelope, her arms crossed over her stomach, legs crossed at the ankles, and her top half bent over so that her forehead came close to touching her knees. All that kept her from falling to the ground was the way her body leaned against the high iron side of the bench.

The doctor in Robert Andrews merged with the loving uncle as he took her into his arms, angling her so he could check her pulse. It beat normally. He lifted her eyelids and knew she wasn't there. Blood on the thorn of the red rose near her feet indicated what had happened.

This wasn't his first experience with spirit travelling. The same kind of disturbing and frightening incident had occurred before. That episode had ended with a positive outcome, but this time it affected the one person in the world he most loved. He hugged her close, trying to still the tremors attacking his body, and it was then his gaze fell on his notes all piled on the table in disarray, totally unlike the way he'd left them.

A rational explanation for the weird events he'd recorded on those pages hadn't yet come to him, no matter how much research he'd done or how he'd racked his brain, questioning, always questioning.

His enquiries hadn't uncovered anything, nor had the many volumes of paranormal information he'd read. As far as he knew, no other place had ever experienced such a miracle. It seemed that Bury possessed the only magic rosebush—make that two bushes—in the world.

Again rechecking Dani's vital signs, he admitted what his brain wanted to refute. She was spirit travelling. Where—in whom—and when—he did not know. What he did know was that if anything happened to her, he'd never forgive himself. Keeping that damn rose bush where she could get at it, leaving all his notes lying around where she'd be able to read them, those errors made this his fault.

"Idiot! Blasted fool idiot!"

She looked so pale and innocent in his arms that he felt weak from the fear of what could happen to her. The resemblance to her mother, his older sister, emerged more strongly when his precious niece lay unmoving.

His sister! Marion… Oh, my God! She would go barmy and blame him for everything. How could he rationalize the rosebush's magic to his bossy, paranoid sibling? And trying to use it, as a reason for her daughter to be in this situation would, quite frankly, never work. In fact, nothing about the truth would pass muster with her. He needed to come up with a credible excuse—and fast—for keeping Dani here, in hiding, with him. Apprehension loomed like "the knowing about a dentist's needle before the filling."

Dani's unruly soft curls tickled his chin, while a whiff of her favourite flowery scent assailed his nostrils. The brilliant colour of her hair, eyebrows, and long reddish lashes highlighted her unblemished white skin.

She was a glimmer of sunshine in his otherwise bland life and workaholic schedule. He knew he'd never have children of his own; the time for him had long passed. But if he had been so blessed, he'd have wanted a child exactly like this smart, inquisitive, spunky girl.

She appeared very young in her present condition, tiny and weak, an impression he knew to be untrue. Dani had developed quickly, retaining her slenderness through athletics, and even at her tender age, she carried herself with attitude.

A knock sounded a moment before Dr. Andrews' housekeeper, Mrs. Dorn, peeked around the large fern near the garden's entrance. "I don't wish to intrude but—Good grief, Dr. Andrews, what's happened 'ere?" She lumbered toward him, her massive body swaying from side to side in a comic kind of wiggle.

"I'm afraid that Dani has slipped into a coma. Nothing to be alarmed about, Mrs. Dorn. I've seen these situations before, and they have a tendency to resolve themselves. We'll be looking after her for the next little while until the effects fade away, but I suggest we tell her mother a bit of a fabrication. I don't think she'd take it too well if we were to admit the truth."

"What is the truth, Doctor?" Inquisitive to a fault, his housekeeper would not be put off easily.

"I believe Dani has had an allergic reaction to the—the rose she pricked her finger on. I've seen it happen before. The effects will wear off in time, but she must be treated specially. By keeping her here, we can give her better care than the overworked staff at the hospital—where, I have no doubt, my sister would demand she be taken."

"Cor, you're right there. What'll you be telling her so she'll leave the child with us?" Mrs. Dorn moved with surprising speed to sit next to the sleeping girl in order to peer more closely.

"There has been a strain of highly infectious flu going around lately. Using that as the explanation for her illness, I can hint that Dani became violently ill while here and mustn't leave and—and spread the germs. You know how Marion is about infections and disease. I think I'll just tell her that the best medicine for the child is for us to keep her here, in a light sleep to, ah, to stop her from scratching and marring her skin."

"Ohhh, that's a good one."

"You think so?"

"Yes sir, it's brilliant, and it'll work with your sister."

"Good. That's got it, then. I'll fib and caution her not to visit. I can tell her that since I've been inoculated, because of working at the hospital, I'm the perfect person to stay with Dani. But for anyone else it would be too dangerous."

A bit thick, Mrs. Dorn's face scrunched up, her head quickly swivelled back and forth, and she said, "'Ere now! This flu the child has is hazardous? I haven't had a shot…" One glance at the doctor's questioning look and raised eyebrows, and the lights came on. "Right-o! I knows how to keep me mouth shut, don't you fret none. We'll take care of our little miss between us, and mum's the word."

So saying, she leaned over the cradled girl who'd always treated her well. Her fleshy fingers gently brushed the ringlets away from Dani's brow.

"A right proper darling she is, Dr. Andrews, always a friendly word and a smile to cheer up me day."

Dr. Andrews looked at the kindly face and, for the first time ever, didn't zero in on the large wart protruding near the end of her nose, but gazed instead into her damp eyes. He smiled reassuringly.

"It'll be simply a matter of time, my dear Mrs. Dorn. We'll have to be patient. I loathe having to lie to my sister, but we wouldn't want to worry her unnecessarily. Come now. You take her feet, and I'll carry her upper half. We'll have her comfy and tucked up in no time. I'll hire one of the nurses from the hospital to stop in each day to do for her, and we'll take care of her the rest of the time between us."

"God love ya, sir, we'll be just fine."

Later, as Dr. Andrews sat near Dani's bed rereading the notes he'd left in the garden, he came to realize that the mixed-up pages were his only hope. He prayed that she'd read them in their entirety and had understood the most important detail—how to get back home.

From now on, until she returned to herself, he would have her body on the bench at twelve noon every Saturday to prick her finger, and hope she was doing the exact same thing wherever she might be. If things worked in the similar way as they did with Lucy McGillicuddy's case, where both people had to prick their fingers at the exact same time, then it should also succeed with Dani.

The crunching noise, of papers being annihilated, had him unclenching his hands. Worry ate away his ability to concentrate and his mind jumped from subject to subject. It finally came to rest on how upset his niece had seemed earlier.

Up till this moment, he'd forgotten about the troubled note in Dani's young voice and the pleading in her eyes. Now the memory plagued him, and he realized she'd never gotten around to confessing her problem. What could have caused her so much distress?

Such a muddle! The anxiety he felt had little to do with him knowing how to look after her, and a lot to do with worrying about whether she might be able to look after herself.

What struck him as most significant was that one of his ongoing questions had been answered, but only in part. Whether or not his private rose bush—the one he himself had propagated from the mother bush near the vicarage—contained the identical formula of the supernatural. He'd wondered and even made some experiments with John Norman's assistance from time to time, but until today the flowering bush had graced his garden as a beautiful decoration with no sign at all of anything unusual. Obviously, it did harbour a similar magic, but he had no idea if that magic would work in the same way as the original rose bush.

His hands went up to link behind his head, knuckles clenched and pure white. The sigh that escaped lasted a long time and echoed back to him, forcing tremors of apprehension.

Chapter Four

Y*es, Yes, Yesss!"*
While her host shut himself off, Dani celebrated. The magic had worked. She'd abandoned her troubles, her home, and even her body to lurk inside another's. A break from the predicament she faced couldn't have come at a better time. The fact that she'd ended up in a man's body didn't fluster her; it only added to the excitement.

She knew from looking at his long-fingered hands—through his own eyes, mind you—that she resided in a younger man somewhat fastidious about nail care.

His jean-clad legs seemed to be muscular, and she did like the stylish shoes he wore. But she couldn't wait to see what he looked like. Faces interested her—they represented possible characters in future stories. She wrote constantly and liked to make up adventurous backgrounds for those people who attracted her most.

Apparently, he could close himself off from her by blanking his thoughts, exactly what he was practising at the moment. Interesting! Could she do the same with him? She'd have to try it.

It felt strange to be a thought process without any power over the muscles of the body. Wait a second. She should test it before taking anything for granted. She lifted his hand to his face and stuck his finger in his nose. He pulled it out and waved it around as if clearing a swarm of mosquitoes.

"Stop that! Look, let's get one thing straight right from the start—"

"You're attracting attention again, talking out loud." Either her words or her sweet tone angered him, because she sensed a quick rise in his inner temperature. Actually, he became quite hot inside. At least he took the hint and clamped his lips shut.

"Quit interrupting me, and quit telling me what to do, and for the love of God give me a break and get the hell—heck—out! I need you here like I need a hole in my head. I can't believe my rotten bad luck—"

"You're rambling and using profanity. But I don't mind—the swearing, that is. Go ahead if you want to."

"Hey! Even if you're only sixteen, you're a female, aren't you? And I'm not a callow kid. I do not swear in front of females."

"Right! You only cuss away inside your mind."

"Right!"

He groaned so loudly that the young biker passing by became distracted and had to swerve at the last minute to miss the bushes.

"How about if I promise to censor your language myself when you mess up. Would you relax then?"

"No! I can stop the habit altogether. It only takes a bit of will power."

She waited, sensing he had more he wanted to say.

"One question, little girl. Do spirits smile?"

" Why do you ask?"

"I've had the urge to say 'wipe that smirk off your face' ever since this conversation began."

He found out to his dismay that spirits also laughed.

As Dani felt him loosen up and his anger recede, she decided enough time had passed for him to get over his snit.

"I suppose we should introduce ourselves, since we'll be living together for a while. My name is Dani."

"Isn't that a boy's name?"

"It's a nickname I made from my real name, Daniell, which I dislike terribly. Names with consonants on the end are not at all attractive. I love names that end in 'ie' or 'y.' Girls called Julie and Christy are always so much cuter than girls with names like Marion or Elizabeth, don't you think?"

"I never thought of it. My mother's name is Elizabeth, and she's beautiful."

"What does everyone call her?"

"Lizzie."

Dani also found out that a chuckle from inside a person is a very warm sound.

"What's your name, and where do you live?"

"Troy Brennan, ma'am. Chicago born and bred."

"I live here in Bury, finished my sixth form just last week, and will probably go on to university next term."

"Why do you say probably? Don't you know for sure?"

"I know what I want, but my parents have other ideas." He sensed her vexation for just a moment, and then she tamped it down like a pro. *"I won't fret about it now, as there are always special circumstances that can bring about changes to the best-laid plans, aren't there?"*

"You mean like having unexpected visitors?"

His sense of humour tickled Dani. *"You're being very reasonable about all this bother."*

"I'm hoping lack of sleep is making me hear voices."

"I'm afraid that isn't what's happening. Why do you keep looking at that woman in the cemetery? She's very beautiful. Is she your girlfriend? Or your wife?"

"No. I'm not married. She's the person I'm here in Bury to interview, but I doubt the moment is right, so I'll wait around."

With him, Dani watched the elegant blonde, who, in the distance, wove in and out of the lush vicarage gardens. When the woman stopped and looked towards where he sat, they could see her expression, lonely and a bit sad until a voice shouted to her from behind the wall. A pretty girl of about nine or ten years old, a petite, golden-haired doll whose ringlets flew in every direction, bounded into sight. She never slowed her racing steps until she'd flung herself up into the waiting arms with a glad cry of "Mummy!"

Following close behind were an older couple, arms linked and strides matching. They didn't rush ahead but drew near in a leisurely manner, as if to give the excited twosome a moment to get caught up with their kisses and hugs. Upon approaching, they sedately greeted the woman before they all turned, clinging together, in the direction from which they'd come.

The blonde stopping to pick up a small case hidden behind some bushes, gave one last glance in Troy's direction, and hurried to catch up.

Troy rose to follow. Sauntering, he stayed many steps behind the laughing, happy group ahead until they slowed for the corner.

As they closed in, Dani recognized the group in front. "Why are we following these people?" *For the first time her voice seemed oddly constricted, as if tears clogged her throat.*

"You okay? You sound funny. I just want to know where she'll be staying, so I can return another day to request an interview."

"I see. Don't you know her name?"

"Yes, it's Ellie Ward, and she's a very well-known author."

"An author. How lucky she is. One day I want to write books myself. The little girl is wonderful, isn't she? Will we meet her?"

"If things go my way, then it's a sure thing."

"You are very presumptuous."

"Do you even know what that big word means, little girl?"

"Yes, big man. It means this tenancy could prove to be rather difficult."

"Go ahead and break the lease anytime you want."

"You'd like that, wouldn't you? I'm afraid, since it's only Monday, you're stuck with me for a few more days."

Dani had carefully read all the notes her uncle had left in the garden, and she knew her only escape would be on a Saturday at twelve noon.

Earlier, she'd recognized her very own parents, and seeing them interact with the person Troy followed had thrown her into a tailspin. She felt as though she'd looked into a mirror at her own future self, where her stylish silhouette was years older and a whole lot prettier.

The little girl calling her "Mommy"—she didn't even want to go there. It was clear she must have travelled into the future. How confusing. Could she possibly be in the same place at the same time without there being repercussions? Would the universe allow this? Just in case, she'd have to stop him from catching up to the group ahead. At that moment, like a direct answer to her prayer, Dani heard a bawling noise.

"Troy, listen! Can you hear it? Someone in the lane here is crying. Something must be wrong."

"None of our business. I need to follow Mrs. Ward. I've been on her trail since Chicago, and I'm not going to lose her now."

Mrs. Ward? She was married?

"It's a child's voice, Troy. A child is in trouble, and we need to check it out."

Troy stopped in his tracks. She used every bit of yearning, persuasive power she had to influence his decision.

"For pity's sake." *He slapped his hands against the sides of his legs, swivelled, and took off down into the shadowy, dark lane.*

Three bigger males, teenagers by their appearance, surrounded a small boy who clung to a cowering puppy. The terrified canine, intent on hiding his muzzle under the lad's arm, appeared to be the object of the skirmish.

"'Ere! Give over, ya sissy. He's ours, we found 'im." Two of the brutes reached over and each grabbed one of the tyke's shoulders.

Brave or just stupid, he didn't back down. "No! You're hurting 'im. I saw you with the cans. You can't tie 'em to his tail, the noise frightens 'im." The small lad whispered the last words from a throat too closed up to enunciate clearly. Tears poured down his face, and a puddle slowly started to form in the dirt under his leg. He trembled, but his intentions were clear. His arms held even more tightly to the whining bundle, while his eyes shut tight.

Without waiting for Troy to speak, Dani jumped in. "Let go of him, you two! You're a right pair of idiots, ain'tcha, pickin' on a nipper, and you three all twice his size."

The leader of the pack sized up Troy, sensing weakness from the tone and the words used. "Don't mess about, mister. Ain't none of your business, this. The punk here has me dog, and I wants 'im back. Me mum brought 'im home for me yesterday—for me birthday."

"You're lyin'. Your mum never did." Incensed, the boy tried to break away from the restraining hands.

"Shut your gob." Neither the pointing finger nor the threats prevented the small boy from speaking up.

"The pup's a stray." Tears didn't halt his words, either. He sensed Troy's protection. Wriggling hard, he escaped from the two who'd been holding him and ran over to stand next to the big man. A hand rubbed the fair hair and settled on the boy's neck in support.

Predictably, the two followers turned to their mouthpiece, waiting to take his lead. Three against one were pretty good odds. Tall as he stood, Troy's presence hadn't been threatening. His tone hadn't scared them, and his relaxed demeanour confused rather than intimidated.

"Aye, there, hang on. The dog's mine, and I want him." Grubby, sandy-coloured hair curtained one half of the insolent face. Mismatched teeth protruded, detracting from any slight attractiveness the braggart might have had if he'd smiled rather than sneered. He had a slight build, still a youth but wiry, muscled, and unafraid.

His two sidekicks were similar in size, both dark-haired, both wary, and both heading to circle around the lone man and boy.

"Troy, they're going to jump you. Maybe we should take the boy and get out of here." *Dani's anxiety brought a smile to Troy's face—not a nice smile, not a smile that would make others respond similarly when they saw it. It was a mean grin full of menace and glee.*

"I've got it covered, Miss Nosy Parker."

Troy gently put the lad behind him and took off his leather jacket. Laying it across the youngster's shoulders, he winked and took a second to ruffle the furry face peering up at him.

He stood, legs solid, braced, and slowly, purposefully, he rolled up the sleeves of his shirt. His obvious lack of concern threw his would-be attackers off guard. They looked at each other, nervous, hesitant, waiting.

"Hey, boys! Smart-assed little shits. Come pick on someone your own size." Troy frowned, the lines in his forehead scrunching together while he flexed his hands and wiggled his fingers. The lower part of his face formed a malicious scowl with absolutely no humour involved. "My golden opportunity for a workout." He pointed at the bigmouth. "You got a problem? You want the dog? Come get him."

No one moved.

Finally, Troy approached the pushy goon. He stared him in the eye, and his intent gaze kept the lowlife from looking away. Without turning or dropping eye contact, he called to the hovering child and asked, "Hey, kid, do you know this jerk's name?"

"Aye, that I do, sir, and his address."

Troy poked his finger into the chest in front of him. "Not so brave now, are ya?"

The touch seemed to galvanize the others into action. Seeing their friend needed help, the two ran forward and were met with a nonchalant readiness. A karate kick to the groin put the first one out of order, and a flat-handed chop to the stomach and a push to have him trip over his partner fixed the second, while the third hung from Troy's arm in a headlock. Gripping his ear, Troy hurled the leader onto the pile of bodies and then stood over the sprawling bunch.

"I'll get your name, creep, and I'll be checking in with the kid from time to time. If I hear of any trouble with my new friend, there'll be hell to pay. Now, get out of my sight."

Within a few seconds the alley was cleared except for the wide-eyed half-pint and his canine trophy.

"Mister, I never saw anyone move that fast. It was jolly well rivetin', it was. Thank you for helping me." He carefully handed Troy first his brown jacket, making sure it didn't touch the ground, and then the puppy.

"Look, kid—"

"Me name's Archie Butcher."

"Right. Archie. Those three won't be returning to hurt you after I leave, will they? 'Cause if you need for me to walk you home, talk with your mom or dad and explain what happened, I can."

"No, it's fine. Me older brother will sort 'em out when I tell 'im what's happened. Once he has a talk with those blighters, they'll leave off. It's the doggy I'm afeared for, sir. Me mum won't have a dog 'cause she's algeric."

"You mean 'allergic.'" Troy's smile invited the boy to smile back, and he did.

"Uh-huh. Allergic. Can you take 'im? Otherwise those bullies will get hold of 'im again. They were going to hurt 'im, maybe kill 'im, ya know."

"So I gathered. Look, I'm just here on a visit, I don't live here, and I can't look after a dog. Isn't there anyone else you can give him to?"

Without thinking, Troy had accepted the furry bundle, hugged him close, and soothed the trembling body. As they were talking, the boy had slowly backed away.

"Thanks, mister. I'll tell me da about you. He'll be wanting to thank you, I'm sure."

One last wave and the boy ran towards the entrance of the lane and disappeared.

"Hey, kid! Come back here!" Troy took three steps as if to follow and then stopped. *"Daw-gonit! First a female invasion and now a damn dog. Why me, Lord?"*

"Troy! You were fantastic. It felt great to experience that episode inside you. Myself, I'm a coward when it comes to anything physical, but you were so calm and controlled. I know you held back when you hit those boys, and I never felt you lose your temper at all or—"

"Don't—talk—to—me." She imagined if he had spoken out loud, it would've been through clenched teeth. "Because of you, I've lost Ellie Ward and gained a scrawny, homeless mutt. What the blasted, damn heck am I going to do with this sorry-looking thing?"

Troy held the pooch up in front of him with one hand and stared into the wet, black, almond-shaped eyes. The scruffy, matted coat looked to be a dirty brown with spots of white in some places. A glance downward confirmed his male status. Ears, too big for the size of his face, flopped over in an adorable way after a few seconds. He whined and arched his body, trying to land his small pink tongue on the cheek of the man glaring at him.

"He's a cutie, Troy. I can't believe you're sorry. In fact, I know inside you're not. You did the only thing possible in the circumstances, helping that boy. You know he wouldn't have given them the dog. And, he would have gotten hurt if—"

He growled. "Do me a favour. Just—be—quiet."

Chapter Five

Robert Andrews, I have had it with you and your excuses. I want to talk to my daughter. This is the second time I've called in two hours, only to be put off by your impertinent housekeeper."

"You mean Mrs. Dorn?"

"Of course I mean Mrs. Dorn. What other housekeeper do you have? Are you being purposely annoying?"

The thought came to him out of nowhere. If voices could cut, he'd be bleeding.

"No, dear. I'm, ah, I'm just very busy right now. I can't discuss this—"

"Don't—you—dare put me off again, or I'll come over there personally and find out what the devil is going on. Where is Daniel?"

"I don't want you getting upset, truly, Marion, but it's best that I keep Dani here with me for a while."

"Excuse me!!?"

"I said that I will be keeping Dani here with me for a short while." His voice escalated annoyingly—on purpose.

She snarled and then replied, "Robert, you are being very difficult. She left the house four hours ago saying she wanted to visit you, and she hasn't returned. What I want to know is—why?"

"Dear, have you heard of the vicious Asian flu going around Manchester? It's a deadly strain, and we've only seen a few cases here in town. The victims have all had to be quarantined to protect—"

"Daniell has this flu? That's what you're telling me, isn't it? I've warned her over and over again not to go to that blasted orphanage to teach soccer to those unhealthy homeless children. But does she listen to me? No!"

Dr. Andrews made comforting noises and then cleared his throat to cut off the tirade. "As soon as I realized her symptoms, I made her go to bed while I had some tests done. The results should be in soon. I was waiting to ring you until after I had them to confirm my diagnosis."

"She has been acting a mite strange lately, now that I think on it. Is she very sick?"

"She's sleeping, Marion, and will be fine in time. But unfortunately we cannot move her. I have to keep her here, where Mrs. Dorn and I will be taking care of her. I've given her a sedative, so she can rest."

"I'll be right over. My poor Daniell will be needing me."

"No, Marion. You cannot come here!" Alarm was evident in the quick response. "The house is now under quarantine. Look, please don't worry. I told you she's in seclusion and sleeping, which is the best thing for her. The flu has some pretty nasty side effects; one is intense itching from the rashes that occur. This could cause horrific scarring. So I'll be keeping her sedated until we see that her temperature has dropped."

Marion's voice rose another few octaves. "She has a temperature?"

"It's not alarmingly high, but a bit more than normal."

"You're saying I can't come and look after her, my own baby?" The woman's voice came through like a child's, scared and weepy.

"It's for the best, my dear. And she isn't a baby but a strong young woman. Look, you mustn't come. I couldn't bear it if you became ill also. It's a much harder battle for the older generation than for the youngsters, and the rashes can be devastating."

"Robert, how horrible! What about you and Mrs. Dorn? You could get the flu, too, couldn't you?"

"I've already been inoculated, working at the hospital, you know, and Mrs. Dorn—she's nursed her, ah, sister, who had it earlier this year, and so she's built up an immunity. I'll bring a special nurse in, Grace Joye, if I can convince her to come. She's the best we have on staff, and she can take over most of Dani's care while I'm away at work. You mustn't worry. We'll give her the best of attention, even better than if she was to go to the hospital."

"What will I tell her father? Henry will be so worried."

"Explain exactly what I've told you, and he'll understand that it's best this way. If he has any concerns, have him call me, and in the meantime know our girl is resting and in good hands. Trust me, Marion. Your child's safe here."

"You know I wouldn't trust anyone else with her. Please call me if you need anything, anything at all. I'll drop off her night things—I'll ring the doorbell and leave the suitcase on the front steps. And I'll get my ladies' group at church to have a prayer sit-in for her."

"That's a wonderful idea. She's young and healthy, and if I thought there could be any danger at all, I promise, I'd let you know. She just needs to rest."

"Thank you, Robert. I don't know what I'd do without you. I'll ring you tomorrow, love. Ta-ra!"

Dr. Andrews lowered the phone, wiped his brow with the handkerchief from his pocket, and sighed long and deep. "I have no doubt," he muttered soulfully.

Chapter Six

Still closed off, occupied with unanswerable questions and weary beyond words, Troy stared at the wiggling pup in his arms, and then his chin dropped comically to his chest.

The time had come to search for a room. He guessed it would be best to shelve all his problems for the moment. After all, the possibility of a girl lurking in his brain, or wherever the hell she lurked, couldn't be real. But then he couldn't dispute the fact that she knew his thoughts without a word being spoken. As crazy as the idea seemed, he felt her. A kind of glow lit his spirit, and as much as he didn't understand, he kinda liked it. The feeling was warm and gentle and—well, nice.

Tucking the pup inside his jacket, he made his way to a local pharmacy to gather the essentials he'd need for the next few days. Then, at a small market nearby, he purchased a few pairs of cheap briefs, some socks, a bit of beef jerky, a newspaper, and, most important, a writing tablet. He walked the two blocks back to the Cozy Inn to book a room, and all the while he steamed in silence.

When the bell over the doorway tinkled to announce an arrival, a middle-aged woman with a bandana tied around her hair looked up from her magazine. Slouched over the counter, she nonchalantly wiped at non-existent dust with the cleaning rag she held.

"Good evening, sir. Can I help you?"

"Yes, ma'am. I'd like to have a room for tonight and possibly the next few days."

She stared at him, and one eyebrow rose as she took in the wiggling bulge in his jacket, the newspapers under his arm, and the small paper bags he carried. "Do you have any other luggage?"

"No." He chuckled. "Impulsive trip. I'm travelling light." His smile faded when it wasn't returned. He glanced around and discovered the interior of a room decorated with themes from nigh-on twenty years before. He remembered the same rose-patterned wallpaper in his grandmother's farmhouse bedroom, and the light fixtures—pink frosted spaghetti-glass globes—were classic early fifties. He shuddered.

The heavy-chested, moustached female called over her shoulder as she walked past him and disappeared down the hallway. "Bunty, you've a customer."

Within minutes, a stunner emerged from a doorway behind the desk and held her hand toward Troy. Her slim hips wiggled with a touch more effort after she had eyeballed and catalogued his charms.

Her busty upper body, clothed in a skin-tight sweater, thrust out invitingly, which together with the way she walked on her high heels could make an observer fear she might at any moment fall forward. "Good evening, sir. I'm Mrs. Hubble. You're wanting a room?" The woman's syrupy attitude, a complete switch from the previous greeter, charmed Troy.

"Yes. For at least one night, maybe more. I've business in town, and I'm not too sure how long it will keep me here." His hand patted and controlled the nuisance hidden underneath his leather bomber jacket.

"I see. I have a nice room at the front overlooking the street, which will suit, I'm sure. Sign here, if you please? We do serve a supper every night in the bar area between five and seven. If you're late there's always snacks in the pub, or a restaurant down the street. It's open until much later."

Troy signed where her red-polished fingernail pointed and then turned the large register back in her direction. "Tonight, I'll eat in my room, if that's possible. Can a tray be carried upstairs? If not, I can come down and get it."

"That'll be fine, ah, Mr. Brennan. I'll bring it upstairs for you myself. Say in half an hour?" She beamed at him, her lipstick-coated lips issuing a subtle challenge.

"Thank you, Mrs. Hubble."

"Please, just call me Bunty. Mrs. Hubble seems so formal, and being as how I'm a widow, the title doesn't really count anymore." She turned and strutted over to the pigeonholes that were fronted with hanging keys. Taking her time, she withdrew a skeleton-shaped one and swivelled around to pass it over the counter.

"There's the stairs, or we have a lift, if you prefer." She pointed to the far end of the room.

Troy accepted her offering. "Thank you, Bunty, I need the exercise." He couldn't help smiling back at the obviousness of his proprietor. He winked and turned in the direction she'd pointed, towards the spiral wooden staircase.

The small upstairs room he entered depressed him somewhat. He missed the customary television set and longed for a private bathroom where he could soak away the aches from the last twenty-four hours. He did thank the gods for the installed wardrobe, where he could store the puppy out of sight when anyone came knocking. Lowering his pal, he put his finger over his lips and whispered, "No barking, or you'll find yourself outside. Got it?"

The small whine of agreement satisfied him.

With a little push on the furry behind, he said. "Go investigate, and no accidents." Then he threw himself over the blue chenille-covered bed, crossed his arms and legs, and sulked.

****

"She's a bit of a tart, isn't she?" The words burst from a life force shut down for far too long. Dani had tried to respect his wishes for silence, but she found it unbearable not being able to speak her mind, or think out loud.

He groaned. "What do you know about tarts? You're a child, and your mother must have told you that children should be seen and not heard."

"Hang on! Since I can't be seen, I claim the right to be heard."

"Of course you do," he said sarcastically.

"You're still angry with me, aren't you? I can feel you simmering and stewing about it."

"I'm not angry!" Troy groaned with disgust. "Fine. Maybe a bit annoyed. I followed that woman all the way from Chicago to Bury, England, and never once did she leave my sight—don't say it!"

"I wasn't going to! It's understood you couldn't follow her into the loo."

"Within reason, she never left my sight. Then you come along and invade me for a few minutes, and all hell breaks loose. Instead of doing what I should have done, which is mind my own business, I end up with a mutt and a cold trail on the one story that could give me everything I want."

His aggrieved tone made Dani feel terrible. The simmering annoyance he couldn't hide burned away inside like the embers in a fireplace. She sympathized with his frustration. If finding Ellie Ward was that important to him, she couldn't withhold information she knew would restore his good mood.

"Look, don't get your knickers in a twist. I know where her parents live here in town. I can show you how to meet up with her again so you can sort things out."

"You do? Why didn't you tell me earlier?"

"If you remember, you were in a serious bother at the time." Working him in the same way she worked her father, she injected a small hurt tone. "You said I couldn't speak."

"Look, I'm sorry, kiddo. I can be a bit of a shi— jerk sometimes. Just ignore me when I get that way. It comes on quickly and goes away just as fast. Can you show me in the morning where Ellie and her family live? Then I'll get busy working the article. If I do my homework, gather background material on her early life here in Bury, it could be a spectacular piece, maybe get picked up by the Associated Press, and I'll have the chance to once again be in print nationally."

A knock sounded on the door, and Troy dove for the dog. He grabbed up some of the beef jerky he'd bought and used it now as an inducement to keep his new pal from complaining too loudly for being put in a dark place. His bundled-up jacket used for a mat worked fine. Moving quickly, he placed the busily chewing puppy on top of the soft material, threw in another few pieces of the treat, and closed the door, concealing the mutt from prying eyes.

"Good thinking!"

"Thank you, ma'am, I aim to please."

"Well, that should delight Mrs. Hubble." The droll wit, a part of her personality that enchanted her uncle, came easily to her.

The resultant smile, plastered over Troy's face, elicited an even bigger one from the widow Hubble as she deposited the fully packed tray on a table in front of the window. She jiggled the tied-back, white organza curtains, giving them an extra swat before she turned to face Troy.

"I trust your room is in order, Mr. Brennan?"

"Thanks so much for bringing the tray up for me. Everything is perfect, and the stew smells great."

"It's very kind of you to say so. If there is anything else we can do to make your stay memorable, please don't hesitate."

The simpering words were spoken in tandem with an obvious come-on. She straightened her shoulders and held them back, arching her bosom, and then she crossed her arms to frame what she wanted to emphasize. Catching his eyes, she smiled in a flirtatious manner while watching his reaction from under her eyelids. An over-application of mascara made them appear false and so weighted her blinking took longer than normal.

"What a silly cow!" Not used to hiding her thoughts, Dani's raging candour prompted Troy's engaging grin.

"No! I'll want nothing more. Thank you, Mrs. Hubble. I'll bring the tray down after I'm done. Good night."

Annoyance flashed across the landlady's features at his sorry-not-interested tone. A loud slam vibrated the floor when she left the room.

"Sorry about that, Dani."

Troy went over and released a happy, wriggling fluff-ball from the cupboard. Then he laid newspapers on the linoleum and placed the little one on top of them. "Okay, Licky-lou, time for your lessons." He pushed the pup's hind end down, over and over again, with the command "stay" until defiance receded. The warm pile of broken-up stewing beef might have had something to do with his obedience, also.

Inside, Dani smiled, and the warmth spread throughout Troy.

"You handled Mrs. Hubble like a pro, actually. And, I'm not a child, Troy, as much as you want to insist that I am. My parents, and especially my uncle, have always treated me beyond my years. It's forced me to mature faster than my peers, and when I think of the silly, immature kids I'm forced to hang around with, I'm jolly glad for it."

"Think again, my girl. It's important to get along with people your own age, or you won't have very much fun growing up, will you?"

"I have friends. Good friends. It's just that most of the students I spend my days with are either dim-witted, and that's being complimentary, or they try hard to look that way to fit in. Popularity is ghastly."

"I see nothing's changed since my days in school." Troy ate and visited at the same time.

"I have a friend. He's a lovely boy—no fancy airs, no vindictiveness like many of the people in our school, adults included. But the other blokes, and even some of the girls, treat him like he's inferior, all because he's shy. It's horrible, it is."

"Is he your boyfriend?" Troy asked, teasing.

"Not really, but I like him and feel sorry for him."

"Sweetheart, you can't right all the wrongs of the world. Sometimes people have to stick up for themselves or be dumped on. It's just the way things are. You need to take care of number one."

"Troy, you can't believe that. It's a disgusting way for people to think, never mind live. We all have a responsibility to help each other—"

"Hey! You think the way you want to. I'll believe what I know is the way things are out there in the big, bad world. And I'll thank you not to try to influence me while you're my resident. Deal?"

"But—"

"Deal?"

"Deal." Dani's mind raced. Could he really be serious?

"Dam—darn right I am. Now go away, sweetheart, and let me eat my supper."

Earlier, her own need for some personal privacy had forced her to delve deep, to find the way to zone him out should she need space. She learned how to shut down their pipeline and exist inside her own sphere where he couldn't tune in. Once she conquered this ability, she felt better.

His startling declaration earlier needed private consideration. What she'd shared with him was the truth. In her family circle she spent much more time with adults than with people her own age. It showed in the way she behaved, her ease with being a good listener, and her tendency to respect everyone else's views.

But his views rang false. "Look after number one." His philosophy baffled and saddened her. Between what he'd just told her and what she knew to be true from her own experience, a wide chasm existed. Had he spoken honestly? Or spouted words to make an impression? Sometimes it was easy to tune in on his true feelings, and other times it didn't work. This time it hadn't worked.

She supposed as they got to know each other better over the next few days she'd learn to read his emotions. Maybe even trust him enough to discuss her dilemma and tell him her secret. Then again, maybe not. Dani couldn't stand the thought that he might make her regret what she'd done. Especially since she'd begun questioning herself about the choices she'd made and whether or not the outcome would be worth the uproar.

Cautiously optimistic, she decided to take her time and just let things ride for now. If she admitted her real identity, would he use that against her in some way? A self-professed jerk should be treated carefully.

Another niggling worry came to mind. The date on the newspapers he'd spread on the floor was July 1978. The day she'd visited her uncle had been ten years earlier.

Not that there hadn't been other obvious changes everywhere they'd gone. For instance, her showing up as a grown woman in the vicarage garden. The time difference was pretty freaky.

Her mind wandered away from a problem too complex to solve. She speculated on how her uncle fared, and how he was dealing with her batty, lovable, overprotective mother. The woman could drive an angel demented, but the whole family loved and protected her from the harshness of reality.

Poor Uncle Robert. And poor Mrs. Dorn! Dani's mood lightened for just a sec when she imagined the shock that woman would suffer upon being told about the spell attached to the roses in the garden.

Now Dani understood why her uncle never let anyone else near them. He pruned and watered them himself and maintained very strict instructions that they were never to be cut for any reason, not for the house or for company.

Thinking about him made her sad again. She missed him, but she also knew what awaited her at home wasn't anything she wanted to rush back to. The longer she could put off returning, the better, because when she did get back, her family would be split apart, and she would be right smack dab in the middle.

Chapter Seven

Hello, Mrs. Dorn. This is Marion Howard again. Is my brother available to come to the telephone? I've called three times before and—"

"Yes, mum, you don't have to tell me. I've answered each time. Run me feet ragged to get to the bloody phone, I have. Sorry. He's not 'ere, and I don't know when he'll be back. He's a busy man, he is."

Standing next to her, Dr. Andrews frowned at Mrs. Dorn's attitude, then nodded agreement when she picked up on his agitation and changed over. She'd tempered her tone and added the last sentence to soften her manner.

"I'm aware of how much extra work my daughter is, Mrs. Dorn, and I wish I could be there myself to look after her. It's very annoying that I'm not allowed anywhere near when she so obviously needs me." A sob could be heard over the line.

The doctor's eyes looked upwards, furrowing his brow. His hands clenched, one over the other, and then lifted to rest against his lips.

Mrs. Dorn's pinkish nose wart appeared prominently against the paleness of her face. She tried to push the receiver toward the doctor, but her action met with resistance. He shook his head quickly and pulled his hands away, as if someone held a gun on him and had given the order "stick 'em up." As added reinforcement, he then swung them behind his back, a mulish look obvious on his face.

With a sigh, Mrs. Dorn answered. "Your Dani is the loveliest lass I know, and doing for her is me pleasure, Mrs. Howard. According to Nurse Joye, young Dani is resting well, her colour is good, and, let me tell you, she's getting the best of care. The doctor has seen to that, he has. He'll ring you as soon as he gets back from the, umm, emergency. As long as it ain't too late!" The doctor's grimace had her adding on the last part.

"See that he does, and thank you, Mrs. Dorn." A sniff lingered as the last sound heard before the miffed housekeeper slammed the phone down.

"Doctor Andrews! A fine howd'yedo! Here—why are you being such a pinhead? I know Mrs. Howard can be difficult, but she is your sister. The blithering woman's distressed about her little girl's sickness, about not being allowed near her, and she deserves your consideration, if just for a few minutes every day."

"You are so right, Mrs. Dorn. Forgive me for foisting this situation onto your most efficient, accommodating shoulders—"

"'Ere now, none of that nonsense. I've done for you for twenty years, and helped you out of many a pickle, but this time, sir, you're out of order. And if you don't soon fix things, I'll be one of your dotty patients meself!"

"Confound it, Mrs. Dorn! My older sister might be a tiny bit overpowering, and for that I'm sorry, but that woman can differentiate between me telling her the truth or not, even over a telephone. I swear there's an inbuilt lie detector located on the frontal lobe of her shrewd brain."

Mrs. Dorn's chubby arms unwound slowly from in front of her considerable chest, and her stance became less stiff. The intractability in her attitude slowly faded. Seeing this, the doctor continued.

"Bear in mind the time I felt wretched over the Pringle suicide, and Marion invited me for dinner? I refused to go—it's true. But I distinctly recall telling her I was a mite tired after working with some specialists from out of London. Admittedly, I might have sounded a wee bit down, but considering the circumstances, those reactions were not unexpected. I was ever so careful not to let on about my mood, or to say anything that would lead her to even suspect a slight case of depression. She arrived an hour later with her suitcase and promptly informed us she was here to make sure I took some time off from work. Do you remember, Mrs. Dorn?"

She nodded, her attitude undergoing a slight change, but she didn't speak.

"Three unbearable days she disrupted our lives. Three of the longest days in memory." The doctor's voice rose perceptibly as the tale continued, and his eyes enlarged to the point of seeming to fill the round wires of his spectacles.

"Oh, Doctor, 'ere now. She behaved quite well, even going as far as to stock up on your favourite Bury Black Puddin's. She carried tea trays to you every hour, checked in on you to be sure you weren't working, had your secretary reschedule all your appointments—all to give you a long-overdue break."

"Yes, and made a mess in your kitchen, changed over all your cupboards, forced me to give said secretary, Doris, a raise to get her to come back to work, and saw to it that, to this very day, I hate any dish associated with pudding."

"To be sure, she was only trying to help, but you can be right, sir. Your sister isn't someone to take lightly. Aye, but look 'ere, Doctor! Lying to her is not on me list of duties. What if we get Nurse Joye to talk with her, calm her fears?"

"Nurse Joye, the sweetest-tempered nurse at the hospital? She isn't up to lying any more than I am. I'm afraid my sister would see through her stuttering explanations at once. If I promise to call Marion every morning with an update, would you be so kind, dear Mrs. Dorn—of course with a healthy recompense for your troubles—to continue attending to the annoying calls she insists on making?"

"Oh, piffle, I guess I can be persuaded. You're a right charming bloke when you turn it on, Doctor. I don't see how you've managed to remain a bachelor all these many years."

"I'm a Swerver, Mrs. Dorn." The twinkle returned to his eyes now that he'd gotten his way over the phone calls.

Mrs. Dorn swung around to go back into the kitchen. As she waddled away Dr. Andrews clearly heard her mutter, "I'd say you're more like a jolly good Hider. And more often than not, I'm your flamin' accomplice."

Chapter Eight

Troy lounged against the trunk of a tree, waiting for the floppy-eared puppy, happily examining the grassy area, to finish his business. He'd bathed the mutt the night before and been pleasantly surprised to find the puppy's light brown coat grew thick, with beautiful golden highlights and white patches around his neck and ears. One day his tail would be a full waving plume, as he most resembled a miniature border collie.

"What are you going to call your friend?" Dani's voice sounded *wistful.*

"I won't have him long enough to name him anything but a pain in the butt." He heard her reflex sigh. *"What?"*

"I've always wanted a dog, but the parents wouldn't have it. First they said our lives were too busy to look after one properly, which didn't stop my yearning, and then my mother discovered she had rather convenient, ah, algerics."

As the smile lit up his face, he felt her answering one inside.

"We always had animals when I grew up—my dad loved his dogs almost as much as us kids. And my mom was a cat person."

"Kids? How many were there in your family?"

"Counting me, there were three boys, and two older sisters. Us boys drove the girls crazy. We snuck up on them with their dates, messed with their stuff, and stole their records. It's a wonder they didn't do away with us and hide the bodies."

"You're so lucky to come from a large family. I'm an only child. I can tell by the warmth you're generating that you loved your life and your sisters."

"Actually, my sister Deb, the closest to me, used to bail me out, when I was a little guy, by eating my potatoes. In those days I hated the things unless they came in the form of a french fry. I'd try coating them with ketchup, which would help a bit, but after a while my throat just clogged up, and I couldn't do it. My dad hated food going to waste and refused to let me go out to play until I'd finished my plate. I'd sit there and pout, feeling very sorry for myself, and Deb would eventually come along and slap me on the back of the noggin for smothering them with ketchup, but she'd always gobble them down. To date, she's still the one with the kindest heart. Deb loves dogs, and she and her husband recently bought a kennel. They raise poodles."

"She's so lucky. When I was seven, my uncle bought me a lovely little black poodle. I begged for a pet every Christmas and every birthday until finally he broke down. According to the veterinarians, poodles don't have the same kind of fur as other dogs, and so we didn't need to concern ourselves with mother's medical problems. I called my poodle Curly."

"Curl—y! No surprise there." A grin slowly spread. He could feel it starting at one corner of his lips, and he finally had to give in and let it all emerge. He lowered his eyes. Walking along, forcing the furry wigglepuss down under his chin while the animal was determined to wash his face, Troy bit down on his bottom lip to realign his mug and stop himself from looking like some happy idiot. *"Did your mom let you keep her?"*

"Yes, she did, but only because her younger brother bought him for me. Uncle Robert is a psychiatrist, also a bachelor, and she dotes on him. I loved that poodle so much…"

"What happened?" He sensed the bad news coming. Her sorrow spread inside, starting with quivers and ending in a tightening of his stomach.

"She became sick. One day after school, while I was playing ball with her, she started foaming at the mouth. I called my uncle in a panic, but nothing helped. She had to be put down. Her sickness came on in a matter of hours. My uncle said it was just one of those flukes

that happen to small animals sometimes. We were together for only a few short months, but my heart broke, and it took weeks for me to get over her death. My uncle offered to get me another, but this time my mother stayed adamant. No more pets!"

"What is it, kid? Whenever you speak of your mother, I sense you morphing from happy-go-lucky to sighing furtively. Don't you get along with her?"

"No one gets along with her. We just get out of her way. Don't misunderstand me. She's a wonderfully loving lady whose demeanour resembles that of a—a Sherman tank. It's easier to give in to her than argue."

"Pretty hard to be your own person when you let another have so much power over your decisions. But then again you're only sixteen, so—"

"Almost seventeen!"

"Right! You're almost an old lady, so I guess your time to take over will come soon enough."

"Sooner than you think!"

"Don't be in too big a hurry, Dani. Enjoy being young while you can. Responsibilities aren't all that much fun. Look, since you missed out, I hereby bequeath this monster to you. Consequently, it's your duty to give him his name, but with one restriction. No respectable male wants a name with an 'ie' ending."

His teasing did the trick. Her essence filled him inside with such a joyful radiance he wondered if others noticed the glow.

"I'll think on it and let you know. Something as important as a name shouldn't be taken too lightly."

"You do that. In the meantime, purchasing a new shirt and jeans are next on my agenda. I can't be walking around in these same clothes much longer. Do you know of a men's store in town where the prices aren't too high? I'm not all that flush right now."

It got to him, knowing he had a whopping big bank account back home and no way to get at the funds unless he worked his way through a lot of red tape. Those things took time, time he didn't have. He'd be damned if he'd ever travel without his check book again.

"I have money. I'll write you a cheque. We can get a blank form at the bank."

"You would do that for me? No hesitation, no questions?" Not that he could take her up on it.

"Of course! We're friends, aren't we?"

"More like roommates, I'd say."

She giggled. "We'll call it my rent payment."

His loud laugh distracted the lady passing by and earned him a lovely smile in return. "The people around here are friendly. Not like Chicago, where the locals are so busy rushing around they have no time to pay attention to anyone else."

"Noticing the friendliness of the locals doesn't seem to be the norm for blokes, especially older ones. You're a people watcher."

"I'm very observant. I have to be, in my profession. And cut out the 'old men' comments, I'm only twenty-nine. Besides, how many men my age do you know? You must spend most of your time with boys."

"True, unfortunately. But I really do prefer adults, and I think I'd like your big city. One day I'll go and see Chicago for myself."

"Chicago's great. I miss the goings on."

"Goings on?"

"Yeah, you know. In the big city something's always going on. I'll be back there as soon as I get my story, and once you leave me and return to where you came from."

Just the thought of being alone again brought an extra swing to his steps. Daydreaming of working at the *Chicago Sun-Times*, he imagined his future office. There would be an outside window, a beat-up overflowing desk, and glazed glass in the top part of his door with his name in gold letters—Troy Brennan, Editor.

The jiggling body in his arms restored his awareness to the surroundings, and the anxious whining had him lowering the pup to some nearby grass immediately. Good thing he'd acted quickly!

While he waited, Troy glanced around him.

"Dani? How about this department store? Do they have inexpensive menswear?"

No answer. His heart skipped a beat.

"Dani? Come out, wherever you are?"

"How the devil should I know? I've never bought men's clothes."
Her grumpiness jolted him. Up till now, he'd taken her cheeriness for granted.

What was up with his trespasser? Shaking off his thoughts, he asked a small boy sitting on the curb close by to watch the pup for a few minutes while he made his way inside.

The general store, filled with clothes for younger men, proved to be exactly what Troy wanted. He grabbed a pair of stylish bell-bottomed jeans and a black T-shirt from the overflowing racks and made his way towards one of the changing rooms. As soon as he opened the curtain and saw the mirrored wall he stopped.

"Hold it! Are you still there?" His voice warned of his seriousness. It was a rougher, no-nonsense tone—one she recognized from when he'd used it on the bullying blokes yesterday.

"Uh-huh! Where else would I be?"

"Don't be cheeky! You can see right now, can't you?"

"Of course I can. I see out of your eyes, don't I?"

"Right! Fine." He closed his eyes, continued into the change room, and stumbled when he stubbed his toe on the wooden chair.

"What in the world are you doing?"

"You're only sixteen. You shouldn't be seeing a man undress."
He hadn't had to worry about her spying in his room, for there wasn't a full-length mirror. He'd taken care never to look at anything she shouldn't be seeing. Not an easy task but doable.

"Number one. Just 'will' me to leave and you'll feel me shut down, because I'll respect your privacy. And number two, yours wouldn't be the first male body I've seen anyway."

"Number one, how about just shutting up instead of shutting down. And number two, what the hel—heck do you mean by not the first male—No, wait. I don't want to know."

"At least let me see you after you're dressed. It's very difficult carrying on conversations with someone you can only see from the inside."

"What does it matter?"

"What if I told you I have a crush on you and I want to see what you look like, especially in your knickers?"

The tight jeans were only halfway up. Vertigo and embarrassment collided, engulfing him at the same time. His knee bashed against the chair and his forehead hit the wall. Muffled swear words and babbles that made no sense, except that the surly meanings were explicit, rang out before he spoke to her again. *"Stop that!"* He sounded angry.

"Stop what?"

Was she giggling? *"Stop saying things like that. You don't have a crush on me. You don't even know me."*

"I know you're extremely kind, that you care about small children and animals, take on burdens even when you don't want to, and—and you're ambitious. You have a wonderful, warm chuckle, and—"

"Enough! For God's sake, my head will swell. Look, sweetie, you're sixteen—"

"Almost seventeen."

"And I'm almost thirty. Besides, you should be with a nice guy your own age."

"I already have."

"What?" Troy's eyes popped open—wide, very wide.

Chapter Nine

*O*hh! You're a smasher, you are."

He stared into the mirror as if he could see into the soul hidden inside him. The ferocious look on his face warned her not to say another word. Instead she silently continued to view his features. His piercing, multifaceted eyes, brown and green, gold and gorgeous, were daunting. In the light from the naked bulb hanging above, his auburn hair gleamed. It was cut quite short on the sides but grew longer and thicker in the front, where he flipped the waves towards the back.

His lean body filled in the jeans the way the manufacturer must have planned for them to be worn when they were designed. Now she knew why she'd caught so many women's glances following him, yearning clear in their expressions. Something niggled at her about his face.

"If you're an American, where did you get those un-American-shaped eyes?"

It took him a while to answer. He made her wait, the silence drawn out. Finally he backed down, and his tone resumed its normal timbre. *"My mother is Hawaiian. They say I take after her."*

"They?"

"Everyone who knows us. I sure as heck don't take after the old man. He's pure Texas, and all male."

"Like your all-American he-man?"

A chuckle broke. "Yeah! Sort of."

"Your mother must be a gorgeous woman."

"I think so. Hold it! Is that a compliment?"

"Not bloody likely—you were born with those eyes, you didn't do anything for them. Therefore the fact that you're a good-looker shouldn't count."

"Good-looker! I hate being teased about how I look. Do you know how many noses I had to flatten to stop that kind of garbage when I was a kid? They soon changed it to Tough Guy. It suited my personality much better."

"So you do take after your, ah, old man."

"Yep! I guess I do." He chuckled, his voice husky with pride.

As Troy took his new garments to the cashier, Dani stopped him.

"Troy. Look at that green shirt, the one on the mannequin just there. You must buy it. Please, for me. It's the perfect colour for you."

"You think so, princess? Fine, I could use another one, and if it'll make you happy, then consider it done."

The stop at the busy pharmacy next door to buy a dog collar and lead earned him high marks. Dani's contentment spread. After his purchases were made, the dog collected and leashed, Troy stopped in the centre of the sidewalk.

"So are you going to keep your word and tell me where Ellie's parents live? It's time I earned my keep. I have to start writing the story I came for. It's why I'm here."

"Do you want to walk, or take the bus?"

"Will they let the pest here on the bus with me?"

"If you carry him, they might."

In no time they were in front of a showpiece home on a secluded lane. It was an elegant Victorian house with rampant ivy covering the walls. A spacious patio could be seen behind hedges, and plant groupings of red roses, purple rhododendrons, and darkish green holly bushes decorated the flagstone walkway. An old coach house stood isolated to one side of the acreage that made up the yard.

A blanket covered with a little girl's precious items lay spread on the spacious lawn in front. Dolls, stuffed toys, and pieces of a pink plastic tea set were strewn everywhere.

Smack dab in the middle of it all sat the small golden-haired imp he'd seen near the vicarage with the older couple the day before.

Troy stopped to look around him and absorb the picturesque scene. The freshly mown lawn leached the air with the fresh-cut smell known to anyone who'd done chores as a youngster. Troy spent a moment inhaling deep breaths and let the memories flood.

With his mind wandering, he didn't pay close attention to the inquisitiveness of a small puppy when he sees someone close to his own size. A wiggle, a circle, a yank, and the happy mutt escaped from his newly acquired collar.

Joyful yips warned the startled little girl that her play would soon be invaded. When she spied the puppy running her way, her arms opened in welcome.

It was love at first hug. Troy and Dani witnessed it together and both smiled—one inside, one out.

He approached slowly, looking around to see if there were other adults present. Watchful to see that the small child didn't show fear of a stranger coming into her space, he stopped in front of her.

He needn't have worried.

"Hello, sir. Is this your dog? What's his name? He's wonderful, isn't he?" In between the words, her tiny hands moved constantly, petting and hugging. Her laughter rang out as the pup's tongue, in rapid progression, worked his way over her face, stopping her from further speech. His shenanigans made her arch her head back and out of the way, while his plump body and scrambling feet climbed up her chest. His paws straddled her throat as if he wanted to embrace her.

Troy, hips cocked, hands in his pockets and head on one side, watched and laughed. His manly roars intermingled with the child's glee. He hunched down to be level with the little girl. She drew him as food would draw a starving animal.

Only he heard Dani's accompanying laughter diminish into sobs.

And then she faded.

What was that all about?

Chapter Ten

N urse Joye! You've arrived. Thank God! I do appreciate your speaking with me, since my brother hasn't returned my numerous calls. I've left message after message, all to no avail." With her voice breaking, the mother's tension filtered over the wire directly into the young nurse's soft heart.

"Mrs. Howard, the doctor feels terrible about his negligence, but he's under extreme pressure right now. He will update you as soon as possible. All I can say is there is no change since you last called. Your daughter is resting comfortably, and all necessary tests have been taken. She's sedated and has twenty-four-hour care."

Mrs. Dorn, leaning against the wall opposite the telephone table, nodded her head in agreement with the words she heard from Nurse Joye's side of the conversation.

The red silk scarf tied around the housekeeper's tightly permed hair had slipped a bit to one side, covering a portion of her forehead, and her flowered, smock-like dress fitted snugly—so snugly that an astute observer might consider she needed to get a larger size or she'd soon burst from the one she wore. Her chubby fingers, interlocked under her gigantic bosom, fidgeted—as if in nervous anticipation of being forced to take the receiver.

Nurse Joye, carefully keeping the unsightly blemish on the left side of her face hidden, smiled in the housekeeper's direction while listening to the fretful voice on the other end of the line. She waved away Mrs. Dorn's anxiety and watched as the heavy woman rolled her eyes.

"Yes, Mrs. Howard. I will ask him to call. Dani's lovely. It's my pleasure. Ta Ra!"

The housekeeper's sigh of relief was obvious as the young woman in white hung up the phone. "Nurse, if the doctor don't speak with her soon, I'll be going off me rocker. Iffen you ask me, the poor dear's got a right to know her daughter's in a coma. I'd want to be told, wouldn't you?"

"For some strange reason, Dr. Andrews is pretty sure that by Saturday Dani will become conscious again and will be fine after that. He's asked us to put Mrs. Howard off until then. How can we say no?"

"Perish the thought. I'd no more go against hisself's wishes than dance naked in Piccadilly Circus."

The picture her words made brought a smile to the face of Nurse Joye. Seconds later a giggle followed, and then a look of surprise. She didn't laugh very often.

"I doubt there'll be any reason to go that far, Mrs. Dorn."

"Yer right, but there's one thing I do know for sure. There'll be the mother of all rows if she ever finds out he's been fibbing her."

"I have no doubt the doctor knows what he's about, Mrs. Dorn. We're merely here to support him and to look after Dani."

"Yes, miss. By the way, the test results have arrived from hospital, and he told me I should pass them on to you as soon as ever they came."

A large brown envelope, previously propped up on the side of the table, changed hands.

Nurse Joye slipped out the pile of forms and looked them over as she walked towards the room housing her patient.

With a sudden muffled exclamation, her slender form stopped dead.

Flipping the pages back to the beginning to check the name on the envelope, she squeaked, coughed to cover it up, then much more slowly continued on her way.

Chapter Eleven

The local establishment pulsed that night, brimful of customers mingling, drinking, and carousing. Situated at the back of the room, the bar area, bordered on one side by stools full of half-sodden adults, was reflected in the mirrored wall behind. It looked to be very busy.

Upon his arrival, Troy spotted a man clumsily packing away his cigarettes and sweeping his money from the counter to his pocket in preparation to leave. Troy wasted no time in weaving his way through the packed tables to grab the empty chair.

Beatles music started up and blasted the eardrums; its discordant sounds intermingled with those of the noisy patrons. A jolt of pleasure struck his midsection, and the homesickness he'd battled since his arrival in Bury faded. When the initial smell of beer gave over to the stench of cigarette smoke, Troy relaxed, comfortable and at peace with the world.

His finger flicked, pointing at the glass in front of the bloke next to him, sufficient information for the blonde working the taps. She nodded, poured him a mug, and passed it over with a naughty wink. The first sip fulfilled his expectation. He groaned from pure pleasure.

"So this is what the inside of the pub looks like. I've wondered."

"Why would you care?"

"Being it's a sanctified adult area, all kids want to know what goes on here. Some of my mates got phony cards and tried to get in, but they were I.D.ed and thrown out."

"And so they should be. It's no place for youngsters."

"I'm a youngster. I'm here."

"Yeah! But you're with me, and if there's any nonsense going on you shouldn't see, I'll close my eyes."

Erupting giggles tickled him. He lowered his head and stared at the beer-foamed glass in his hand so no one could see the silly grin fighting to appear on his face.

Dani, the bane of his existence, made him laugh more than anyone else he'd ever known. And she was only sixteen years old.

"I'm not a child, you know. And I'm almost seventeen."

"So tell me, Miss Methuselah, how did you get inside me? Are you ever going to explain? I'm thinking to take out a long-term lease if you're planning to homestead."

She teased right back. *"You'll have to co-sign for me, 'cause I'm underage."*

"Whoa! I've never met anyone who can play the age game better than you. You're an adult when it suits you. On the other hand, reverting back to childhood when you feel the need doesn't bother you at all."

He loved hearing her cheeky laughter, but not nearly as much as he liked the warmth flooding over his internal self. Exuberance filled him, and he had to admit to getting hooked on the high.

"You are so easy, Troy. I'm gonna hate to leave you. But I guess I'll have to, since tomorrow's Saturday, and that's the day we'll be able to undo the switch. Right. Here goes—and don't interrupt, no matter how silly it seems. The fact is—well, it really is the rose bush."

"You're still trying to feed me that baloney. The rose bush! I thought we settled that subject. Next you'll be saying it's magical."

"It is." Her voice strongly emphasised the last word.

He filtered through his senses systematically. And was forced to accept one thing. She was telling the truth. A magic rose bush? *"Holy cow!"*

"According to my uncle's notes, if I understood them correctly, and I think I did, I read them twice and—"

"Dani…"

"Right! He'll have my body near his rose bush—the one I pricked my finger on, at precisely twelve noon each Saturday until the changeover occurs to get me back there. He'll prick my finger in hopes that you will also prick yours at the same time. He knows I'm aware of the magic and how it works, because he'll know I read all his notes about a similar case he investigated last year. I accidentally knocked them off his table, the notes that is, and probably didn't get them back in their correct order. It's what started this whole thing."

"And you're sure it'll happen?"

"No. But it's what I gathered from going through his papers, and it worked for two other women who had the same experience."

"Great! Tomorrow! We'll be there early."

****

He had hurt her feelings.

She shut herself off, hiding away so he couldn't feel the devastating ache that clutched at her and made her gasp. Tears, a physical reaction to release overwhelming pain, weren't available to her. Emotions too advanced for a young girl tore away rose-coloured glasses, wounding, maturing. Her almost seventeen-year-old psyche had started connecting to him in a way that confused her. Every moment she'd shared his life, little bits of her soul had shifted to him until there wasn't much left he didn't own.

She'd seen the flirty invitations in the eyes of other women, the smiles in response to his winking. Awareness of his good-looking exterior satisfied her superficial shallowness. The triviality of that upset her, but only a little.

His loving nature, the person inside, had watered the seeds of affection she'd begun to feel. And his gentleness had nurtured those sentiments into a full-blown infatuation.

The fact that their time together was limited and becoming shorter with every passing moment obviously bothered him not at all.

It was a blow to realize that. While she suffered at the thought of leaving him, her imminent vacating of the premises pleased him—the simple-minded jerk. For her, the looming separation tore at her heartstrings, leaving it wide open, exposing a ghastly emptiness that terrified.

His chuckle caught her attention.

The blonde bartender, in her too-tight, too-low, peasant-styled blouse, had leaned over the counter, providing an eyeful to anyone who watched. Jiggles of flesh accompanied each movement, dragging the eyes exactly where she intended for them to go. Fluttering her overly made-up, gooey-blues at Troy and studiously wiping the wet surface, she pointed her red-tipped finger at the empty mug in front of him. Troy, no different from every other male in the vicinity, tore his gaze from the public display of her bosoms, lifted it to her face, then grinned and nodded.

"You fancy her?" The words poured from Dani before she could close off the spout.

"What's wrong with her? She's very attractive."

"Don't be daft! She's a mite too sluttish for my liking, she is."

"What's with the strong accent all of a sudden?"

"You caught me unaware. I wasn't paying attention for a few minutes, and you go and get into…oh, never mind."

"I go and get into what?"

"Mischief! That's what! Does every woman you meet give you the green light, encourage you, fawn over you?"

"Pretty much. I like women. Nothing wrong with that. You're a woman. Don't you think I should respond positively to the overtures of friendship these ladies dispense so flatteringly?"

For a short time his using the term *"woman"* in describing her stopped her tirade, but not for long. *"Flatter-… They bloody drool over you. It's sickening, is what it is. You should be ashamed."*

"Aw, sweetheart. I'm only teasing you. Look, I'm a friendly kinda guy. Nothing wrong with that, is there? But I'm pretty choosey when it comes to whom I date and when."

A sickening sensation hit her all at once. "Is there someone in your life now, at home, in Chicago?"

"Nope, just me hanging with a lot of good buddies. I've been more than friends with a few great gals, but with me being away so often, they get bored and find someone who sticks around. Lately, I've been spending most of my time with the newspaper crowd in Chicago. I guess it's why I want a desk job in the industry. I've been freelancing for too many years."

"Are you an investigative reporter?"

"Uh-huh! After a couple years in college, I couldn't stop the restlessness from taking over and decided to get my learning on the streets. I pick a topic of interest involving a specific crime, or ongoing political corruption, or even a possible scandal, and I write an exposé that can take months to work on. I've been in so many different countries I've had to add a back page in my passport. Hiding, being undercover, seeing the meanness and dishonesty in the world has all but left me burnt out. It's time I settled down in one place to build my career."

"You're a truth bloodhound."

"I've never heard it put quite like that before, but I guess it's better than being called a nosy pri-, er, jerk. After I got shot during my last sojourn in a country not my home, writing about a story that wasn't based on my own people, I took it as a sign—time to go stateside and stay there. Since then I've been hanging around the city, until this story about Ellie Ward broke. I knew it could be the one to put me behind a desk at the Chicago Sun-Times. I had to get it at all costs, even if it meant travelling again."

"You were shot? Where?"

"In Thailand…"

"Not that where—where in your body? It must've hurt something wicked."

"In my shoulder, and yes—it did hurt something wicked. But I got a great story, so I'm not complaining about a little scratch."

"You love the business, don't you? I can feel that radiating throughout your system every time anything to do with journalism comes into our conversation."

Before he could answer, a man sitting at a table just behind them cussed at the fellow next to him. Fists swung and glasses flew everywhere.

"Oh, oh! Time to get you outta here." He started to rise.

"Don't hurry on my account. I'm sure they'll sort things out. Remember, an author needs to experience every aspect of life if she wants to be able to write convincingly."

"Not sixteen-year-old authors."

"Almost seventeen!"

Wavering on the stool next to him, an old drunk grabbed Troy's arm. "Aye, there, hang on, mate, what's yer hurry? They'll settle down."

Troy released the gripping fingers by lowering his shoulder and leaning back on his stool. The spittle from his neighbour, now out of range, sprayed the bar instead.

"Hey, pal, time for me to call it a night. It's been a long day." Troy made as if to rise again but hesitated, knowing his answering grin gave the fellow a green light to carry on.

"Cor! You're a Yank. I need ta buy you a pint. Me brother's a dockworker in America, and he's always blithering on about his cushy job and his mates. Says they're a fine bunch of lads, he does."

"Where is your brother living?"

"In the United States."

"There are fifty of them, which one does he live in?"

"Fifty what?"

"States. Is he in the eastern part of the country or in the west?"

Grinning slyly, the balding man slapped his hand down hard on the wooden surface in front of him. "He's in the state of Baltimore."

Beginning to enjoy himself, Troy settled back down and nodded when the blonde bartender's eyebrow rose. "Baltimore is a city. It's in the state of Maryland. Your brother's lucky—it's a beautiful city."

"Who's in Maryland? What's a beautiful city? I don't know is on third." The chap even looked a bit like Abbott—or was it Costello?

Troy laughed, lifted his mug at the twinkle-eyed sot next to him, and settled in for a visit.

An hour later Troy made his way to his room, knowing his four-legged friend would be expecting a walk and a treat to nibble, if preceding evenings were any indication of their nightly routine.

It was during the walk that Dani finally spoke up.

"You stayed to talk with that inebriated old boozer. Why? He was obnoxious."

"No! Not obnoxious, honey, just lonely. He needed to talk."

Oh, God! She was going to miss him!

Chapter Twelve

Nurse Joye followed Dr. Andrews into their young patient's room. "Did you get the results from the second set of tests yet, Doctor?" She eyed him, noting the shattered look on his face when reminded of the first test's results. With hands clasped tightly, she waited.

"No, my dear. Nothing so far. I'm sure there's an error in the earlier ones we received, a mix-up of names, or some such nonsense." He moved closer to Dani. Unaware of the turmoil those around her suffered, she lay solitary, uncaring—comatose.

Flattened curls diminished the size of her face, leaving her features starkly pronounced. The few tiny freckles sprinkled across her straight nose had become more noticeable, enhanced by the paleness of her skin. Even her cheeks, translucent in the dim light from the small blue bedside lamp, looked overwhelmed by the long auburn lashes. The whiteness of the pillowcase, a crude frame, reminded all who saw her that she lay in her sickbed.

Doctor Andrews gently lifted the hand not attached to the intravenous tubing and smoothed her skin before he took her pulse. To give him privacy, Nurse Joye walked to the window overlooking the garden. She opened it, letting in the fresh air to billow the sheer ivory lace curtains.

From force of habit, she kept her face carefully angled as she approached the bed. Her trained eye surveyed the sparkling-clean room, double-checking her housekeeping efforts. The antique brass bedstead gleamed from constant polishing, and the faint hint of the air freshener she'd used earlier lingered and added to the fresh smell. The large vase of garden flowers, reflected in the dresser's mirror, gave her pleasure and brightened the otherwise melancholic atmosphere. Visually, the room presented a pleasant scene, but emotionally it radiated anxiety.

"She's doing as well as can be expected, Nurse." Doctor Andrews stepped back from his patient and lowered his bulk to sprawl in the rocking chair next to the bed. With his elbows resting on each wooden arm, the tips of his fingers met together to form a tower that covered most of his face. He rocked, closed his eyes, and sighed, the noise loud in the otherwise silent room.

Nurse Joye moved near and patted his shoulder, concern apparent in her gentleness. She admired Dr. Andrews and had always appreciated his chivalrous manner for her delicate sensibilities over the large, unsightly birthmark on her left cheek. He invariably remembered to place himself so he faced her right side, and he never forced her to make eye contact for an overly long period.

"Would you like to tell me what the real truth is about Dani, Robert? I'm most terribly sorry for her condition, but I know there's something, well, strange going on, and since I trust you implicitly, I haven't asked. Maybe it would make you feel better to share, and I'm happy to listen."

"You've been wonderful, Grace. My sister might not know how lucky we were that you were available, but I do." He hummed another sigh, long and low. "I could tell you the truth, but then you'd likely think me bonkers and have me institutionalized." His weak smile and heavy grunt contained enough sadness that she quickly admonished him.

"Doctor, you are one of the sanest, most competent men I have ever worked with in your field. If there is something unorthodox going on, then I'd wager it isn't because of a lack of skill on your part."

"No, it has nothing to do with me. Actually, it's about a case that Dr. John Norman brought to my attention a few years back. We collaborated to help a young woman in a strange, very uncommon…umm, rather difficult situation." Not being a man who normally had trouble expressing himself, his hesitation in choosing his words sparked her interest.

"I know John. He's a good doctor."

"Yes, he is. We handled that particular case with positive results, and since then there have been similar incidents that have popped up. Look, I'll give you my personal notes and various reports to read, but I must be able to rely on your discretion."

He didn't trust her? Dismay attacked until she noticed the stark anxiety on her mentor's face. The poor man hadn't slept well for days and wasn't himself. Her sympathy split the bonds of friendship wide enough to let devotion settle in.

He admonished himself at once. "What am I saying? Of course you're trustworthy. I'm sorry, Grace. I'm that worried about my niece, I forgot for a moment who I was talking to."

"Doctor, you know I'd never let you down." The shock in her voice fractured his last vestige of resistance.

"If Dr. Norman weren't on holidays, I'd call him in, but he and Lucy, his wife, are on a cruise and can't be reached. Therefore, your help in dealing with this situation could be critical to a successful outcome. I'll go and get the case notes, then leave you to study them in peace. But when you're finished, I have no doubt we'll have a lot to discuss. Trust me, Grace, and keep in mind that I'm not insane."

She smiled, thinking he intended to tease.

He stopped at the doorway, his back to her, his palm clasping the handle. She waited, and for the first time in the years she'd known and admired him, she noticed his shoulders were stooped and his movements stiff.

The tension so apparent in the troubled man now attacked her also. Uneasiness, like a shroud, encircled her. Silence reverberated. Then he opened the door and stepped forward, letting it close behind him with a soft thud.

****

Dr. Andrews hurried from the sick room straight to his office, aiming for the locked bottom drawer where his most critically important files were stored. But first he plonked down in his leather chair and took a few minutes simply to breathe.

Grace Joye had the distinction of being the best nurse he'd ever known, a natural who'd adopted the career God had put her on the earth to do. The perfect match! A girl with a big, soft heart looking after the sick and the sad in the world. The injured, desperate for a gentle touch, cared little about the cruel twist fate had played on her face. By putting his trust in her, the pressure would be halved. That alone would be a marvellous help.

He shuffled the mess on his desk and double-checked the calendar. Tomorrow was Saturday. He had no choice but to let her in on the secret. At exactly noon, he'd need her to help him with Dani's body at the rosebush. If naught transpired... God forbid. He'd be a basket case. The thought of dealing with his sister for another week generated such panic that he felt his stomach recoil. Quickly he dug in his drawer for the bottle of antacids.

Having Grace as his accomplice would be even more vital should Dani remain in the coma. And if the second set of test results proved the first ones correct, Dani would eventually need as many supporters in her corner as possible. Good grief! Just thinking about that scared him into a state of pure misery. On the other hand, could it by why she'd needed to talk to him so desperately?

The ringing phone shocked him out of his meditation and back into the present hellish situation. Reflex forced his hand to lift the receiver before the warnings, nattering in his brain, kicked in. Aggrieved by his carelessness, he nevertheless feigned pleasure.

"Hello, my dear. Yes, I'm glad you caught me, also."

His sigh, the loudest yet today, resonated.

"No, I didn't moan, Marion. The desk drawer sticks and makes an awful racket."

Chapter Thirteen

Dew embellished the grass with a million diamonds, while the birds sang their songs to welcome Troy as he stepped from the inn and filled his lungs.

'We didn't need to leave this early to get to the vicarage bench. I've a strange feeling you're a bit keen to get rid of me.'

Since their time was coming to an end soon, Troy chose not to hurt her feelings. His natural instincts of gallantry and his basic impulse to be nice, to reassure, kicked in.

'Look, brat, I'll give you the straight goods. You've been very considerate about my privacy, not bugging me all the time, and I appreciate it.'

'So all the whistling and smiling means you're only having me on!'

'I wouldn't go that far, kiddo.' Outright lying didn't sit easy with him, and anyway she'd know. How she did it, he couldn't be sure, but she seemed to know most of what he felt. If he lied, guilt, the emotion he most disliked, would attack, and he had no doubt, she'd call him on it.

From as far back as he remembered fibbing registered as the worst sin in his family. They were big on punishment for the offence. He'd learnt early that his nose might not grow but his backside would surely be blistered.

'I don't lie, either. Or hardly ever. It can be tricky not to hurt feelings and still stay out of trouble.'

'Tell me about it!'

He sauntered along the sidewalk, aiming to hit the little pub, just a street over, that made the best breakfast in town.

Eggs, bacon, sausages, fried bread, mushrooms, and baked beans would sit well with him this fine morning.

Sometime later an astonished Dani commented, "I don't know how you can eat all that food and not gain weight. You must be lucky."

"I come from good genes. No one in my family has a weight problem. Plus, I never stop moving. Guess I'm a bit hyperactive, if the truth be known."

"Me, too. Drives my mum round the bend. Where are we going?"

"Time to head over to the vicarage, my little roomie, and wait for the moment of truth."

"You still don't believe me about the bush?"

"Since it's all we have to go on, I'm pretty well forced to." He felt vibes of frustration jangling throughout his system and smiled. "Okay, settle down. Let's just say…"

In the distance a scream split the balmy morning atmosphere. Other screams and yells joined in until ignoring the noise became impossible. Troy lowered his head and listened. Drifting whiffs of smoke grabbed his attention.

Swivelling towards the sounds, he started off at a run. Black billows stained the blue sky above and turned the white fluffy clouds to a horrible grey. From a block away he could smell the stench of a burning building, and the closer he got, the more it intensified. Many others ran with him, all having the same goal in mind.

Fear, obvious on their faces, caught him up in its tentacles. Utterances of "Oh, my Lord!", "What in the world!" and "Call for help!" added to the catastrophic tone.

"Oh, no! It's the Kingsly boarding house that's on fire. Troy, it's mostly full of seniors." Dani's horror was obvious.

On approach, the place looked like a huge, older-style mansion, but the sign in front boasted rooms for rent and, in smaller letters, *Home Care.*

Smoke streamed from the dormer windows of the upper story, and flames burst free from the confines of the roof, where sections of tiles exploded and plunged down into the interior. Bits of sooty debris shot out like blackened hailstones.

Troy could taste the grit on his lips, and he blinked to clear his irritated eyes. The stench of fear and fire intermingled. Heat seared his skin, warning that the monster had taken over—it had control.

People, some still in their nightclothes, poured out the double front doors, a few walking on their own while others used walkers, canes or caring shoulders.

Aged victims shuffled along like lost souls. Others, less fortunate, were in wheelchairs lined up on the sidewalk; bodies dumped without care, hanging every which way, many close to falling over.

Troy scanned the scene and felt his horror merge with Dani's. Her whispered words jabbed his heart. *"My God, these poor, poor people."*

One woman, tears flowing, screamed for someone to help find her cat. Still others zigzagged over the grass, calling names of friends and loved ones. Neighbourhood children intermingled amongst the adults, creating more chaos. Barking dogs added to the overall confusion. A black mutt gave chase to a frenzied kitten, stopping at the bottom of freedom's tree to whine at the escapee.

A white-haired man, wobbly, confused, and crying, called for Mary, over and over. His eyes streamed from a mixture of smoke and tears, and his hand knuckled to try and clear away the wetness. He searched every which way until, overcome, the poor fellow crumpled to his knees, falling directly in Troy's path.

Troy felt Dani's sympathy. It overwhelmed, cutting through his insides, slashing any resistance he might have felt about stopping to help the poor old guy.

As he leaned over to support the elderly grandpa, Dani spoke before he had a chance to even form the words.

"Sir, let me help you. Are you hurt?" Gentleness rang in tones not quite his.

"Me missus, she went to the laundry room to do the wash. I can't find her. I don't know if she got out." Sobs blocked his ability to speak further. His trembling hands sought the strong ones helping him, as if by touch he could convey his torment.

"Where is the laundry room?" Troy took over, his tones firm, unruffled, intense.

"In the basement, sir. There's an outside entrance."

"Can you show me where it is?"

"Yes, sir." Getting to his feet with difficulty but perseverance, the man held to Troy's arm and shuffled across the driveway to the side of the house. He pointed his finger at a small, veiled door, hidden by bushes and nowhere near the congested area. "It will be through this entrance, at the end of the hallway, first door on the left. But this way's always kept locked."

"Stay here and wait for us—uh, me." Troy led the elderly man to a large boulder out of the danger zone and helped him sit down. With a glance at the nearby bed of flowers, he spotted a sizable rock that filled the palm of his hand. He approached the door the old man had pointed out and smashed his weapon through the glass, then reached inside to undo the lock.

"Mary! Mary!" Dani's words echoed in Troy's voice. "Where are you? Mary?" Calling forced deeper breathing, and the deadly air soon claimed victory. Dani stopped.

Clouds of smoke mushroomed, becoming thicker, drawn by the fresh oxygen from the open door. Troy took off his green shirt, wrapped it over the lower half of his face, and put his sunglasses on to protect his eyes. The instant gloom made vision difficult, but since he knew his destination, he didn't hesitate. He lurched forward, making his way directly towards the laundry room.

The noise of the fire was much louder here and much more frightening than from outside the building. The sounds of collapsing walls, shattering glass, and roaring flames blasted his eardrums. Smaller explosions nearby urged him to hurry. When the sky outside the one small window darkened and blackened clouds began to obscure his precious light, Troy knew he had very little time.

Before he reached the end of the hall, he nearly tripped over the body of an older woman sprawled at an awkward angle across the floor. Without the meagre light from that tiny overhead window, Troy would certainly never have seen her.

He dropped to his hands and knees beside the white-haired lady where she lay next to a heap of cloth. Lowering his glasses, he got really close. Blood streamed from a cut on her forehead. Ashen, blue-veined skin scared him into checking for a pulse.

"Troy, she's alive. My God, the poor dear is dreadfully pale. We'll have to take care. Can you carry her?"

Breathing was becoming more difficult for Troy. He tried to take shallow breaths so he wouldn't cough or draw smoke into his already afflicted lungs. *"I don't think so. It's difficult breathing, and if I try to stand and pick her up, I'm scared we'll be overcome. Dani, I don't know what the hell I was thinking, bringing you in here, taking such a crazy chance with your life."*

"Give over. I wanted to come. How could we ignore the old bloke's grief? We have to save her. For him. But I don't think we can drag her. She's bleeding a lot and her leg's angled strangely. What can we do?"

With sudden realization, Troy saw that the soft heap pooled on the floor by Mary was a quilt. He scooted over, grabbed it, and flipped it across the prone body, then awkwardly rolled the woman into a cocoon and onto her back in seconds. Now fully enclosed in a pink-flowered shroud, she became easier to move. By grabbing one end and twisting it, he could haul it over his shoulder. Then he crawled, slithered, and wiggled, with the blanket skid bringing up the rear.

Flames burst from a room on his right, encouraging him to move even faster. The tail end of the quilt flapped open, sliding through red embers. Like a tease, a flame caught, only to fizzle out again. The open door loomed about ten feet ahead. Choking, gagging, hot tears pouring from his eyes, he found in Dani the encouragement and strength that kept him going.

"Troy, love, almost there. You're wonderful. My God! You're fantastic. Don't stop now. Here's the door. You've done it! I love you, you ruddy great darling, do you hear me?"

"I hear you. You're screaming so loud it's a wonder I'm not deaf. Couldn't have done it without you, and I'm rather fond of you too, brat."

Gnarled waiting hands helped Troy pull his precious cargo through the last foot of the hallway and over the sill. The sobbing entreaties that had coaxed the exhausted young man through the final effort of the rescue stopped as he collapsed—his strength gone, used up, depleted.

Troy lay face down on the cool grass, concentrating on controlling his breathing by pure will power. Coughing hurt, so he took small breaths and swallowed repeatedly, trying to bring moisture into his dry throat.

Cradled in loving arms, Mary soon came around. She looked up into the rheumy eyes of her man, and she smiled. "There ya are, you old tosser." The words, whispered in a voice raw and grating, produced a relieved smile.

Hearing her speak, Troy scuttled over to where the old couple were cuddled together. As he approached, two sets of streaming, red-rimmed eyes peered his way. The old man reached out to Troy's cheek and patted as one would a child.

"God love ya, sir!"

Chapter Fourteen

D r. Andrews, nervous and prayerful, checked his watch once more. Nurse Joye flashed him a sympathetic look. The minutes sped by, showing twelve and then twelve-oh-one and twelve-oh-two. They'd pricked the girl's finger more than once, but nothing had happened. Dani's body remained lax, supported on both sides, filling the space between them. Apprehension, like a living entity, surrounded the bench in the doctor's garden.

Dani's curls, free in the breeze, bounced around her head, the golden-red spirals wild and unbound. Dr. Andrews brushed them away from her face, his hand noticeably shaking.

"Confound it, Grace, I'm most terribly sorry, but it doesn't look as if she's returning to us this week."

Unknown to those on the bench, Mrs. Dorn had hovered behind the fern plant that somewhat blocked the doorway. Eyes gaping, ears tuned to catch every word, with both hands covering her mouth, she had waited. When she heard the doctor's admission, her left foot stamped down hard, and then her right followed as she danced out her temper. "Bloody hell," she whispered, and headed to her kitchen and the hidden bottle of gin she kept under the sink.

"It's just not working. I know you think I'm quite mad, my dear, and I don't blame you, but I truly believe she will return to us, and in this exact manner."

"Since no one else has come up with a solid reason for why this girl is in the state she's in, and after reading your reports on the other vicarage bench cases, I'm inclined to put my faith in you, Doctor. We can carry on this week and try again next Saturday."

"Thank you, Grace. You realize these next few days will test the patience of all of us. My sister is getting more demanding every day. She's determined to come and see her daughter, and I can't say I blame her. My only hope is to keep playing on my "uncle" status, along with my professional credentials. If we can convince her to leave Dani where she is and not interfere for just one more week, chances are good that the girl will reappear next Saturday. If she doesn't, then I'll have to gi-gi-give over and admit my duplicity."

Grace reached to pat his arm, lending unspoken support.

Depressed and shaken, his mind wandered. He revisited the gut-wrenching feelings he'd had as a lad at boarding school, waiting hours for the headmaster when they caught him smoking. He'd had the same sick feeling in his stomach then as he did now. While rubbing his chest, he reached to the inside pocket of his vest for his medicine. The amount of heartburn medication he'd used just this past week was more than he'd used in the whole previous year. And from the looks of it, he'd have to buy a couple more bottles to have on hand.

"Doctor, I'm sure your sister wouldn't blame you if the truth were made known to her. How could she?"

All colour left his face. He squinted, hesitated, then swallowed another mouthful from the small brown bottle. "The fact is, she would not only blame me but hold me in contempt for trying to feed her hogwash about a magic rose bush." How could he ever explain his family's dynamics to an outsider?

Marion, at ten years of age, had decided that her new baby brother would be her special responsibility, and no one could dissuade her. She took over his care while he still wore diapers. His mother, thinking it was adorable the way her oldest daughter played at being his mummy, and having three others to take care of, stepped aside and let her have her way. The girl literally became his warden—so much so that he was probably the only fellow in his campus who had looked forward to the end of holidays and returning to school. Marion's uncanny knack of seeing through his nonsense, trapping him in lies, and cutting him off at the knees still had the power to render him speechless.

With his right hand he rubbed the back of his neck as he arched his spine. This week would be pure hell.

Chapter Fifteen

"T *roy, quit sulking! You can't blame me that we missed our twelve o'clock deadline. I didn't start the fire. And you know we couldn't leave the old man alone after they took Mary and the others to the hospital in the ambulance. We had no choice. With the shape he was in, we had to go in the taxi with him. Anyway, you wanted to come as much as I did."*

"Dani, please, just—shut up!"

"Why am I not surprised? Every time something happens you don't like, you tell me to shut my trap. Now that's grown up, isn't it? An educated world traveller such as yourself showing the younger, less sophisticated person how to react in stressful moments. I'll be taking notes, for sure."

"Dani, I'm warning you. Fade, go away, leave me alone to deal, or you're liable to get an inside scoop on what a grown man looks like throwing a temper tantrum any two-year-old would envy."

"Rolling on the ground, beating your fists, and screaming at the top of your lungs? Now that's something I'd stick around for."

"You're incorrigible."

"I like to think so."

"And a brat!"

"Uh-huh!"

"And a royal pain in the ass."

"Cussing? You are ticked. I'll forgive you. Being a royal anything to a Brit is rather pleasing."

"Oh, shut up!"

"I believe we already covered that. Considering you're a reporter, your use of the English language leaves a lot to be desired, my man."

"I am not your man." Abrupt words spoken in a clipped inner voice.

"I beg to differ." The smirk showed in her tone.

"You know you're really beginning to get on my nerves."

"My cue! I'll be here when you're in a better mood."

"Don't hold your—my—breath!"

Dani loved squaring off with Troy. By fencing words with her, he treated her with the same respect he'd give an equal. Plus, his sense of humour fit well with hers. She didn't constantly have to bite her tongue, or in this instance curb her thoughts.

Knowing she'd be forced to spend this next week with him made her happier than she could ever remember. Her feelings for him were changing, growing stronger, and this would give her time to try and understand what they all meant. When she'd told him she loved him, as they'd rescued Mary, the words had resonated with an honesty that needed to be explored.

She'd messed up at home and knew she had a load of bother to face, knew it wouldn't go away. But still, she felt as if fate had stepped in to give her seven more days of sanity.

Until recently, she'd abided by the rules, lived under her mother's strict regime, and found her own avenues to enjoy life through her writing and her friends. Her uncle played a big role in her day-to-day existence, being there for her whenever she had a need to let loose. Her father also ranked high on her list of people with whom she most liked to spend quality time. They enjoyed many a wonderful day together, often going to London to see shows followed by treats of restaurant meals and unlimited shopping.

But none of them had ever made her as happy as Troy. Being a part of him, watching and evaluating his behaviour, helped her to truly "get" the person inside. And that person was lovely. Not a mean or thoughtless bone in his body.

How could she ever want to leave him? She'd never before felt so safe.

On every occasion when he'd asked about her background or tried to trick her into telling him about her home, she'd refused to reveal any information whatsoever. Fearing he would want to investigate her private life, she knew she couldn't allow that to happen. She was quite aware of the time jump she'd made, and her relationship to the people he'd met in Bury so far. However, if he found out her secret, that she was, in reality, Ellie Ward—or would be in ten years using that name as her pseudonym—and that she was the very woman he'd come so far to interview, he'd never forgive her for not telling him.

Yet if she admitted what she knew, everything would change. And since she had no idea of what was going to happen in her future, because for her it hadn't even happened yet, it wasn't as if she could tell him anything about the incident in Chicago anyway. Gosh, just thinking about it gave her a headache.

Naughty—yes, definitely. And a little unkind—maybe, but she wanted this next week. She could help him with his job, if he'd let her. What a grand opportunity to learn how a successful writer works and thinks. As long as he approved, she'd absorb every nuance of his skills that he would share.

Lastly, she knew he had laughed it off when she teased about having a crush on him, but in all truth she felt quite sappy over the good-looking bloke. Every minute she spent lodged inside with his wonderful spirit was, to her, total bliss.

****

Troy threw away the mangled rose—it hadn't had any effect on him whatsoever—and jerked upright from the vicarage bench. He stood for a moment, hands on hips, legs wide and head down, thinking. He'd argued with Dani that they needed to try to reverse the spell despite being late, but she had been right. It hadn't worked. She was still with him, and he fumed about wasting the time. What a fool's errand! Niggling doubts entered his mind, questioning whether or not she knew what she was talking about, but since he had nothing else to go on, no one else to ask, he'd have to trust her. He stomped back in the direction of the hospital.

Anger festered, but only a little. It was the worry that bothered him more. He worried about her family and the fears they must be suffering with their Dani in a coma. If only she'd tell him something about herself, so he'd be able to contact them and assure them that…what? That she still existed? That she'd taken up residence inside of him for a while? Okay, maybe not such a good idea. Especially since she'd be no help at all. It was clear to him that this setback pleased her.

He'd felt her relief when the magic hadn't taken, sensed she was keeping something from him but knew she had no intentions of sharing her secrets just yet. And did he really want to hear them? Getting more involved didn't seem like a smart move.

Maybe he needed to step back, but then again, in their circumstances wouldn't that be a mite difficult? He knew she'd developed a schoolgirl crush on him. What scared him silly was that, without meaning to, he'd begun to feel quite attached to her, also. What a mess!

Another week of living with her would try his restraint to the limit. She could be very engaging, and he'd never had anyone look up to him the way she did, or make him feel tall as a mountain, either, for that matter. He liked it. Who wouldn't, for goodness sake? He was a softie who'd never had much time for romance and sometimes felt cheated in that part of his life.

Of course, he'd had lady friends; what decent-looking guy his age hadn't? But that's all they were. Women. Linked together in one word. No one stood out from the others, because he hadn't let his feelings become involved. With Dani, he'd had no choice. She fit him so perfectly that he'd begun to rely on her being there, inside him, a part of him.

Oh, God! What in holy hell was he thinking? She was a seventeen-year-old virgin. He was a man of the world, more than ten years older. This was crazy. As hard as it would be to stop his fantasies, he had to. What if she zeroed in on his thoughts? Then where would he be?

He needed to concentrate on his work. Being broke upset him daily. The thought of having to call his brothers to pitch in and get him out of this fix was enough to make him break out in hives. He'd be suffering their teasing at every family gathering for years.

Not gonna happen!

Add all that to the fact he still didn't have the story he'd come to England for, and it became understandable that his disposition wasn't the best. Time to get to work and stop mooning around over his little soul mate.

His plans for the next few days were simple. Visit with the victims of the fire to get their stories. Then find Ellie Ward and get her to talk with him. He shoved his hands in his pockets and swivelled his neck from side to side, stretching his muscles. Aggravation rode him hard.

Who knew his life could become so complicated in just a short while? One day a single bachelor without a care in the world, following a great lead—the next, a broke, botched-the-job reporter with an adopted puppy and invaded by a mystical, endearing, demon teenager. What the hell was that all about?

****

Hospital noises swirled in the background as soon as he entered the old building. Various voices over the PA system called for specific doctors and nurses. Cries of children, groans of adults, and the commotion that exists inside every ER clamoured all around him. A lone floorwasher aimlessly swiped at the grey tiles with a wet mop, stopping every so often to dunk the dirty strands back into the pail of water nearby. Cleaning agents overpowered most of the other smells, but pain and fear had their own scent that nothing could cover.

Unembellished heartbreak, screamed in an old woman's voice, perked up his ears. His reporter genes kicked in. Glancing around, he saw a multitude of stories hovering everywhere. They called out to him—to the part of him that was full of questions aching to be asked.

Wanting to understand.

Needing to learn.

The folks who had endured tragedies today were chock full of painful anecdotes waiting to come to light and be shared, and he was just the person to collect them. Local papers normally bought freelance work if it ranked high in quality and interest, and his work had placed among some of the best. Articles on behind-the-scenes action, special coverage, and stories of the heart always sold.

He evaluated his interviewing prospects. Grandpa, who'd introduced himself in the taxi as Edmund Conway, would be his introduction into the piece. In this specific review, Troy could add a lot of background filler, thanks to being a part of the action himself. Descriptions from others were fine, but having had a first-hand view of the tragedies at the fire would help big-time. Experiencing the feeling of fear, the heat of the blaze and the atmosphere from inside the burning building would bring a special kind of reality to his writing.

He found Edmund resting in the visitor's room, praying and waiting to hear the doctor's diagnosis on Mary. His head of messy white hair leaned against the back of the sofa, while his eyes stared at the empty grey ceiling. Low murmured prayers, whispered in a raw voice, could be heard if one took the time to listen. Troy sat next to the old fellow and put his hand over the ones clenched and trembling. As soon as Edmund looked over and saw Troy, he started to babble. His worries came across in his words, and his fear came through in the way he clutched Troy's hand.

Compassion struck just as it always did when Troy faced the heartbreak and terror of others. He decided now might be just the perfect moment to take Edmund's mind off what had happened earlier. He'd query the fellow and get him to reminisce—good medicine for a worried soul. Besides, it would be necessary background for the piece he'd be writing.

Dani returned just then. "Troy, you're not serious? How can you even think of questioning him at a time like this? It's—it's indecent."

He not only heard Dani's horror—he felt it. She opened herself up to him completely, and he experienced her instinctive shock. Her repugnance created a sickness in his stomach that forced his muscles to tighten and the saliva to build up in his mouth. Sadness swept over his spirit, and he had to blink repeatedly to stop the sensation from overflowing to leave traces on his cheeks.

"Hey, little girl, hold on there. I'll not hassle the old guy; I'll just get him to talk. Dani, it's my job."

"Have some sensitivity. He's worried sick about his wife. He doesn't need anyone badgering at him now."

"Folks will want to read about what happened. They have a right to know more than bare facts. They care about people—people like Mary and Edmund. It's my job to help them see the individuals

involved in the tragedy, not just an old building that burned down. Try and understand?"

"Don't the victims have rights also, like their right to privacy during such a painful time?"

"Look, sweetheart, you have to have faith in my integrity. This is my job, what I do for a living, and I'm good at it. Trust me!"

"I do—but promise me you'll be careful."

He sighed.

He waited, not saying a word. He felt her re-assessing, thoughts speeding through with an astuteness that surprised him, made him proud. Seconds built into a minute, and still—he didn't speak.

"Sorry! I do trust you, ever so much."

"Thank you."

An hour later, an hour in which Troy took copious notes, the bustling doctor arrived in front of Troy and Edmund with the good news.

"Edmund, Mary wrenched her ankle quite severely and sustained mainly first-degree burns. The smoke inhalation at her age worries us somewhat, but the main reason we're keeping her in hospital is because she was unconscious at the time of rescue. There's some minor pain from the knock on her head, and we'd like her to stay here with us under observation. If you'd like to remain with her, you'd be welcome. She's fretting for you, so whenever you're ready, come to Room 201."

Edmund had reached for the doctor's hand at the beginning of his speech and never did let it go until the younger man kindly put his arm around the old fellow and began to lead him to Mary's room. Troy followed to peek in on her himself.

Still in shock from the disaster of losing everything, and unnerved from her close call with death, the pale old woman lay swathed in a white hospital gown, with a bandage the same colour wrapped around her head.

Physically, her condition looked better than some of the others he'd seen in the hallways and on stretchers. All in all, it was excellent news for the Conways, at least about Mary's health. But what about their home?

Everything Troy gleaned from Edmund's ramblings pointed to one conclusion. All the inhabitants of the Kingsly boarding house had co-existed for years, living as a large, extended family. They'd shared with each other through thick and thin, good times and bad. Now disaster had struck, and nothing could be worse. They would be homeless, many without funds to help themselves, without relatives to take them in.

"My God, Troy! Whatever are they going to do? These poor people need someone to come to their aid!"

Chapter Sixteen

I jolly well know it's been a week, Mrs. Howard, but Dani is still not recovered from the rash. The doctor says as long as she has them sores, she's infectious."

"I know what my brother says, Mrs. Dorn. I still insist on speaking to Daniell. I doubt if I'll catch anything over the phone." The acid in her voice seemed to burn through the wires.

Yanking the receiver away from her ear, Mrs. Dorn exploded in a violent whisper, her hand over the mouthpiece. "Bloody hell! The stupid cow never lets up!"

The agitated mother to whom she referred didn't hear the housekeeper spout off and demanded her attention once more.

"Mrs. Dorn? Hel-lo? Are you still there?"

"Hang on, luv. I dropped something. Now, what were you saying? Oh, yes, you wanted to talk to Dani. She can't talk to you, as you very well know. It were the doctor's idea to keep her doped up to stop her scratching, and if you ask me, it was a smashing idea." Agitation was evident in her words, but her slippered foot kicking the wall emphasized it.

Roused by the thumping, Nurse Joye stayed secreted behind the slightly opened sickroom door while spying on the conversation. She hung back until she grasped that her help was vital, then revealed herself and sped toward the frustrated woman by the black wall phone in the hallway.

Mrs. Dorn looked up at the nurse and grimaced. The small red knob at the end of her nose stood out grotesquely, and her narrowed eyes snapped with indignation. Obviously at the end of her tether, Mrs. Dorn needed rescuing.

"I'm most annoyed with my brother, to tell you the truth, Mrs. Dorn. I don't see why he can't keep her conscious long enough for me to have a proper conversation with her. I've asked around at the hospital, checked with my friends, even enquired at my doctor's office, and so far no one has been able to tell me a thing about this so-called virus. I shan't be put off much longer. I'm very concerned."

"Iffen you ask me—"

Nurse Joye plucked the phone from Mrs. Dorn's hand and put it behind her own back while she waited for the larger woman to extricate her arm from the twisted cord.

She spoke softly. "Mrs. Dorn, I'll take this call. You go and make a nice cuppa and calm down. I'll be in to see you as soon as possible." The housekeeper looked fit to be tied. It took a few seconds for her to close her mouth and nod. She stomped toward the kitchen, her satin slippers slapping the hardwood floor with each step.

"I'm terribly sorry, Mrs. Howard. Nurse Joye here. Mrs. Dorn had to go to the kitchen to—to stop her pudding from boiling over. I couldn't help overhearing part of the conversation, and I gather you're troubled about Dani."

"Nurse Joye, thank goodness. Sometimes I feel you're the only sane voice I can talk to in that house. I keep praying Daniell will call and tell me she's back to normal, but I've heard nothing. If I didn't telephone each day for updates, I don't believe I'd ever hear from Robert. I'm going mad with worry. She's my baby, she's..." Sobs from the anguished mother echoed straight into the single woman's heart.

Tears clogged Nurse Joye's eyes and shivers darted every which way throughout her body. Her voice, reflecting her distress, wobbled until she got herself under control.

"Mrs. Howard, please don't upset yourself this way," she murmured, speaking with the velvet tones of a born caregiver. "You know how much Robert loves his niece, and what a wonderful doctor he is. You must believe he's doing everything in his power to make Dani as comfortable as possible. It's the reason he's kept her here, in such lovely surroundings, rather than the cold atmosphere of the hospital."

"That's exactly what my husband tells me, and I am grateful. Please don't misunderstand. It's just so hard not being able to see her and be with her. Is her condition improving at all?" Marion's fretfulness had receded slightly, but the mournful tones of a woman kept away from her sick child remained.

Connecting with that expressed pain left Nurse Joye no other recourse but to give in to the obvious plea for reassurance. "My dear, we're hoping to have her up and around by Saturday. She'll still be weak, but at least you'll see her then."

"Goodness, that's days away. I only hope I can last that long."

Finally, after many more minutes of evasive tactics, Grace hung up the phone and leaned back against the wall, her hand covering her cheek in a common reflex during moments of stress. She closed her eyes and inhaled deeply. Lying was abhorrent to her, and normally she wouldn't allow herself to be put in a position where it became necessary. But in this case she had no other option.

Robert knew his sister extremely well, and Grace had to concur with his assessment. If he'd tried to explain to Marion what he'd told Grace, she had no doubt in her mind, none at all, that the frenzied woman would not only have her daughter into a clinic immediately but would also be seeking professional care for her brother.

It would be disastrous for Dani to be removed from the vicinity of the mysterious roses. Grace firmly believed the only way to get that girl back to her normal self was to have her body by that specific bush at noon on Saturday. With luck and prayers, all would go according to plan. She made the sign of the cross. Asking assistance from a higher presence wouldn't hurt at all.

Aware of her duties, she peeked in on Dani to assure herself all was well. Then, satisfied of her patient's comfort, she headed toward the kitchen to tackle Mrs. Dorn. Before entering the room she smoothed her hands over her proper white uniform and forced her shoulders to relax.

Mrs. Dorn, bent over and rummaging in the cupboards under the sink, jumped a foot when she realized the nurse stood in the kitchen behind her.

"Strewth! I didn't see ya there, miss. You startled me, ya did." She put back the odd-looking container and straightened to face the nurse.

"Mrs. Dorn, do you have any children?"

"No, but I have a sweet little kitty."

"With all due respect, my dear, I don't believe it's quite the same thing."

"Not exactly, but Pearl's getting on. She misses me something fierce, according to me sister, who is cat-sitting her while I'm staying here to assist the doctor."

The woman literally oozed righteous virtue when stating her employer's need for her services. She always spoke the doctor's name with a reverence that indicated her position, as his housekeeper, was probably a bragging tool with her family and her pals.

"If you have a sister, who I'm sure you care about, you should be able to understand how difficult it is for Marion Howard to have Dani, a beloved daughter, sick and out of her reach. Any mother would be frantic, and she is particularly vulnerable, according to Dr. Andrews. After years of trying to conceive, she'd given up the possibility of ever having children. So Dani was something of a miracle."

Mrs. Dorn's head lowered a bit more with each of Nurse Joye's points until she resembled a castigated child. "I know I can be a bit full on sometimes. Look 'ere, that girl *is* a miracle, a lovely lass, respectful and kind whenever she comes to visit himself. Always takes a few minutes to come in and wish me a good day and beg for one of me special cookies."

"If you like her so much, you'll want to do what's best for her and her mother, right?"

As if Grace hadn't interrupted, the woman ranted on. "It were the doctor's idea to have me stay and help with her care, and I'm happy to do it. But taking the mickey out of his sister is wearing a bit thin. She won't give over, hounds me until I'm flaming ratty."

All the time she talked, Mrs. Dorn filled the copper kettle, fetched china cups and saucers, and set the table for two. Lovely teacakes, which she'd made and decorated with different colours of icing, were arranged on a pretty platter and placed on the white lace doily covering the well-scrubbed wooden table.

A cozy rocker and footstool positioned near the fireplace looked to be the woman's retreat, and the basket next to it, filled with bright red wool and knitting needles, her pastime.

Multiple plants hung from the ceiling by the bay window in fashionable holders. Asparagus ferns, variegated spider plants, and many pots of colourful violets crammed the smaller spaces. Frilly yellow curtains framed the bright area and produced a pleasing atmosphere in an otherwise utilitarian room.

As a background for the large-boned, cranky woman, whose support stockings were rolled at her ankles and familiar red kerchief shielded bobby-pinned hair, the room didn't quite fit. Until, that is, a person looked deeper and noticed the obvious pride she took in her surroundings.

Grace appraised the spotless room and smiled. Her glance settled on Mrs. Dorn. The wrapping on the outside of a parcel didn't always reflect the jewels hidden inside, a lesson Grace knew well. It had been drilled into her through many years of living with her own misery.

Getting back to the matter at hand, Grace said, "Mrs. Dorn, we really must try to have more patience. Can I count on you to keep your temper with Mrs. Howard, or shall you feel better if I talked with her from now on?"

"Honestly? The cheek of the woman gets to me some days, but me blasted foot's aching like the dickens today, and I'm a might touchy. I fancy I'll be back to me normal happy nature tomorrow, see if I'm not."

"Thank you, Mrs. Dorn. I'm not much good at, ah, telling fibs. Therefore, I do rely on you."

A booming laugh reverberated across the table. "Telling porkies doesn't faze me a-tall. It's the woman's fancy airs that are a bother. I only hope she doesn't push me too far." With a large sigh, the housekeeper plonked herself down across from the slender girl in white and began to pour the tea.

Chapter Seventeen

Bunty Hubble's usual seductive greeting was noticeably absent when Troy finally trudged back to the Cozy Inn that night. In fact, her smouldering glare levelled him, stopping him in his tracks.

"Your—animal—is tied in the back garden, Mr. Brennan, and will not be allowed inside in the future." She tilted towards him, her finger waving in warning, her anger very apparent.

"Buddy! We forgot all about the poor baby. Troy, he'll be frightened, left alone for so long. Do something."

"Bunty, I apologise for my thoughtlessness. I truly forgot about the poor little pup. You see, I got involved in a fire not far from here. A shocking situation—"

The word "fire" caught the woman's attention. She scanned the dirty, blackened figure leaning tiredly against the counter. Then she moved, a whirlwind of competency.

"Hang on, what's happened to you? Come and sit down." She ducked under the lift-up section of the reception desk and moved over to guide Troy to the brown leather sofa crammed between two overflowing plant stands. "You're injured? You poor man, you look exhausted. You must have been involved in the Kingsly fire. Such a catastrophe! Those sad misfortunates have no place to go. My heart breaks for them."

"You're right, Bunty. It was a bad scene. I got drawn into their predicament and ended up going to the hospital. It's why I forgot about Buddy."

"Buddy?"

"The pup. He must have been in a sorry state, being left alone so long. I'd hoped to get him to his new owner before he became a problem."

"Ooch! He's no problem whatsoever, poor wee little thing. He seemed scared, and I was miffed, thinking you'd hidden him and weren't caring about any mess he'd make. But he never did—make a mess, that is. In fact, if I hadn't gone into the wardrobe to put the extra cover away, I'd never have even known the little devil hid there. Quiet as a mouse, he was. He'll be fine in the room with you, and if you need to go out, just leave him down in the garden. I'll be happy to keep an eye on him for you in the future."

"You are one sweet woman, Bunty. Thank you." Troy cocked his head, stared straight at her, and smiled, a smile he'd used most of his life in moments when someone touched him. This smile started from his heart, connected with his eyes, and travelled to his lips with such sweetness that an instant bond of friendship swelled between them.

Flustered and pink-faced, Bunty said, "I try, Mr. Brennan." This time when she leaned towards him, she reached over and very gently patted his shoulder. "Now you go on out to the garden and get your Buddy, take him up with you, and I'll get Cook to fix you a nice tray of supper."

The woman's sincere empathy earned Dani's grudging respect. "Why, she's really very nice, Troy. She genuinely cares about the fire victims, and she was sweet about Buddy."

"Why are you so surprised, little one? Most people are kind-hearted and care more than they let on. You're way too young to have such a blasé, distrustful attitude. You must have learned it from someone else. And I'd stake my life on it that you got the biggest lessons from your mother."

"Troy!"

****

The supper tray, now empty, sat in front of Troy on the room's only table. A white linen cloth lay scrunched up next to the rosebud vase where one perfect yellow flower rested. Before he ate, the overwhelming odour of lamb chop and mashed potatoes had dominated, but now the faint sweet scent of the rose drifted through.

Gazing out the window, Troy watched the slow traffic moving along the right side of the street, driven by people seated on the right side of the vehicle—all wrong to him.

The narrow cobblestone road, a picturesque addition to the scene for a man used to concrete and asphalt, glistened from the rain shower washing it clean. Window baskets, full of colour and beauty, graced many of the street's smaller shops and were being watered simultaneously. Sporadic rays of late sunshine broke through the misty droplets, forming arcs of brilliant rainbow beauty.

A sigh filled him, not his own, but still it vibrated around inside, leaving him feeling sad, a sensation he hadn't felt in years. He looked down and spotted the small furball plucking a dainty paw at his pant leg, eyes peeking through tufts of fur and long black lashes. Adoration challenged Troy's returning stare.

Dani took over. *"Buddy!"* Strong arms reached down and gentle hands lifted the small pup, cradling him as one would a baby, rocking the tiny mite back and forth. Intense sensations of misery deepened to overcome Troy, encouraging him to speak words he'd never intended to say. Words he'd been shying away from, because he knew that, once spoken, they couldn't be unsaid. Words that would involve him even more in the life of a mere girl whose increasing importance scared the hell out of him.

Her yearnings spread like wild vines interweaving themselves around his heart. She interested him like no one else ever had, but he stopped the words, bit down on his lower lip, and swallowed those treacherous urges to let her confide.

Silence grew, eventually becoming comfortable, togetherness carried to a whole new level. Sitting and petting the sleeping puppy, watching the world go by, two souls merged for a short time, melding in a way very few people ever have the fortune to experience.

The room darkened as the night sky slowly replaced daylight. Shadows loomed and streetlamps came on to throw their auras around people meandering along the sidewalks. Sounds of voices, though muted, added a sense of fellowship to the scene. It broke into their aloneness.

Total relaxation engulfed the man who slouched comfortably in the easy chair, embracing a warm furry body and sheltering a tortured young soul.

"Troy? I've respected your need to recuperate from today's disaster, and I've stayed in the background tonight as much as I could. But since we'll be together for another week, I just have to share. I can't possibly keep this secret hidden for seven more days."

"Sure you can."

"I'm serious, Troy. There's a huge crisis looming in my life, and if I don't tell someone, I'll bust. And you're my perfect someone."

"I'm nobody's perfect someone. I don't even want to be a someone—"

"Troy, please."

"I know, Dani. Look, I've been hoping you'd work out whatever your predicament is on your own, but I feel the buzzing going on in your—my—head, and it's constant. Your anxiety echoes loud and clear, sweetheart. It's just that I'm not sure I really want to know what it is. For a guy who keeps to himself, this sharing of my body has been tough enough for me to get used to, but sharing emotions—"

"Quit talking. You're just hoping you'll stop me. I want to get your feedback on my situation. I need help, Troy, and you're the only person I can ask."

"Can't you go to your uncle, or ask your minister, or tell a girlfriend, when you get back on Saturday? God forbid, don't go to your mum."

"I did decide to tell my uncle, even though he's never been able to hide anything from my mother. But then this happened. I'm afraid my life is going to undergo a very big change."

"It can't be all that bad. After all, how much trouble can a young girl get herself into?" The question rippled outwards, and returned to slap him in the face. The Oh-My-Good-God-No! sensation followed. Before he could say a word, she came clean.

"I'm pregnant!"

Unthinking, he yelled out loud, and the sound of his angry "No!" reverberated, pulling him upright, scaring the sleeping puppy, who scrambled from his lap to slide under the bed, his tiny rump wriggling desperately.

"You're pregnant? Are you sure?"

"Oh, yeah!"

"How the hell did that happen?"

"You don't know? Humm—let me see, how to explain. I behaved rather naughty with a sex-starved fellow who put his male appendage in my vagina—"

"That's enough!"

"Not quite, but you'll know the rest, I'm sure."

"Don't be a smart-ass. I want to know who—and why!" He'd lost control. Rage pulsated through him.

"Oh-oh. You're cussing. That's a really bad sign, isn't it?" The sobs he heard mixed in with her words didn't help.

"I only control my swearing in front of ladies."

"Ouch! Troy—that hurt!"

"You ain't heard nothin' yet, sweetheart. Wait'll your family and friends find out."

"From them I'd expect censure, but not from you. From you I expected—more." He reacted as if hit with a large brick to the side of his head. He sat back and twined his fingers together

in front of his mouth, as if to stop it from opening. He swallowed the bile swimming in his throat, but the nausea eating away at his stomach wasn't quite as easy to quell.

He counted slowly: one, two, three…until he reached ten. Leaning back in the chair, he swiped his cold hand across his lower face, wishing he could close off his mind as one would close off a tap. The shock of her announcement had stunned him so much that every emotion running through him had been as visible to her as pictures on a motion picture screen.

She waited, playing him at his own game.

"Tell me about the father." His hard-won calm pleased him.

"He's my friend, someone I've known for years. Troy, he was such a sad fellow. He lacked self-confidence, had no self-worth, I mean to the point of being borderline suicidal. You should see him now, strutting around the school, nobody's bully-boy any longer."

"You mean to tell me you went to bed with some guy to boost his self-esteem?"

"No, I made love with him to save his life."

"One, two—"

"I never believed people actually did that. Count to ten, I mean. Does it help?"

"What do you think?"

"It calms you. It's incredible, really. I'll have to try it. Maybe when I come clean with my mother."

"Can you count to a million?" When he chuckled, the tension gripping his core finally started to unwind. *"Does this loser know about the baby?"*

"Not yet! He'd want to do the right thing, and that's the last thing I want."

"Heaven forbid you should want to do the right thing."

She ignored his satirical shudder and instead giggled, a sound filled with the relief of sharing. "Before letting the situation take place—you know, making the decision to let him go ahead—I'd decided the encounter would help him enormously and at the same time benefit my writing. I mean, how can an author truly write about love and 'doing it' if she's never experienced 'it' herself?"

"None of your characters intend to rob a bank, do they?" His hand first pantomimed holding a gun, and then he waved his finger around in circles near his head as if he could express, by movement alone, that she was a lunatic.

"Now you're just being silly."

"Am I?" Unhappiness festered inside him, while the pounding in his head increased. Finally he broke the silence. *"Do you love him?"*

"No…. But the change in him—that I loved."

Chapter Eighteen

D ani shrank into the sphere where she was untouchable, shut down communications, and left Troy his personal space to deal with the bomb she'd just dropped.

Looking back over the last few months, she realized how foolish she'd been to allow things to get out of hand the way they had. Barry, her baby's father, a nice enough lad, was exactly that—a lad. After living intimately with Troy, she knew how a grown man reacted when being threatened. Barry had a lot to learn in the catch-up years until he reached Troy's age.

Since grade school, Barry had been her on-again-off-again friend. Aching for his unhappiness, pity mushrooming every time she'd come across him being bullied, she'd tried to help bolster his low opinion of his worth. She'd even gone as far as intervening, sticking up for him, fighting for him. The more she stepped in, however, the more his morale sank, so she stopped. But year after year he became worse, until he simply began wallowing in the murkiness of his self-pity.

This behaviour more than annoyed her: it was abhorrent to a gutsy girl like Dani. Her mother might be a possessive clinger, but she made Dani aware by this goofy conduct that she was the most important person in her world.

Her father, a quiet retiring character but nevertheless a strong ally whenever Dani had reached the point of suffocation from being over-mothered, reinforced her value both as a daughter and as a person by his gentle, loving manner. And her Uncle Robert instilled in her the importance of demanding the same respect you gave to others.

Barry's parents were the complete opposite. Both busy workaholics, they remained unaware of the misery poor Barry suffered.

As the two youngsters grew older, Dani witnessed many incidents where the other students' pranks cut Barry deeply, goading him past endurance and, lately, poking at his masculinity. It had torn at her heart to see how much lower this past year had brought him—how unhappy he appeared.

Then, three months ago, she'd come upon two of the bigger, more popular blokes at the school giving him a thrashing. Seems he'd messed up a homework project they'd forced on him.

"Here, what are you doing?" She'd broken into the fray and demanded attention. "Let go of him."

They stopped hitting him, but using their young muscular bodies they trapped him, crushing him between them. They continued to poke at him with their elbows, proof she had no power over anything they wished to do.

"The little moron let us down. We asked him for one small favour, and he screwed it up."

"Rubbish! Stop that. Stop hitting him; he doesn't have to be doing your work. Do it yourself."

"You stay outta this, Dani. It ain't none of your bloody business." The taller of the two got a mean look on his face and stepped towards her. Partially hidden by long strands of greasy hair, obvious cruelty shone from his beady eyes.

"Well, I'm making it my business." Dani had always disliked Nigel Brown, the lad who continued to advance towards her slowly, menacingly. He stopped when she blocked his way. Then, forced to look up, she felt small, intimidated, and angry for feeling such things.

"What's it matter to you? The poof's a bleedin' chump. What do you care what we do to him?"

She smelt the bad breath of a cigarette smoker. "Of course I care. He's my boyfriend. Let him go, and leave him be."

Nigel pushed even closer to her, rubbing his chest against her breasts as he said, "He's not fit to be your boyfriend. He's scum. You want a real man, come with me. I'll take good care of ya." Dark stringy waves framed a pretty-boy face, but the mean expression spoilt what could have been attractive features.

Fed up, Dani pushed him away. "Barry's worth ten of you," she said. From the corner of her eye she watched the reaction of her words wash over Barry's homely face. He looked dumbfounded but took the opportunity to wrench himself out of the other boy's grasp. Then he moved aside and waited, afraid to step up but not running off.

"Barry is more of a man than you'll ever be, you big bully. He's smart and strong, and one day he'll be someone to be reckoned with. You wait and see. On the other hand, you will most likely be a kept man. Kept by the local authorities behind bars in a prison somewhere."

Bullying rage flashed. Warning signals started in her stomach, butterflies battling and acid churning, but she didn't look away. Her eyes never wavered, never flinched, and never stopped glaring her disgust.

Long seconds passed. Finally, with a middle finger showing his disdain and a sneering grin plastered over his red face, Nigel swung around and lumbered in the opposite direction. The copycat slowly followed, his shrug a clear indication he wasn't sure what had just gone down, but neither was he willing to question his pal's authority or his decision to walk away.

Barry, sheepish, approached warily, caution as obvious as a neon sign flashing. "What'd you do that for? They'll be after me even more now, calling me a liar and such."

"Tell them it isn't a lie. I'll confirm it. We can be seen together and—and hold hands. Maybe go to the films and to the café for lunch."

Dani reached up and pushed his thick blonde hair behind his ears. With a little more grooming, he'd be quite handsome. His big brown eyes were encircled by long curling eyelashes. If he'd look a person straight on, as he did with Dani, they'd be able to see his kind heart shining through.

"They'll know, Dani. Look at me! Why would any girl want to be seen with the likes of me? God's honest truth! It's not going to make sense."

"It's better than letting them thrash you. Come on, Barry. We'll go on a date Friday night, and then it won't be a lie, will it? You'll get yourself done up, and I'll dress to kill, and we'll make a smashing couple."

They'd gone on that date and then another and another. Slowly, Barry stopped slinking around and began to walk upright, straight-backed, a tall strong body revealed. But one thing kept coming up between them.

Repeatedly, he'd question her spending so much time with him. "It's a pity relationship. You really have no use for me—you just feel sorry for me. It's true, ain't it?"

"Give over, Barry. We've been friends for years, since we were little tots. I like you. I really do. We have lots of fun."

"It's not enough. Dani, I love you. And I want more than holding hands, and pecks goodnight. Please, Dani, let me. I need you to."

The truth behind Barry's words never registered with him, but it did with Dani. She sensed his need to feel vindicated as a desirable, normal male. He couldn't accept himself as worthy without her acceptance of him as a sexual partner, and bighearted Dani couldn't withstand his desperation, couldn't add to his rejection list. Until she proved his value by loving him all the way, he'd continue to doubt, to query—to deny. Time after time she'd seen him regress into the black funk where he'd question everything about himself.

And so, without thought of any consequences, she'd wrapped her young, strong arms around him and held on as he became a man and she became a mum.

Chapter Nineteen

Nurse Joye stopped in the doorway of the dimly lit sickroom and peeked in, listening. Mrs. Dorn muttered all the while she gently wiped the pale face of the still girl. She wore an expression of devotion as her gnarled hands wrung the water from the soft cloth.

"Poor wee lass! Yer flamin' mum would drive a saint to drink, she would. I don't know as how you've lived with her all these years without clobbering her with a ruddy great stick. She's rung up four times today, and it's only the supper hour. I don't know how long the doctor and I can hold her off—that I don't. You have to come back to us, dearie, for the doctor's sake and my sanity."

Reddish gold curls, springing every which way, were tenderly brushed back from the girl's forehead, but to no avail. They sprang back into place, loops pre-programmed to twist and coil and frustrate anyone trying to control them.

"Flubbin' her off is wearing me down. I've run out of stories to keep her satisfied. I'm thinkin' to pretend she's got the wrong number if she calls one more time this evening."

A deep breath in preparation for a loud sigh inflated the old housekeeper's body, swelling her by at least one size. She released it with such moaning that the giggle escaping from snoopy Grace Joye broke into the heartfelt noise and brought Mrs. Dorn's head swinging around. She caught the nurse in the act of trying to hold back her hilarity by covering the offending mouth.

Mrs. Dorn rose and swelled to her great height of five feet. Her eyes narrowed, her hands gripped her ample hips, and a smile twitched at her lips.

"So, miss, you think it's funny that the windbag and her hoity-toity manners are driving me demented?"

"I'm sorry, Mrs. Dorn. I know it's naughty of me to laugh. Please don't be angry. You've been wonderful about taking on the phone duty. Doctor Andrews told me just yesterday that he didn't know what we would do without you."

"That's what keeps me going along with this nonsense." She turned to look at the patient. "What will he do if the lass doesn't come back to us?"

"Don't even mention such a possibility. He's been glued to his reports. Working day and night on very little sleep. He's tried to examine everything he can get his hands on pertaining to this phenomenon. He's so pale and exhausted, he'll need caring for himself if this Saturday doesn't bring Dani home."

"I've read the case notes, you know. Couldn't help meself."

"I suppose he wouldn't have left them where you could get them if he didn't trust you implicitly."

"I wouldn't be in his shoes for any amount of money in the world. Iffen he has to tell his sister that her pregnant daughter's body lies in a coma while her spirit is holidaying in someone else's, there'll be jolly hell to pay. Add to everything else, he has no idea *where* the lass is at the moment, or *whose* body she's occupying. I'm thinking we'll surely be visiting him in his own hospital bed—while he's in a body cast, more'n likely."

The smile slowly faded from the nurse's features. "Put like that, Mrs. Dorn, I wouldn't want to be in his shoes, either!"

Chapter Twenty

Troy had risen early, enjoying the brisk chilliness of the dawn. He ate a full English breakfast and didn't know what rated higher, the appearance of the food or the delicious smells of ham and eggs wafting from his plate. All the while he devoured the meal, he chatted up Bunty to learn about the latest gossip on the fire.

Noting her early morning effusiveness, he decided to expand their topics of conversation to include the person foremost on his mind, Ellie Ward.

"Bunty, I wonder if you could help me? I've been trying to meet up with Bury's star author, Ellie Ward. I'd like to arrange an interview, but it seems impossible to get through to her personally. I've tried numerous times to call her phone, but either no one's home or a woman, an extremely unpleasant woman, answers and puts me off. Do you know how a fellow could get to meet her?"

"Ellie's a bit of a recluse, Troy. She very seldom agrees to any form of publicity. And when she's here in Bury it's usually because she's working on her latest manuscript. While she's writing, she's not available to anyone, sometimes for weeks on end. Except of course to her family."

"Does she live here primarily? I'm asking because not long ago, in Chicago, she saved the life of a young girl. I'd very much like to discuss that incident with her, get her point of view on what happened. You know, have her share her feelings with the readers."

"She's a heroine? I'm not at all surprised. Actually, she lives in Chicago part of the year. It's only during the holidays, when her daughter visits her grandparents, that Ellie spends so much of her time here in Bury." The smile, which lit up Bunty's face while talking about the famous author, clicked with Troy.

"Do you know her? Could you arrange for us to meet?"

"I know her. We go to the same church. For some unknown reason I've never understood, she's treated me as a personal friend, but I'd never presume on that friendship."

Bunty's brightly coloured lips closed tight, a sure signal that she would say no more on this specific topic. Familiar with the reactions of humans to nosiness and uncomfortable questions, Troy backed off. With a jaunty smile, he thanked her for the meal.

"You're away, then? No more lollygagging with the likes of me? Looks as if you've a special destination."

Troy winked at her presumptuousness and fed her curiosity.

"A fine howdyado. A bloke can't pull anything over on you today, Miss Smarty Pants." Armed with a pocketful of sharpened pencils and a notebook under his arm, he gently pinched her nose and left.

On the far side of the street, he passed a tobacco shop he hadn't noticed before and glanced in the window. On display sat a large black-and-white photograph of Ellie Ward, the very woman he'd been trying to find. Piles of her latest book, *Come Find Me*—an apt title if he ever saw one—flanked the picture. The setup presented an artistic exhibit, but his eyes were drawn to her image.

Her soft expression dazzled him.

Her rioting curls made him smile.

But her eyes mesmerized, seeming to burn into his soul as though they connected directly with him.

And then the unforeseen happened. A woman stepped from the shop's doorway, pivoted, and made her way across to the other side of the street. It took Troy a moment to realize who she was. As soon as it kicked in, he started after her.

"Here we go again, pursuing poor Ellie." Dani's tone resounded with cheeky sarcasm. All the while he'd been with Bunty silence had reigned. Now, when he'd prefer to be on his own, she'd returned to badger.

"Come on, Dani. The woman's famous, a true heroine. She's the reason I'm even here. This could be the proverbial scoop of the year. After I get her to open up and share her story, I'll send it off to the Sun-Times. They'll offer me a job, maybe even make me their ace reporter. Besides, people need to know what made her act the way she did. It's important."

"That's rubbish. You'd persecute this poor woman because she's brave?"

"I'm not persecuting her, as you so indelicately put it."

"What do you call sneaking around, following her everywhere, asking questions you've no business to? Aren't you planning on revealing her whereabouts to the whole world? You know all she wants is her privacy."

"Okay! Just maybe you're somewhat right, but the world needs heroes, and I'm a reporter. It's my job to get the story. People have the right to know what made her step in and fight. Stop humming in my own head. It's beginning to bug me."

"Good! What did this superwoman do to earn such a lofty title as heroine?"

"First of all, she happened to be in the wrong place at the wrong time, and second, she didn't follow the basic, more intelligent rules of today."

"Which are?"

"Don't get involved. And never when there's danger."

"You're one to talk." Her teasing snort encouraged him to continue.

"Yeah, well, I'm an idiot. Trust me. It's best to ignore trouble around you, stay away from dangerous situations and let others worry about themselves. Ignoring these proven principles, Ellie Ward single-handedly stopped a bank holdup."

"And that's bad how?"

"The thieves were armed killers and known to the police from four other similar jobs they'd recently pulled in the city. Bank customers died at each of the other robberies, and the two suspects, both brutal murderers and both with long records, had been taken very seriously."

"What did Ellie do?" The intensity of emotion ringing in her voice surprised Troy, but he replied with the details.

"She talked them into swapping herself as hostage with the hysterical teenager they'd first grabbed. When the guy agreed and seized her instead, she pulled some fancy karate move and flipped him in front of her to take the bullet his partner shot her way. Then she hurled a marble pen stand from the counter at the gunman, who'd decided to flee, and knocked him unconscious."

"Bless my soul, you're right. She is crazy."

"I didn't say she was crazy."

"You said she didn't follow the rules of intelligence."

"True, I did say that. But crazy she isn't."

"You're quibbling semantics."

"Dan-i?"

She knew he was losing patience.

"Okay, okay! Then what happened?"

"She snuck out the side door during the ensuing commotion, and the bank customers have been singing her praises ever since, wanting to give her a commendation for her bravery. Everyone from the president of the bank to the President of the country wants to thank her personally for saving so many lives. But at first no one could discover her identity."

"You did."

He smiled. "I'm a good reporter."

"Right. Who told you?"

"The kid she saved ended up with her purse. She didn't want to tell me, but I can be a persuasive son-of-a-gun when I have to be."

"Her being female didn't hurt, either, I'd wager. So you and your silver tongue got hold of the purse and—"

"Actually, no. The kid wouldn't give it up. She gave me a business card from the pocket of Ellie's bag, and it had her picture on it. Turns out she's a famous author, something the kid didn't realize. But the lead wasn't so hot, because there happened to be a news photographer at the bank at the same time as the robbery went down. He'd had the foresight to set his video camera on top of one of the marble counters before hitting the floor, and he let the tape run during the whole incident. That night the film showed live on the late news."

"Poor Ellie couldn't catch a break, could she?"

"The whole world saw her, so incognito wasn't an option anymore. The news hounds were after her."

"You talk like they're a different breed. Aren't you one of them?
"

"Dani, I have principles. Some of those old dogs would chew off their own legs to get at a story."

"Whereas you'd just fly from one continent to another."

"I had to. I have a feeling this meeting will change my whole life, get me the job I want, and at the same time show the world that ordinary people can be special. We can all be... Never mind. I'm rambling."

But Dani knew he wasn't. He had come close to telling her what she'd already suspected. This man cared. Not just about the story—he cared about the truth. It lured him, like a Hershey bar lures a chocoholic. *"What happened next?"*

"She left her home and went to a hotel. The place she picked offered some protection, as did the police, but with a story as hot as this one, someone was bound to either sneak inside or get the facts by other methods."

"You."

"Why not? I'm fed up with freelance work. It's time I settle down and put my career on track, get a desk job, and stay in one place for more than a week. She could be my ticket to success."

"Your meal ticket, so to speak."

"You make it sound terrible. People want to know details. Who is this woman? What's her story? What the hell possessed her to do what she did? It's important for them to understand."

"You think so. You keep saying it, so you must believe that rubbish. Well, I don't. I think people should respect her wishes for solitude and privacy and leave her the hell alone. That's what I think."

"What do you know? You're just a kid. Oww! Stop that screeching."

"You're bonkers, is what you are. I might be only seventeen, but I have more insight into human kindness, more integrity—"

"You're still sixteen."

"Troy, you make me livid... Oh, bugger it!"

She shut down. This time it felt like she'd squeezed into a tiny puddle of hurt and lodged herself in a place that made swallowing difficult. He rubbed his chest instinctively, but the horrible feeling wouldn't fade. It was as if he were a small boy again. One who'd angered a mom who was the love of his entire universe. In those days, all he'd think about was how to fix things and get back into her good graces.

He stopped in the middle of the sidewalk and swung around, looking in all directions. He'd been so caught up in his bickering with Dani, Ellie had disappeared, and he hadn't even noticed.

Enough! He had a job to do, and it was high time he got on with it. He had to eat and pay for his lodging, so his choices were limited. He had to work.

Purposefully, he made his way towards the hospital.

"You're still planning to interview the fire victims? Even after what we've talked about? I wouldn't have believed you'd be this

heartless, disturbing those poor people the day after such a tragedy."
Dani, her tone aggrieved, borderline nagging, had just enough pain ringing through to stop him dead in his tracks.

"You don't understand, Dani."

"No, you don't understand. Those people have lost everything. They need time to heal, and they need to be left alone to do so."

"I disagree. I think they need to know that someone cares."

"Why? Do you care? You know nothing about them."

"I will after today. Trust me, and let me do my job, or stay out of my way."

Chaos in the hospital impeded him, making it difficult to discover where the victims from the fire had been taken. He finally coaxed a student nurse to take him to the ward where most of them were housed.

Trolleys full of linens, medications, and used food trays lined the hallway. The smells of congealed soup and stale bread mingled with the strong perfume of a cleaning solvent—Eau du Pine Sol, a fragrance he remembered from childhood, from living with a mother who cleaned diligently every day and took a great deal of pride in her modest home.

High counters, behind which the nurses convened with charts and ringing phones, were laden with colourful plants and flowers. Arrayed in numerous displays, tiny white envelopes on sticks poking out from each of them, they waited to find their new homes. The vivid colours, a welcome distraction from the surrounding beiges and greys, added a cheerful note.

The nurses, all in starched white, looked harried and ignored the man who cunningly portrayed himself as a legitimate visitor. Being able to slip into the background, a requirement for any good newspaperman, alleviated suspicion from the staff.

He veered into the first ward, ignored the curtained-off area in front, and made his way over to where an elderly woman lay in a bed by the window. Hair the colour of snow spread every which way over the matching pillow. Her sunken eyes were open as she stared blankly at the view of the city and of trees being blown about by the strong winds. Troy approached slowly and waited.

She finally turned to him. "Who are you?" Her tone sounded harsh, miserable—tragically lifeless.

At first Troy couldn't speak for the turmoil filling his mind. Dani's presence, still ranting, destroyed his ability until he cut her off.

"My name is Troy Brennan. I'm a reporter from Chicago, an—"

"You cheeky bugger! How did you get in here? I have nothing to say to you." Tears appeared and streamed down sunken cheeks as the woman's agitation increased. Her clenched hands beat on the spread wrapped around her tiny frame. Anger spilled over, as if her body carried more than it could contain. "My Harry is dead." Wailing the words seemed to break something up inside her, loosening a dam of sorrow.

"Ma'am, I'm so sorry. Was he one of the victims from the fire?" The velvet voice of the man left no doubt to its listener—he felt for her loss. A voice that could wrap itself around a sick, sorry soul with such tenderness could never be questioned for its authenticity. A person just knew. He cared.

She reached out her hand, which he grasped gently in both of his. "My Harry was killed helping his mate who lived in the room next to us. The old fool thought he could work a miracle. I told him there wasn't time to go back, but did he listen to me?" Spoken in her clogged, teary voice, the words were difficult to understand. Troy sat near her, patting her hand, giving the impression he had all the time in the world to wait until she felt stronger.

She used her hanky to mop up, then mutilated it between her arthritic fingers. Her sigh cut his heart into ribbons and left him wishing he could take on her pain. "That devil never heard a word I said half the time, he went his own way, and that's the truth. But he was my man, and we had sixty years together." She turned to Troy. "What's left for me now?"

"What would Harry tell you if he heard you saying such things?"

A tiny grimace appeared, probably as close to a smile as she could handle at the moment. She swiped at her eyes with her free hand, like a child who's been forgiven. She sniffed.

"He'd probably say something like 'faggots and peas puddin', lass. Give over now and move on'."

Troy smiled and nodded. "Your Harry sounds like one smart man."

"He was that. Why, he drove taxi for over fifty years. Even delivered two babies, he did. One's named after him."

"A boy, I hope!"

A chuckle burst out before the old woman could stop it. She smacked his hand. "You're a fine piece of work, ya naughty devil."

Flashing the old lady his most beguiling smile, the one that had gotten him behind the scenes many times in his career, Troy leaned forward so she could see his face. He wanted there to be no doubt about his intentions.

"Do you think Harry would want the folks here in Bury to know he cared so much for a friend that he gave his life to try and save him?"

She listened intently.

"Do you believe that reading his story could one day possibly spur someone else to step up and help another like Harry tried to do?"

She thought for a few seconds and then nodded.

"And do you really want to go through this pain alone?"

"I am alone."

"You don't have to be. Tell me your story. I'll write it tonight, and tomorrow you'll get to read it before anyone else. We'll let the world know about the man you lived with and loved. Once you realize the truth—that when others read this piece they'll feel your sadness—then you're not alone."

The stimulus of sharing her history, a concept now firmly anchored, replaced the look of sorrow with one of interest.

"Sharpen your pencil, lad. We've got a lot of writing to do."

Chapter Twenty-One

The black-clad woman snuck up the hallway unnoticed and tiptoed into the sickroom where Dani lay still as death. Covered by a white chenille spread tucked around her shoulders, the teen appeared tiny and frail and very sick. Thank goodness for the fiery curls that haloed her ashen face. They saved her from being totally colourless.

Marion's brilliant brainstorm of sending a flower delivery to the front door when she knew Mrs. Dorn would be alone had gotten her through the side door and up the stairs undetected. The plans for her siege had given her something to occupy her mind and had saved her sanity. She'd missed her daughter's presence every minute of every long, lonely day. Knowing her girl rested close by only made it more unbearable.

All she needed was a few seconds to look at her, to see for herself how she fared. No touching or taking any silly chances on catching the virus. She didn't want to upset her brother, because she truly approved of his taking the initiative to care for his niece. She knew in her heart how much he loved Daniell. Even as a child the redheaded sprite would follow him around and her tiny arms would reach for him whenever he came into the room. They had a wonderful bond.

Jealousy had never entered the picture because she'd always thought of Robert as a special gift sent just for her, a focus for all her pent-up affection. It seemed only natural for him to share a similar connection with her daughter Daniell.

As she approached the bed, the intravenous setup attached to her girl gave the first hint that something didn't add up. In fact, the lifelines monitoring the girl's vitals threw her into a complete frenzy.

The resultant screams brought Mrs. Dorn puffing into the room, clutching her immense bosom, her hair scarf slipping to cover half her frightened face.

"Bleedin' hell, woman! Shut yer gob! You near scared me half to death." Rapid breathing, pouring sweat, and a face devoid of any colour hinted at a potential heart attack, which could excuse her lack of respect to a mother near collapse.

Marion stopped the horrific noise in the only manner she could. She clapped her hands over her mouth and pressed. Then, visibly shaking, she leaned over Dani and tenderly pushed the silky tresses away from the girl's forehead. She tried to feel her temperature, the first thing any mother thinks of when she deals with a sick child.

Her voice thick with emotion, she faced Mrs. Dorn and pleaded, "Call an ambulance!"

"'Ere now, don't be daft. Wait for the doctor. He'll be here in a jiffy. He can set you straight, mum."

"Set me straight?" The woman's voice reached screaming proportions in three words. "Mrs. Dorn, you are fired! If you touch my daughter again, I will have you arrested." Her voice sank with every word she spat out, the eeriness of her tone compelling the housekeeper to believe that she meant exactly what she said. "Pack up your belongings and leave this house."

"It were all your brother's idea to keep this from you. I—"

"Quite frankly, I don't give a damn whose idea it was. Get out!"

Recognizing pending hysteria, Mrs. Dorn gave up the good fight and bolted as quickly as her girth would allow.

Before she could reach the telephone, Marion pushed her aside and grabbed at the receiver herself. The ensuing struggle's outcome would never be questioned. A mother's love overrode a woman's loyalty every time.

****

The ambulance, with its precious cargo, left before Doctor Andrews arrived home. When he did, he found his housekeeper, wretched, gulping a cup of tea at the table in the kitchen.

"Mrs. Dorn, how could you let her take Dani away? Today is Friday—you knew the importance of keeping her here until tomorrow."

Mrs. Dorn, feeling hard done by and not in a mood to be blamed, scowled at the shaken man, no sympathy at all on her countenance. She slapped the table in front of her, knocking her tea mug over, releasing a surprising odour of gin.

Uncaring, she stood and leaned towards the distraught man, whose eyes widened at the menace he faced.

She spat angry words directly at him.

"Aye, there, hang on. Don't you start! It were your sister's idea to call the ambulance. I tried to stop her. But she'd have none of it. Tried clobbering me with the telephone, she did. Fired me—then did her damnedest to kill me. Ruddy woman near gave me a heart attack, screeching and carrying on."

All the while she ranted, her hand clutched a bag of ice and dabbed at her forehead, where a lump encircled by a red welt had begun to form.

Nurse Joye arrived just then to see the doctor cowering under the scorn of his furious housekeeper.

"What has happened? Mrs. Dorn, my dear, you've been hurt? Here, let me help you."

The young nurse, starched uniform crackling, rushed forward. She threw off her cape and, reaching her arms towards the older woman, steered her into the empty chair behind her. Kindheartedly she guided her to sit down.

All the while, tender words were spoken to a recipient in dire need of them, balm to a bruised and worried soul.

"Dani's gone." Dr. Andrews, not to be overlooked, drew her attention to himself. His voice portrayed his grief over the dreadfulness of the situation he now found himself in. His glasses, perched crookedly on the end of his nose, had a smudge, and that small imperfection appeared somehow precious to the nurse, who hadn't yet taken in the meaning of his words.

Once she did, she plopped into an empty chair at the table. Dumbfounded, she looked first at the doctor's unhappy scowl and then to Mrs. Dorn's even more miserable countenance. Her hand, which had automatically moved to cover her face, stopped in midair and then dropped to her lap.

"No! Oh, my God, no. I'm so sorry. She seemed fine when I left. What in the world happened?" Blue eyes, brilliant blue, beautifully sparkling blue, not often seen because she tended to keep her face averted, filled with tears.

Both people at the table reached out to her at the same time, but Dr. Andrews spoke first.

"No, Grace, Dani's fine. She's just been taken away. Marion played a trick on poor Mrs. Dorn. She crept in the garden door while our fine friend here accepted a delivery of flowers at the front. My sneaky sister found Dani in the coma and called an ambulance. They took her to the hospital."

"Thank God!" Grace's hands crisscrossed her chest in relief. Her eyes closed for seconds while a pretty smile lit up her face.

Both occupants at the table stared her way with eyebrows raised and waited. It only took a few seconds until the direness of the situation dawned on her.

"Oh! My goodness! But this is Friday! What in the world are we going to do?"

Chapter Twenty-Two

On Friday, deadline for the local rag, Troy returned to his room late and utterly exhausted. Buddy, ecstatic to see him, wiggled and yelped joyfully. His furry little body gyrated and danced every which way, while his tail swung in circles that should have had him airborne. He wouldn't settle down until the big man cuddled and soothed him.

Dani broke in before he had a chance. "Aw, baby, it's okay. We're here now. You're not alone anymore. Troy, he's so happy to see you. It's been days since we've been able to do more than take him for quick walks. Thank the Lord that Bunty's become smitten with him, or he'd have been alone all this time."

"I know. But who knew so many of the folks would want to share their stories. Once Susie decided Harry's story needed to be written, it became a catalyst to the others. Not that I'm complaining, mind you. I've made a bundle selling to the Manchester newspapers, and now that London has picked up on the editorials, it'll be an even bigger scoop."

"As if you wrote them for the money. Troy, you're a big fake. The only reason those people shared their tales with you was because they knew in their hearts that you cared about them. And about what they were going through." Pride rang clearly in her tone as she bickered with him. Over the last few days the growing attraction between them had been hinted at but not openly discussed. She dwelt in the warmth of his attentiveness, and he blossomed under her admiration.

"Oh, so you're not mad at me any longer? A guy trying to do his job, and what do I get in return—hassled and put down, that's what!" His poor-little-ole-me performance made her laugh.

"You know how much I loved seeing you at work. I've apologized enough for trying to stop you from doing your job. You're a genius, achieving exactly what you were born to do—make the world see people as individuals."

"If you understand that, then you truly get what I'm aiming for when I write these stories."

"I do. I've learnt more about the true meaning of journalism and about you personally in this week than ever. You, Troy, are a talented and kind man."

"Sure, the kind you'd like to—"

"Don't joke. You'll make me cry. As it is, I'm trying desperately not to get depressed. We've been ignoring the fact that it's Friday today. I suppose we should talk about it."

"Look, let's go out for a nice meal at the pub and—"

"No! Troy, we can't put this off any longer. I want to discuss it now."

"Just like a woman. I suppose you won't let me get any rest until you get your way. I have a fact, too, one we shouldn't ignore. My fact is—I don't want to talk."

****

The truth of this announcement hit Troy hard. He shut Dani off so he could be alone to explore his rioting emotions. Then he accepted another truth. He didn't want to talk about Dani leaving him, because he couldn't imagine life without her sweetness within. Just the thought of losing her wrenched his insides and made him angry at the twist fate had played.

He threw himself onto the bed and interlocked his hands behind his head. Angry words spewed out of him, sounding loud in the empty of the room. "Son of a bitch!"

To finally meet a female he'd like to share his life with, and—what? She was a seventeen-year-old mother-to-be, for heaven's sake. The bizarre circumstances were what movies were made from, not real life. How the hell did he let her get to him so deeply that to lose her tomorrow would be like losing his soul's best friend?

He stood up to pace, circling the room over and over. Buddy tried to keep up but soon lay down exhausted, his short puppy legs quivering. Beyond the open window, the lights of the restaurants and pubs on each side of the street went out one after another. Still he walked. Weariness took second place to grief.

It took Dani a huge amount of will to break through the mental walls he had erected. His overwhelming fatigue finally enabled her to succeed. She'd zeroed in on his grief, his feelings for her, and he knew she was aware of all he'd been going through. The wash of love that came with her returning presence soothed the ache somewhat.

"Troy, I have a huge request. If you refuse, it'll destroy me. So please say you will."

"What is it, sweetheart?"

"Promise me you will, and then I'll tell you."

"Excuse me? You want me to promise something when I have no idea what I'm—"

"Please?"

"What the hel—heck! Okay, I promise."

"My birthday is next Saturday. There will be a party at my Uncle Robert's house. He holds one for me every year. Will you come?"

He hesitated.

"I know you still have to get Ellie Ward's story, which will keep you occupied. The next few days will fly by, and then we'll be together

again. I'll need this next week to—to organize. Make some special arrangements for the future."

Her voice wobbled and ended up full of tears. He could no more refuse her request than he could have stopped blinking.

"Dani, you know I'll be there. And I'll give you your week to organize—but more importantly, you need to take a spell to see how you really feel when we aren't together. You're young, and it's all right if you change your mind." He was the adult, and he needed to give her some space. And the understanding that if she found at the end of the week that things were different, then it would be okay.

"I'll never change, Troy. You can feel my love; you know how strong it is. I'll be waiting on Saturday, believe me—believe in me."

"Staying away from you this week will be the hardest thing I've ever taken on. But when I do come calling, it'll be to collect my heart, because you'll be holding it. You know that, don't you? We'll talk about the future then. I'll give you all the time you need to grow up, as long as you understand what's most important—you're going to be mine one day soon."

"I will always be yours. Never, ever doubt it. You need to get some rest now. Everything will work out, you'll see. I promise."

****

As soon as Troy lay down, he passed out, leaving Dani alone to contemplate the future. Separating from this man would be like tearing herself in two. The secret she still couldn't share with him started the tears. Who knew a spirit could cry? The more she contemplated the coming years, the more she worried. Pain revved up to such intensity that it frightened her. His body tossed and turned, agitated from her angst.

Calm down! For pity's sake, you will see him in time, touch him—make love. But she knew that never again would she be part of him, to experience his every thought and emotion.

The ultimate bond was when he'd opened to her. As he began to trust, he'd let her come into his personal space more and more often—little by little. Prickly as he could be, she adored him and tried never to take advantage. She just filled him chocker-block full of love, so that at times, looking in the mirror, he appeared dazed as he sensed her watching.

To study him gave her immense joy. She saw a handsome man, no doubt, but it wasn't his face that delighted her as much as what she saw on that face. Intelligence and kindness shone from his devastating eyes— eyes where fall colours blended in a warm mixture. They nestled between thick eyelashes, enhanced by a cheeky attitude.

Over their time together, she'd experienced his personality's pendulum from one extreme to the other. Anger revealed at unnecessary cruelty. Bravery, and humour, along with his unending gentleness displayed during special moments. Troy was a full package. Nothing missing that a woman would need to make her the happiest in the world.

When she'd told him he was a kind man, she meant it with everything she was now and would be one day.

He was a kind man. The kind, pray God, she would marry in the future. The distant future. By her calculations, one week would pass for him, but for her, it would be ten long, lonely years.

Chapter Twenty-Three

Dr. Andrews returned to the kitchen, a satisfied smirk on his face.

"Room 405 is empty. I've reserved it for Mrs. Henrietta Dorn, who will be arriving at eight p.m. suffering from a nervous breakdown due to the stress of a devastating fall and subsequent blow to the head."

"You mean, due to being decked by your barmy sister with a telephone and choked with the cord." Mrs. Dorn caught the amused glance that passed between Nurse Joye and her boss.

For a moment, grumpiness gave her the look of a dried prune with eyes and a painted mouth, but once she caught on to the comical picture her muttered words had painted, she started to laugh. And when Mrs. Dorn laughed, people always laughed along with her, she was that contagious.

Since Marion had barred Robert access to Dani, she'd forced them to take strong measures to get to her.

News that the room they sought for their nefarious strategy would be empty had triggered their relief. After a little while, they all calmed down. Plans needed to be made.

Dr. Andrews began. "The quietest time on this particular ward at night is between four and five a.m. I've determined that you must create a disturbance at precisely four-thirty, my dear." This was said with a look at his housekeeper, who nodded in agreement. "Your room is at the furthest end of the hall and around the corner from Dani's. If you can make such a din as to bring both night nurses on duty to deal with you, then Grace and I can get to

Dani and take her out to the parking lot, where I'll have my car waiting."

"Sure, and if you're successful, this house'll be the first place your daft sister will send the coppers to look for her."

"Mrs. Dorn's right, Robert. We can't bring her here."

"Not immediately, no. We'll have to drive around with her for a while until the coast is clear."

"I have a better idea. Why don't we take her to my apartment? It's ground floor, with easy access to get the wheelchair through the door."

"Wonderful idea. Thank you, Grace." Dr. Andrews beamed at the younger woman and even reached out and patted her hand. Then he turned to the watchful gaze of the other woman present. "Mrs. Dorn, I have no doubt that by the morning the nurses will be happy to have me arrive and sign you out of the hospital. If you could make your way here by taxicab, we'll telephone periodically to find out when the coast is clear."

"You'll be going to the hospital?" Mrs. Dorn asked, surprised.

"I'll need to do my rounds. If I want them to believe in my innocence, I must appear to be following my normal routine."

"Meanwhile," Grace interrupted, "I'll keep her at my place until you fetch us to return here for noon." Nurse Joye's calm voice reassured the other two like nothing else could. Her manner made the ludicrous plans under discussion seem doable.

"Robert? Does your sister know about Dani's condition? About the baby, I mean?" Grace's concerned expression left no doubt that her question wasn't one of curiosity. Compassion shone in her blue eyes—eyes that through the course of these current events had unknowingly taken to looking straight at a person instead of continuously downwards. She bit on the side of her lower lip while awaiting the doctor's reply.

"Thanks to Mrs. Dorn's quick reflexes and smart thinking, Marion didn't get our charts. Therefore, the test results will have to be searched for again at the hospital. I'm hoping they won't have found that particular bit of information. It will have to come out sooner or later, but I believe it's important for Dani herself to share that bit of happy news with her mother."

"The poor wee darling!" Mrs. Dorn's heartfelt pity had the other two again smiling at each other. This time their cheek went unnoticed by the woman who sat shaking her head, the growth on her nose seeming more exposed on a face filled with pure sympathy.

****

In the bewitching hours between late night and early morning, Dr. Andrews and Nurse Joye cowered in the staircase exit directly across from Dani's room. They peeked through the upper section of the door, their images distorted by heavy, mottled glass. Five minutes before, the big clock over the nurse's station had shown four-thirty.

The ward slept, as did the nurse sitting at the desk, her face cupped in her supporting hand, elbow propped on the blotter, cap askew.

The other nurse, holding a small torch, made the rounds at the far end of the hall. Her light glowed faintly against the white walls. Her uniformed figure illuminated in the shadows looked to be much larger.

Carefully Dr. Andrews had twisted the knob and pushed the door open slightly, enough for them to be able to hear the anticipated ruckus. The humming of various types of machines echoed as the background music to a sleeping ward. A cough sounded and turned into a hacking gargle, then quieted.

The minute hand crept to the next digit, and then the next, which prompted the two to look at each other enquiringly.

Dr. Andrews' perplexed frown asked the question. Grace, in her nurse's uniform, shrugged and turned back to see the minute hand flip once again, and then again. Muscles already tense became sore as the two bent figures strained to hear something—anything—to indicate Mrs. Dorn hadn't fallen asleep.

First came a mighty crash. Then a wailing curse as the words "Bloody Hell," screamed in a furious male voice, exploded into the silence.

"Uh-oh!" Dr. Andrews whispered, and then he watched.

Sleeping Beauty at the desk flipped the chair backward with such force that she ended up rolling into the filing cabinet behind her and banging her head on an open drawer. "Ow! Blast and damn," she said, restraining her hand in midair before she slammed the cabinet shut and woke the ward.

With one final rub to the wounded area, she straightened herself, patted her cap back into place, and bolted, reaching the area across from 405 at the same moment the other nurse arrived. Both entered and were lost from view. Dr. Andrews and Nurse Joye scurried out of the stairwell and into Dani's darkened room.

"It were a woman, a bloomin' ghost. Godforsaken thing looked mad." The enraged male wouldn't be soothed. His voice carried quite clearly to where the two kidnappers were at work. They also heard the murmuring sounds from both the nurses, obviously trying to calm the enraged fellow.

"Don't shush me. She stood right there, I tell you. Batty thing wanted to kiss me. She swelled up and started flapping all over the place. For the love of God, I'm not making this up. It happened just like I said."

Nurse Joye crept behind Dr. Andrews and helped him unhook Dani's hospital equipment. Angry exclamations could still be heard from the other side of the partially opened door.

She whispered. "What in the world has Mrs. Dorn managed to do?" A giggle burst through, and she slapped a hand over her mouth.

He looked up and noticed the gleeful expression she wore. "I can't begin to imagine." He chuckled, sounding very much like a young lad engaged in a prank. "Why, you little devil, you're enjoying this whole adventure, aren't you?"

"I've never had the opportunity to be involved in such tomfoolery before. I must say, it's great fun—as long as we don't get caught."

"Bite your tongue, my dear." He scooped Dani's slightness into his arms. Wrapped carefully in the hospital blanket, she lay inert, looking endearingly helpless. He waited for a signal from Nurse Joye, who peeked out the door to make sure the path was clear.

"This blasted hospital promised me peace and quiet. I'm at the end of me tether, I tell you." Irate, and letting the world know it, the angry sufferer ranted on.

The nurses seemed to be losing their patience. Aware that the uproar would affect others if they didn't soon put a stop to it, they spoke firmly. "Sir, quiet down. There is no one in your room. You must have imagined it."

"Right! Tell that to the spook—"

His tirade ceased to matter after the stairway door closed behind the two body snatchers.

Chapter Twenty-Four

T roy, quit acting like such an ass. We'll be together again a week from now at my birthday party. You do have my uncle's address in your pocket?"

"It's engraved on my—"

"And don't be snippy."

"Yes, your royal highness."

"You're impossible! I've tried talking with you all morning, and you won't let me in. What is wrong with you? First you allow me a glimpse of what's in your heart; then you act like a moron who's sorry for sharing your sensitivity. I thought I was the kid here! Can't our last few moments together be happy ones?"

Troy sat on the vicarage bench, one ankle resting on the opposite knee. His arm lay along the bench's back. To an onlooker he resembled a confident man at ease, mellow.

Inside, he endured a mishmash of anxieties, stomach-eating fear and enough sorrow as to swallow him whole. Hiding his feelings from Dani had to be the most difficult task he'd ever taken on, but he knew how important it was that she be worry-free when she left him. His extreme unhappiness would only add to the already full load of despair she'd be carrying back with her. A bit of healthy anger towards his behaviour appeared much more appropriate than heartbreak.

She stopped speaking.

He waited, hating the silent treatment.

The breeze picked up, rustling the foliage around him. The rosebush's dark leaves stirred overhead, creating a perpetual melody as the wind blew them every which way.

Sunlight streamed through the canopy, dappling the ground below—shadow, then light. All three colours of the roses, red, pink, and white, bloomed with brilliance against the emerald background enfolding them, nestling them, emphasizing them.

He breathed in deeply, enjoying the aroma and atmosphere of the garden as much as the busy butterflies attracted to the petals' landing strips.

Finally, he cleared his throat, a hint. Still she refused to answer.

"Okay, you're right! I am being a jackass. I guess I'll miss your nagging, and I'm too damn stubborn to admit it."

"Be still, my heart. How can you expect a mere girl to be able to withstand such touching sentiments and overwhelming gushiness?"

"Listen here, Brat. You're lucky I'm even talking to you. First you invade a guy's privacy, you take over his life, and then you leave him broken-hearted. And I'm supposed to be nice?"

"Oh, Troy, you do have a way with words." The edge left her tone as she melted.

"Seriously, sweetheart, take care when you get back to your old life. I know your mother worries you, but since you'll soon be a mother yourself, you'll have to stand up to her. Be your own boss as much as possible. It'll be difficult, there's no doubt, but I also have no doubt of your abilities."

"Difficult? You have no idea. Thank God I've learned some very good lessons from you."

"You have? What?" His pleasure could be heard in his voice.

"Let's see. There's stubbornness, great swear words, how many beers it takes before you get a buzz—"

"Smarty-pants! You just wait till next Saturday. I'll teach you a lot more things."

"Things like what?" She crooned the words, picking up on his sudden switch from friend to lover.

He opened, allowing the sexual craving that pulsed in his system to rampage throughout his entire self. The image of two people entwined and making love, swept from him to her. His body, now fully aware, swelled and became involved.

"Oh, God, I can't wait." Her voice broke.

With Dani, the sexual pull felt different for him, more intense. There was a flagrant need, absolutely, but also much more of an emotional affinity. Probably because this time he loved.

Troy realized he'd gone too far. How could he get through this next week if he didn't control his yearning? He had to let her go. He firmly steered the conversation back to where it had been.

"Baby, your family loves you, especially your mother. She'll do what's right in the end because you're what matters, you and the little miracle in your tummy." Firm words she'd need to remember when she faced her mother alone.

He looked at his watch and noted the minutes galloping by.

"I can't bear to leave you."

"Dani, it's only one short week. We can do it."

"No, wait—"

"We have to start the magic." So saying, he reached up to the roses above and hesitated. *"What's your favourite colour?"*

"I don't want to go back yet. We can have one more week together. You don't know everything about me—"

"Not a good idea, Babe. Your family will be destroyed if you don't show up today. They don't know what's happened to you."

"I don't care. My uncle is a very determined man. He'll be here next week, and the one after that, if necessary."

"Dani! You're not thinking clearly. Now, what's your favourite colour?" He heard her sigh long and low.

She finally answered, *"Red. It's the rose that symbolizes love."*

He reached up and plucked a perfect red bloom with a wicked-looking thorn exposed on the crooked stem.

"Until next Saturday—be good, sweetheart."

He jabbed.

Chapter Twenty-Five

Nerves clamoured all Saturday morning as Dani's caretakers pulled off her kidnapping without a hitch. When the appointed hour arrived, the garden was a riot of colour. Busy birds hoping for lunch tweeted and whistled, creating a lovely atmosphere. Sunlight streamed through the branches overhead and left a variety of shifting designs on the worn cobblestones of the patio floor.

Dr. Andrews, tired and drawn, supported Dani's body while Nurse Joye fussed about with the intravenous paraphernalia. Finally, with everything in order, she sat, the teen on the bench sandwiched between her and the doctor. Reaching up, she gently pushed the wind-blown curls behind ears too small to restrain such weightiness. The fragrance of the teen-trendy shampoo and crème rinse used just that morning tickled her nose as a few red strands flicked past her cheek. She caressed the girl's face and then leaned back against the bench with a deep breath, purposely folding her hands, relaxed.

The picture of Dani's head nestled against her uncle's chest loosened something in the young blemished nurse. Restraints she hadn't know existed were unravelling. Normally she'd have sat with the right side of her face toward the doctor, but numerous tasks had kept her too busy to worry. Her hand started its automatic ascent, but at the last minute she stopped. Instead of covering her face, she pretended to straighten her cap.

"Don't worry so, Robert. I'm sure this week the magic will work, and Dani will be back with us."

"She could be anywhere, in any time period, in any body. What's been so difficult for me is that I have no idea if she's safe, unhappy, in danger... Do you know how frustrating it's been, not knowing? This whole bizarre state of affairs has been perfectly hellish, Grace."

Having been with him since the beginning, she knew what he'd gone through. She supposed he felt responsible for planting the bush in his own garden. If haggard features and pain-filled eyes were any indication of his inner apprehension, then the way he swilled indigestion medication was understandable.

"I do understand. We've been forced to use these underhanded tactics, and it's made life rather difficult."

He groaned and looked even worse. "I know."

"If you're worried about your sister returning, Mrs. Dorn has gone to make sure the doors are locked. We shan't be disturbed."

"Locked doors wouldn't stop Marion if she truly believed we had Dani in this house. But her two earlier searches convinced her we didn't. Now she's terrorizing the police station, stirring them up, driving them crazy."

"She's a mother with a cause. She loves her daughter."

"Cor, you're right there. And I love her. I've hated lying to her all this while, listening to her heartbreak, watching her fall apart."

"Yes, I know. I've seen the torment on your face whenever she's called. The last few days have been awfully hard on all of us. This latest debacle has been the worst, both for you and your sister. And for Mrs. Dorn, I wager."

A reluctant smile replaced the frown he'd worn. "She's a wonder. Imagine her accosting that patient last night, then hiding behind the curtains until the nurses calmed him down. She said it took hours."

"Maybe ten minutes."

"Not by Mrs. Dorn's timer."

"Whatever possessed her to try and kiss him?"

"Seems that didn't actually happen. She leaned over him to whisper the word 'boo,' hoping he'd wake up. When he did, he jumped, instinctively raising his head, and their faces collided. Her story."

"Wrapping herself in a sheet was a stroke of genius." Nurse Joye openly grinned at the man grinning back, two conspirators enjoying a moment.

"Mrs. Dorn's eccentricities have earned her a big raise and a week's holiday. I don't know what I'd have done without her."

Just then Mrs. Dorn appeared. She'd obviously overheard his last words, but she said nothing. She didn't have to. Agreement was expressed by her crafty half-smile and nodding. She pulled out a garden chair to perch on and then pointed at her watch.

The lovely red rose, lying innocently on the garden table, beckoned. Dr. Andrews lifted it and pricked the girl's limp finger. All three people held their breath. Whispers of disjointed prayers floated between them.

Dr. Andrews crossed himself, held up his watch arm and said, "Our Father—"

Nurse Joyce also crossed herself and repeated for what seemed like the hundredth time, "Holy Mary—"

Mrs. Dorn raised her hands prayer-like, and kicked in with, "Now I lay me—"

Dani did nothing. Not a movement, not even a sigh!

One minute passed. Still nothing. The second hand on Dr. Andrews' timepiece crawled. He gave up staring at his watch and instead checked Dani's eyes, looking for some sign that she'd returned. Nothing! He looked at the other two anxiously watching, waiting, and shook his head.

Mrs. Dorn started to cry—big gulping sobs. Water gushed from her protruding eyes like a pot boiling over. "I

can't take anymore. I've been spinnin' in me knickers too...
Ere now, what's that?"

Three pairs of eyes, all disbelieving, stared at the twitching body of the young teenager.

"Good grief! Sh-she's coming back to us," Dr. Andrews whispered, a decided hitch in his voice.

"Thank you, Lord." Grace's voice quivered

Mrs. Dorn spoke the loudest. "Lord love a duck, it worked." Instantly her face cleared, the waterworks stopping as if by magic. "Our sassy little madam's going to get a piece of me mind just as soon as she's up to it, I'm warning you now." Mrs. Dorn put her apron to good use mopping her face.

Chapter Twenty-Six

Troy missed Dani so much he couldn't sleep or eat. The emptiness she'd left behind did fill up—with painful longings, endless soul-searching, and one-sided discussions. A week! Who knew that seven days could seem like infinity?

The local paper hounded him for more of his articles, and this kept him going—losing himself in other people's lives. The tragedy of the fire inspired him. He'd never written better, or put more of his brilliant talent into every detail, every word. His genius was stretched to the max as he focused the readers, willing them to put themselves into the lives of those who were now homeless, terrified and in pain. Newspaper sales skyrocketed, and everyone talked about the event. What would happen to those poor lost souls?

Others who had suffered in the fire, and had read Susie's narrative about her Harry, searched Troy out. Many had similar tales to share. It seemed, when written by Troy, memories became chronicles of the ordinary person who needed to be remembered.

That evening when he returned to the Inn, Bunty was leaning on the counter, reading the local daily. As soon as the bell jingled indicating a customer, she looked up inquiringly, then relaxed when she saw who entered.

"Troy, did you read this special coverage today on the front page, the comments made by Ellie Ward?"

"No! What does she have to say?"

"Other than the fact that her latest novel was released a mite early and had to be pulled off the shelves until next week, she made another announcement that has most of us townsfolk agog. The darling girl secretly bought a property called The Gardens a few years ago and now plans to turn it into a care facility for the Kingsly folks. They'll have a place to go to when they're ready to leave the hospital. A place where they can all live together again."

He could tell what Bunty thought of the idea. Her face glowed with pride for one of their own. "I gather you're in favour of this happening?"

"Well, of course I am, and all the others I've talked with today feel the same way."

"What is this place you mentioned, The Gardens?"

"Right. You wouldn't know about that old abandoned property. A few years back, a crazy Yank—no insult intended…."

"None taken."

"The daft blighter decided to build a swanky resort outside of town as a getaway for Hollywood stars. It was to be top-o'-the-line. He didn't foresee that we don't do things in the same manner here like they do in your country. When the job didn't go his way, he shut it down half-finished, and left. Never seen hide nor hair of him again. Not long after, it was listed for sale, with no takers. Big ol' white elephant, if you ask me." Disgust rang in her voice.

"So you think it's a bad idea for Ellie to have offered this particular property for the Home?"

"Crikey, no. I think it's a jolly good idea. It'll take some work, but the bulk of the construction is finished, and the fancy large gardens won't need much restoring. The stall came about over the fixtures and novelty items the silly sod demanded be shipped from all over the world. Workers to install such vulgar luxuries couldn't be found hereabouts. I rather think he became discouraged at our bugger-it attitude."

A smile spread over Troy's face as the chuckle, he'd tried to hold back broke through. For a short time he looked like the same lighthearted fellow Bunty remembered from a few days ago.

"I gather the place is close to town and fairly large, then."

"Oh, it's huge. But if we keep to the basics for the improvements, the townsfolk will kick in as many free hours of volunteer labour as it will take to have it finished up in a hurry. I've no doubt it'll be a smashing place for the old dears to live." Her manicured finger pointed to the large photograph on page one. "Good on her, I say. Considering all she's had to overcome, she's a darling lass. Always has been."

Her voice rang with the truth as she saw it, and her manner substantiated her belief. The community was proud of Ellie. Troy couldn't pass up the chance to quiz Bunty further about the person who'd originally brought him to this small borough. He'd put her story on the back burner, but his intention had always been to find her eventually and get her to talk to him.

"What do you mean, after all she's overcome?"

Bunty's pride in the celebrated and popular author took over, and she couldn't resist the chance to brag. "The poor girl dealt with some huge obstacles as a teenager. Folks around here thought her a piece of work and were ever so vindictive about her improprieties. Me, I've never set myself up to judge anyone, but regrettably not everyone felt the same. She had it rough and came through the worst of it as the lovely person you see today."

Bunty didn't gossip. He had to give her credit for that much. But he kinda wished she did, he had so many questions.

"Is Ellie married now?"

"Never was."

"She has a little girl."

"Yes. Amy. She's a sweet child."

"I met her, and I know what you mean. She's a lovely little girl. Takes after her mum, does she?"

"In looks and personality. Amy has a million questions, just like Ellie always did when she wasn't much older. I guess it comes with the territory, being as how she's a best-selling author. Her books are sold worldwide. She's quite famous, you know. And it never went to her head. We're all very proud of her."

Reminded of whom they were discussing, Bunty's eyes narrowed. She backed away from the counter she'd been contentedly leaning on. And she shut down. He saw it in her eyes. Before that could happen, he had one last question.

"Since I've started writing on behalf of the victims, do you think she'd give me an interview about her plans for the new home? It would be a perfect ending for the columns, to let the world know the town has come through so well in this critical period."

Eyebrows puckered and wrinkles appeared while Bunty considered his request.

"I could give you her unlisted number if you want to try making an appointment."

"That would be wonderful. Thank you." He waited while she took a paper, wrote down the number, and passed it to him. He gave her the smile most women would sigh over before he went straight to his room to make the call.

For some strange reason the sadness that lurked inside him lifted when he heard Ellie Ward's voice.

"Hello?" A low, husky drawl answered after the second ring.

"Am I speaking with Ellie Ward?" He'd assumed she would be the one to answer the phone, but politeness demanded he ask.

An obvious note of caution could be heard. "Yes?"

"My name is Troy Brennan. I'd like to speak with you about your plans for the care home at The Gardens. I've been publishing stories about the victims from the fire for the last few days. Getting an interview with you on your perceptions and why you stepped in would be a great followup. Maybe you've read some of my work in the local papers?"

Either his name or his opening speech seemed to sway her away from her initial attitude. Gentleness invaded her voice and the crispness faded. She spoke so softly he strained to hear her words.

"Yes, I've read everything you've written, and I'm very impressed. Can you come to my office tomorrow, in the morning? Say eleven, shall we? Come around to the back at my parents' home, and you'll see the office door. I believe you know where they live. You've visited before—or so I've been told. We'll have lots of time to talk then." As an afterthought, she quickly added, "Of course that's if the time is convenient for you." Velvet oozed from her softened tones.

"I'd be happy to." Inside, his pulse quickened while his nerves started an uprising. *What was that all about?* "See you then," he answered. His tone, in contrast, came across as very businesslike.

Chapter Twenty-Seven

Daniell lay on her sickbed; still attached to the medical equipment she'd need for a day or so to monitor her vital signs. "Uncle Robert, you've got to believe me. I'm so terribly sorry for all the trouble I caused you." The pleading in her eyes, proof of her sincerity, touched him as always.

"I know, darling. I'm honoured that you chose to come to me with your troubles in the first place. But that said, I should be shot for negligence, leaving my notes lying around for you to find and—"

"No, Uncle. It was entirely my fault. That day, I would have done anything to avoid having to deal with my problems. But I've changed, grown up, and I'll work things out."

"You know I'll be here to give you all the help you need. And don't mind your mum. She'll come around."

"I still can't believe how badly she acted yesterday when she barged into the garden. If I hadn't been so weak, I would have stopped her. I'm only sorry she took out her anger on the wrong person and slugged Mrs. Dorn. It wasn't the poor old dear's fault she was forced to lie. Do you think she'll ever forgive us, and return to work here?"

"She's already back. Seems after 'the poor old dear' slammed out, she waited in the back garden until your mother left. Then my crafty employee accepted a rather large pay increase for her black eye, with two extra weeks of paid holidays thrown in to cover her pain and suffering. And my solemn promise to get the house key back from your mother turned out to be the clincher." He felt a silly grin creep over his face and couldn't stop it. *What would he do without that gin-toting woman to look after him?*

"It must have been a nightmare, keeping mother away for so long. I did try to come back last week but—I, I can't talk about it." He watched her trying to swallow the lump that clogged her throat. She choked, coughing intensely. Racking sobs interspersed with the irritated spasms. She was a mess.

Dr. Andrews, captivated by the various hues in her drenched amber-green eyes, gathered her gently into his arms. He rocked the slight body back and forth. This child, whom he loved more than anyone else, had the power to turn him inside out and upside down. He wasn't surprised at the rush of sympathy throbbing throughout his body. He'd never heard this sweet girl cry with such heartbreak, and he couldn't take it. His own eyes filled with sympathy.

"Dani, my dear, your mother will come to accept the baby. She needs time to recognize that not everything in life must conform to her expectations."

"Yes, I know. With your help, Uncle Robert, I'll get through these coming months until my little Amy is born. It's the next ten years that are making me cry."

"Ten years?"

"Yes. I met a man."

"You met a man?" Moments passed. "And?"

"I lived with him, inside him, and we fell in love. He's everything any woman could possibly ask for in a life partner. And he's coming for me."

Dr. Andrews waited for her to continue, a ploy he used often in his profession. She stayed silent, so he urged her with words. "He's coming…"

"To my birthday party."

"I look forward to meeting him; it's only a week away."

She groaned her next words. "My *twenty-seventh* birthday party." Her shaking hands reached to cover her eyes as the deluge started once more.

"Oh, my dear. I'm ever so sorry." He hugged her again as she became lost in her grief. Her body's weakness added to her inability to gain control, but eventually the span lengthened between her hiccupping sobs, signifying she was nearly empty. When exhaustion invaded, the battle was lost.

She slept while he watched and ruminated about her out-of-body experience. She had to have travelled forward in time and met this man at some point in the future—ten years in the future, according to her words. He had no doubt she'd ultimately tell him all about this person and he'd follow up on the chap in his own way. In the meantime, she'd need him to be on her side. Poor baby. He leaned over to brush the wayward curls from her damp cheeks.

Baby!

She mentioned having a baby girl called Amy. Oh, well, then, how lovely! He couldn't wait to share his glad tidings with Grace and Mrs. Dorn. It might be enough to get the housekeeper to stop glaring at him from her blackened eye.

In his favourite position, Doctor Andrews slouched in the rocking chair next to Dani's bed and watched over her while she slept, a routine he'd started many nights ago. She didn't know it yet, but he had dire warnings that needed to be passed on. His chest felt tight from his heart's heaviness. He didn't want to alarm her, but it was imperative she grasp the importance of his words.

She must not even think to change the future. No matter what might have happened while she time-travelled, it must be left to follow its natural outcome. He didn't relish explaining this to the child. Her intelligence was never in question, but the concept would be difficult for anyone to fully realize and accept. He unlinked his cramped fingers from behind his head and lowered them to the arms of his chair.

His sister's threat to leave Dani with him—supposedly because her ruined status was his fault—appeared to be the only plus he could look forward to. Even though he knew Marion wouldn't stick to her caveat, he'd have this special girl under his protection for a bit longer. He'd care for her and lend his support, guide and spoil, love and...

My God! Ten years!

Chapter Twenty-Eight

Troy brought Buddy along to his meeting with Ellie. Since Dani left, he'd expected the pup to become more of a hindrance, holding him back, always there—a constant reminder. Instead, the furry little bugger soothed him, a link to his spirit-friend.

Striding along at the end of his lead as if he owned the world, Buddy behaved impeccably—that is, until he saw the house where they were headed. After that he pulled, gasping and whining. He knew who would be there waiting for him, and he wasn't disappointed.

The minute they rounded the corner, Troy spied the little golden-haired princess skipping rope.

"Buddy!" She sprinted towards them; the rope lay on the grass forgotten. "Mr. Brennan, you brought him to see me. I'm so glad!" She spoke the truth, if her huge smile and shining eyes were anything to go by.

She looked at Troy, her questioning plea obvious, and his nod became answer enough. Scooping up the bundle of conniptions, she kissed and hugged and laughed. Her delight was reciprocated. Troy stood with his hands on his hips, waiting, enjoying every minute of the exuberant, mutual love affair in front of him.

Finally, Amy tucked the pup's body under her chin, and with a sigh he nestled right in. Eyes, the colour of amber, golden brown centres encircled by flashes of emeralds and lighter greens, pleaded with Troy. He knew what she wanted before she asked.

"Sweetheart, could you look after Buddy for me while I speak with your mother? I have an appointment with her, and I'd appreciate it if you could take him for a walk or play with him a bit. He doesn't get to play very often, and puppies need good times, too."

"You did name him Buddy. Your friend liked my suggestion?"

"My friend knew as soon as she heard it that the name suited him perfectly. Even he likes it." Troy gently grasped the pup's muzzle and shook it. "Since I started calling him by that name, he comes every time. When I tried Jehoshaphat, he just ignored me."

Amy burst into giggles. "I don't blame him."

"Okay, you're right. It wasn't so great. Then I tried Beelzebub… Why are you laughing? Beelzebub is a great name for him—it's a devil's name." Her peals of delighted chortles banished his mock gruffness and started the smile. The one every female he'd ever known couldn't resist. She couldn't, either. She threw herself into his arms, an expression of her delight, and he scooped her up, doggie and all.

She smelt wonderful, like sunshine and flowers—and everything a single man yearns to one day have for his very own.

"I hate to infringe on this happy reunion, but I do believe we have an appointment. Mr. Brennan, I presume?"

Troy slowly lowered his precious cargo and turned to see the woman he'd gambled his future on. He knew she was slender from the video he'd watched over and over, as well as from the glimpse he'd had of her a few days ago in town. But face-to-face created a whole different impression.

She was beautifully delicate, with eyes the same colour as her daughter's, only a whole lot bigger, more skilfully accentuated, more intense. Her earlier blondeness was mysteriously gone. Enlivened now to naturally reddish tones, her hair emerged as a striking mass of curls the wind loved. He wondered what it would look like without the yellow ribbon restraining the hotchpotch of wildness.

As a backdrop, the day's bright rays cast a radiance of gold all around her, which stopped him dead while he looked his fill. The flowing yellow sundress, fused to every luscious curve, added to the vision of a woman loved by the sun.

She stared back, surveying him from top to bottom. A smile emerged and lit her delicate features until every inch of her face became engulfed by it. He'd never seen anyone beam with such radiance, as if happiness shone from within.

His first instinct was to hold out his arms. *What the hell…?*

Hypnotized, he drowned in her spell while everything else faded. Even time seemed to stand still. Finally, seeming to tear her gaze from his, she twisted towards her daughter and spoke. "Amy, darling, don't… ahh hog the dog. I want my share."

"Funny, Mum." The sprite made a face, then skipped over to her mother and passed on the wiggling bundle. "Isn't he just like I described? Do you think I could keep him? Mr. Brennan, you did tell me you needed to find Buddy a good home. Remember?"

Ellie lifted the pup and became instantly adored. She turned away, and Troy heard her whispering but couldn't make out anything she said. The frenzied whining and tail-wagging indicated Buddy loved whatever nonsense she was sharing. He'd found another favourite person.

"If I could keep him, he'd be my playmate while you're working, Mum. You wouldn't have to feel bad for leaving me alone so much."

Troy hid his grin. It was obvious the little minx would use any ammunition in her arsenal. He remembered from his childhood that guilt—always a good weapon and understood by most children—worked miracles.

"I'll think about it, Amy, love, but for now I must take Mr. Brennan away. I'm sure he'll let you look after Buddy while we're having our meeting." An eyebrow the exact colour of her hair arched as she looked his way. She waited and waited, hummed, and waited even longer.

A tiny hand snuck into his and the tug of small fingers brought him back to the moment. "Sure, whatever. I'm your guy."

"My daughter wants your dog, Troy. I'm not sure she meant for you to be part of the package." Her teasing struck a chord. His name had come out so smoothly it went unnoticed.

Troy ducked down to be on the same level as the child who—without any shyness—snaked her arms around his neck. She gave him the same adoring look as she had given to Buddy earlier. His heart slid open and in she went. Another person to care for.

"Little one, he's yours with my blessings—if your mom agrees." He added the last bit when he heard the throat clearing that was meant for him to hear.

He stood. His hand slyly rubbed the kiss the little heart-stopper had left on his cheek before hurrying away with her precious bundle.

"Troy…" The woman caught herself, coughed, and readjusted her tone. "Mr. Brennan, how very kind of you. Amy adores animals, and she's wanted a pet for years. I'd love to have a dog, but I'm afraid that, because of my mother's allergies, it hasn't been possible. But I do believe our living accommodations will be changing soon and should remove that particular problem. Can I ask you to hold onto the puppy for another week or so until my arrangements are complete?"

"Please, go ahead and call me Troy. And sure, it's no problem, Ellie. I can hold onto the little fellow for a while longer." He flashed the grin he'd perfected in years of effective use and watched as the strangely devious look she wore deepened.

What the hell was that all about?

Chapter Twenty-Nine

While Troy inspected her office, Dani took a moment
to gather herself. She hid her face behind trembling
fingers and shielded her eyes. How could he not have
recognized her? For heaven's sake, she'd all but jumped into
his arms. Disappointment raged, curdling her zeal for this
meeting.

She watched him inspect her room and tried to see it
through his eyes. The white walls and carpeting made the
small office appear larger. Clutter loomed everywhere, but
in an organized fashion. Reference books piled on the side
of her large worktable battled with mounds of loose papers
for supremacy. The very latest in typewriters, its importance
defined by being set on its own matching side-section,
mocked an older model now relegated to a corner on the
floor. The businesslike black leather chair looked huge, but
the plush cushioning allowed her to snuggle in any way she
wanted—sometimes sprawling, sometimes sitting correctly,
and many times curled in a ball while hugging his picture
and crying.

Only two items decorated the walls: one, a beautiful
enlarged photograph of Amy as a small toddler frolicking in
a field of daisies; the other a print of Monet's most famous
painting, *Water Lilies*. Three inches of whiter wall showed
around the second image, an obvious inconsistency. It
indicated that another, larger frame had hung there recently.

The gigantic picture window she faced—detailed with
twelve-inch grids—overlooked the tidy gardens at the back
of the house, where multiple fruit trees and a luxurious

meadow lay. This vision compelled the eye and enhanced the room, a world to gaze at while the wheels turned, the ideas flowed and words became a story.

If the far wall cupboards hadn't been left open showing the numerous shelves stocked from top to bottom with books, books, and more books, the space would have seemed almost barren.

Dani regretted that he'd caught her at the end of her most recent project and therefore at a time when the whirlwind seemed the worst. In another few days, with the manuscript finished, her office would undergo its usual thorough cleaning to put it back to perfect order until she started work on the next episode.

She watched his eyes travel around the room and waited uneasily for his verdict. If he didn't appreciate the understated but alluring beauty of her favourite space, she'd be devastated.

His gaze settled on the panes of gleaming glass. She heard his indrawn breath—and a whispered "Wow!"—and was satisfied. The aesthetic effect of the massive floor-to-ceiling window seemed to have the same sway on him as it did on her.

With a merry smile, she went to the bookcase and slid open a panel where folding chairs were housed. Fetching him a seat took only a minute. When she turned back, she caught him reaching for the copy of her latest novel, *Come Find Me*. The cover, designed to her specifications, had vines of vibrant red roses in the background, and a red-haired woman's slender body, wearing a gorgeous white gown, illustrated in profile. Dani quickly slipped the novel out of his hands and held it against her chest protectively. He mustn't read the dedication.

"They accidentally released the book ahead of schedule. I had specified that it not be sent out for sale until later in the month. In fact, I had to ask the local bookstore to clear them from the window until I gave permission for him to sell them. Wanting to take advantage of some upsetting publicity that's being raging about a silly incident in Chicago, my publisher released the book early despite my explicit instructions."

"Could I speak to you about that incident? I..."

Her hand, held upwards in his direction, stopped his words. She shook her head to let him know exactly what her intentions were. Body language didn't need an interpreter; hers came across loud and clear. "No!"

"Why not?"

"Excuse me!"

"Why not, and don't say, 'Because I said so.' Even my mother didn't stop me with that answer." He grinned teasingly.

"Because I don't want to talk about it. Does that satisfy you, Mr. Can't-take-no-for-an-answer?"

"Were you injured? Is that why you can't talk about it?"

"No. And I can talk about it if I so choose."

"So—choose."

"Why should I?"

"Because people want to know about what happened, what made you take the risks you did, if you were scared—"

"I was terrified."

"Then why?"

"Because!" The word exploded. "Someone once showed me that you have to help those less fortunate. Even if it means taking the chance of personal injury. It's up to each and every one of us to help those in trouble." Ellie's eyes grew big, and her hands gripped the book she now clutched tightly, her knuckles white. "The girl in the bank— she was such a small girl, helpless. She wet herself. I saw it. I..." The shaking started, building into shudders, and Ellie was forced to drop the book on the chair nearby and put her arms around herself.

"Ellie, I'm sorry. You were right. You don't have to talk about it. Not now!" Troy's hand reached toward her, his expression regretful, full of compassion.

"Maybe never."

"Maybe." His voice caressed. The look in his gorgeous brown eyes was balm to her bruised and lonely spirit.

Her thoughts wandered as she lost herself in his gaze. He looked haggard and sad, and she knew why. He missed his soul mate, Dani. Missed the very person who stood in front of him except he didn't know it. He didn't know her. What a bizarre situation!

Standing near him, she felt drawn in a way she hadn't expected to feel. It reminded her of when a baby's gaze is ensnared by its mother's voice, lured by special ties to the one person in its world who loves it unconditionally.

Earlier, she'd spied on him as he'd played with Amy and Buddy, and it had been all she could do to keep from running to him and saying. "Look at me. God! Troy, please—recognize who I am. I've waited forever." But the moment passed.

After existing without him for ten years, she had her plans firmly set. If he had known her, everything would have fallen into place naturally. But that wasn't the case. Therefore, she would follow the course she'd already decided on.

Her promise to her uncle that she wouldn't ever tamper with the proper order had been hard, but necessary. It was now no longer pertinent, but still she needed to use these next few days to her advantage.

Troy had fallen in love with her seventeen-year-old spirit, but she'd grown up. Could she make him fall in love with her all over again, win his heart a second time? His loving her as Dani wasn't enough for her now, and she sensed it. There were ten years of layers added on and she just wasn't that girl anymore. She wanted Troy to fall for the woman he saw today.

The problem was that Dani held his heart. And the man was anything but fickle. What in the world was she to do? Not throwing herself into his arms and spilling the whole story, explaining her years of celibacy, loneliness, and heartache, took every ounce of willpower she'd attained over the purgatory of the last ten years. How she did it, she'd never know, but she managed to conquer her vulnerability.

Achieving status and acceptance as a best-selling author had taken a decade of hard work and discipline; however, some were born to write. She fell into that category.

Still, existing for ten years without him in her life had taken so much out of her. It had exhausted her stamina and turned her into a recluse.

Living her romantic experiments through the pages of her steamy novels could no longer be tolerated. She wanted a real man, her dream man—Troy.

He cut into her musings. "Ellie? I'm sorry. I didn't mean to upset you. Look, why don't we go ahead and talk about The Gardens and your plans for the care home. After all, it's why you agreed to see me today."

"Ellie?" He hesitated. "Are you there?" He waved a hand in front of her face.

When she drifted back, she couldn't hide the hunger, and she knew exactly when it registered.

His eyes narrowed, and his attitude underwent a distinct change. He backed away, mentally and physically.

She smarted from the rejection while at the same time she understood it.

Unlike her, he'd said goodbye only yesterday to the one he loved.

Chapter Thirty

S he must be a witch!

Troy couldn't conceive of any other reason for his unexpected reaction to Ellie Ward. Sprawled on his bed, pillows doubled behind him, he contemplated how she'd made him feel. Buddy shared the moment. His snout angled over his master's stomach, while Troy stroked and fondled the blissful pup.

Today Ellie Ward had captivated him beyond anything he'd ever before experienced. As their time together passed, her telling glances had driven him crazy. Crazy with lust! He knew the attraction couldn't be anything but carnal cravings. His heart already belonged to Dani—of that he had no doubt whatsoever.

That young miss had made him feel things he'd never dreamed he could be capable of. For his own protection, he'd always been a surface person—he might even say superficial—but all that had changed while Dani was with him. He loved her, pure and simple. And come Saturday, he would be meeting her in person. He yearned for the time to speed past, and a budding expectancy took root when he pictured their reunion.

Funny, he'd never asked her what she looked like. In all the talking and sharing they'd done, not once did that seem important. Now, with this distance between them, the question arose, making him wonder. He supposed he'd built his own image of her—ethereal and lovely and familiar.

His thoughts drifted to the many volumes of poetry and classics he'd read over the years, ones that glorified spiritual love, and he now understood their message. The truth stared him in the face. It didn't matter to him what she looked like. He'd experienced the most important part of her—a beautiful heart. How did he get so lucky?

Brooding, he scanned the room. The emptiness clamoured—palpable—like a living entity. Strange! The space felt cold without her sharing, her laughter—her warmth. Saturday couldn't come quickly enough.

It would be her birthday. Seventeen! Without her there to pooh-hoo his squeamishness at their age difference, he took a few seconds to examine his discomfort. But he quickly pushed it away again. They'd settled all that. He wouldn't look for problems ahead of time. If there were any, he'd deal with them as they surfaced. Think birthday presents. A girl her age would be difficult to buy for, and what he chose had to be something special.

Intuitively, he skipped to Ellie, sensing she could help him find a present. Females knew what other girls liked. No, wait. He had it, the perfect gift. He'd get an autographed copy of Ellie Ward's latest bestseller for a girl who dreamt of emulating her. Now that would be undeniably unique.

Nope! None of that! He intended to stay as far away from that redheaded temptress as possible. She was trouble with a capital No-Way!

His hand raked through his hair, a sure sign of exasperation. Admit it. She scared him silly. The truth was, he'd even made up his mind to give up trying for the interview about the bank robbery. Giving up on any story soured his soul and was definitely not his style. Nonetheless, her sensibilities warranted his consideration—and his distance. The lady sincerely did not want to share her ordeal, and his taste for the story had changed. With any other article, opposition only spurred him on; this woman's painful memories turned him mushy.

The local rag, the newspaper that had bought his special interest accounts of the recent fire victims, had contacted him earlier in the day with a proposition from the international press. They wanted the stories to go national and beyond. This would be the boost to his career he'd been looking for when he pursued the Ellie Ward scoop.

When he called the *Chicago Sun-Times* and offered them a deal, they jumped at his suggestion to be the first stateside paper to run the in-depth articles. In addition, he'd been asked to stop by to talk with them as soon as he returned home.

He glanced down at the pup whining for attention.

"It's one sweet deal, Buddy-Boy. I'll be a journalist working for one of the best newspapers around."

A paw shot out to shake—a trick Dani had taught the goofy mutt. It brought a smile flashing across Troy's face—enough of an invitation for the wiggling ball of fur to head-butt him with a seeking tongue aimed for his nose. Scooping the baby close, he whispered. "We'll be with her soon, Boy. Only five days to go."

Chapter Thirty-One

Uncle Robert, he wouldn't even look at me," Dani wailed as she ran towards him and flung herself against the startled man who'd risen at the sight of her distress. The doctor, as always, had been working diligently, papers strewn every which way around his garden table.

Her voice lowered to a theatrical whisper. "I acted the flirt, doing everything I knew to lead him on, and he stayed true to that stupid little girl."

"My dear, that stupid little girl is you." His arms gathered her close, while he patted her back.

"I'm so miffed. I am. I don't want him to love her. She's the past."

"Not for him."

"Confound it! She's a young girl! I need him to fall for me as the woman I am today. And it has to happen before my birthday." Sniffing, she pulled away, searched out a tissue from her pocket and swiped at her damp cheeks. "He's everything I knew he'd be, Uncle Robert. He's wonderful. You should have seen him with Amy. She's already in love with him. Talks about him and Buddy constantly. Mother's been wearing a sour look for days."

"Give the man a chance, Dani. In his mind, you left him only the other day. He'll need time to adapt…"

"There is no time!" She stamped her foot, and her voice rose to a yell. "I only have this week to attract him." Looking over at the quivering leaves of the greenery leading to the house, she snarled in that direction. "Come out of there, Mrs. Dorn, and give us a hand here. I've no patience today for your shenanigans."

Mrs. Dorn sauntered out, sputtering. "The dust behind there is frightful."

"Not possible, Mrs. Dorn. You dust there whenever Uncle Robert and I are visiting in this courtyard, which is quite often, isn't it?"

"Well! I never!" Indignantly, Mrs. Dorn puffed up, gaining inches in height, and the girth of her rotund body swelled.

"Yes, you do! All the time!" Dani was past caring about tweaking feelings. "Look, I need all the help I can get. So, Mrs. Dorn, if you have any suggestions for me, speak up now."

"Bosoms." The housekeeper replied promptly.

"What?" The doctor exploded.

"Excuse me?"

She had the attention of both uncle and niece.

"Yes, bosoms. You have lovely ones. In my day, they were one of the greatest assets for a girl to—"

"Bosoms? Mrs. Dorn, I beg to differ. You're labelling us men as insensitive louts caring for only a woman's physical attributes over the loveliness of her spirit. I'm sorry, but I must disagree."

"Oh, posh! There ain't a man alive as can ignore a fine pair of bosoms, and, lovie"—she pointed her podgy finger at Dani's chest, while the younger woman reacted by covering that part of her anatomy with both hands—"yours are one of the finest pair I've seen in me life. Dress them up, and wiggle them under his nose, and he'll be all over ya. Trust me." As she talked, Mrs. Dorn put her own hands under her large chest, and lifted the massive weight, jiggling it around a little to make her point.

The doctor's eyes widened and were quickly averted as he plunked back in his chair so hastily it came close to toppling over. Redness riddled his cheeks, and he bellowed. "Mrs. Dorn!"

"Doctor, don't you start. This ain't no time to bicker. This child needs to get her fellow to come courting. There's not much chance without a strong reason for him to all of a sudden switch from Dani to, ah, well—Ellie."

"I would never resort to that type of trickery, Mrs. Dorn." Dani couldn't help the silly grin that refused to be controlled.

"Then more fool you. Dani-love. Most females use those tricks very effectively."

"Don't you understand? It's not my body I want him to fall for, it's me."

"Same thing! He's already smitten with your, ah, youthful heart, and that part of you's only gotten better over the years. Act the naughty bimbo for a few days, and catch his attention. Like I said before, he'll be all over ya."

Doctor Andrews harrumphed, interrupting. "It is not the same thing, Mrs. Dorn, not at all. I'd like to think that the modern man has more sense than to allow his libido control over his behaviour."

"Piffle!"

"Piffle? Mrs. Dorn!" The doctor shot up from his chair, carelessly scattering more papers, his aggravation obvious. "Is it my understanding that you are telling my niece to act the tart to attract her man?"

"Yes, sir!" Mrs. Dorn's Cheshire grin provoked. A curler hung out from under her kerchief, dangling by a few hairs. Her double chin jiggled and her eyes twinkled. "Yes, sir," she repeated. Her hands fisted on each ample hip.

He suddenly relented. "You know, that just might work." He sat back down, rested his chin on his hand, and nodded.

Mrs. Dorn sniffed the air. "Me Yorkshire puddin'!" She hustled into the house to save her specialty dish from burning.

Dani waited until she left before turning on her uncle with an unbecoming scowl. "Did you mean that, or were you trying to pacify the woman who makes the best food in town?"

"I meant it. Every once in a while, the dotty old dear makes sense, even if I hate to agree. There aren't many days left. We know he fell for you without seeing what you looked like. Your essence, so to speak, attracted him, and in that you haven't changed. I guess now you need to see if he's attracted to the outer package. To your body."

"My bosoms," she sighed.

"Your bosoms," he agreed.

Chapter Thirty-Two

Dani slumped in her large black chair, seemingly mesmerized by the charming view from her office window. She'd been staring in the same direction without movement for so long that the slim leg curled under her weight tingled. She groaned, straightened, and massaged.

The steaming coffee next to her had cooled, but the aroma still soothed. She reached out to take a sip.

She'd been waiting all day in hopes that Troy would make the first move, except it didn't look like the blighter would. Phoning him, initiating a meeting, compromised her normal rules of behaviour, but in this case she was rather pressed for time.

Seeing him yesterday had only reinforced the love she'd nurtured for ten long years. She had plunged deeper into being absolutely and unequivocally dotty over the man.

When he'd approached, she'd started quivering. Shivers attacked, and warmth spread throughout her lower regions. Her breasts had swelled with anticipation. Close to him she felt such a consuming kind of madness that she had to tighten her stomach muscles and breathe deeply to control the fever. Readily accepting the truth that stared her in the face, she admitted to an intense eagerness for sexual activity—the sooner the better.

Yesterday, her irrepressible longing to touch him had to be clamped down. She'd spent so many evenings alone, just her with his scrapbook, that being near him was almost more than she could bear. Flashbacks and memories paled in comparison to the flesh-and-blood man.

When he'd looked at her with those incredibly warm, intense eyes, restraint flew out the window. Every bit of strength she possessed was called into play to stop herself from behaving like her daughter and flinging her body into his arms.

It became a battle of willpower for her not to kiss the dimple that flashed whenever he grinned in the sexy way he'd perfected. For her not to stroke the muscles in his arm or run her fingers over the tattoo imprinted there.

She remembered the day she'd snooped in the mirror and asked him about the words engraved on his arm. He rubbed at them almost reverently, then explained that on one of his excursions into India he'd met a brilliant body artist who talked him into accepting a gift of his work as payment for favours rendered.

At the time, he was touched by the offer but couldn't decide what type of artwork he would want to wear for the rest of his life. Stalling, he reached into his pocket and pulled out an American dollar to pay for a bottle of water from a street urchin. The perfect words hit him immediately.

In God We Trust, scripted across his forearm, was entwined amongst an incredible design of what looked to be doves, because of the wings—or were they angels? Imagination had taken over as she'd stared at his tattoo, and she still wasn't sure what the old man had drawn. She only knew Troy wore the work of a genius on his body, a masterpiece of which he seemed proud.

The day before, the edge of the drawing had teased her from under the rolled-up sleeve of his favoured green shirt, their shirt, the one she'd begged him to buy. Tiny burn holes from the fire could be seen here and there in the fabric. They taunted her, reminding her that what happened only a few days ago for Troy had been stored in her memory banks for a decade. The love and craving that raged throughout her body to balance her on the edge of madness had to be hidden by turning away from him.

Those very reminiscences had her hand hovering over the telephone. Ten years of enduring, waiting, controlling the urge to make contact, galvanized her to take action.

Licking her dry lips, reaching, her hand trembling, she took a couple of deep breaths to stop the panic in her flip-floppy stomach. She swallowed some of her coffee, now cold, and started her relaxing technique—one, two… Then she dialled the numbers that would connect her to her heart.

His voice reacted on her taut nerves, and she dropped the receiver into her lap. Grappling with the cord, she finally lifted it back to her ear only to find it upside down. Gritting her teeth, she fixed it in place properly and croaked.

"Hi!"

Wow, brilliant! Words from a best-selling author!

"Hello. Can I help you? Hel-lo! Who's speaking?" She plainly heard a smile in his voice. Gathering her senses, not an easy task, she blocked out her nervousness and answered. "Sorry, it's Ellie. Ellie Ward. I'm calling to offer you the interview you wanted about the bank incident in Chicago. I've changed my mind. I guess you're right, and people are interested in what happened that…"

"Hold it! You were perfectly clear. No way were you comfortable sharing your story. I respect you for your stance and wouldn't dream of taking advantage. But thanks for the call."

"No, wait! Hold it! I've changed my mind." What is wrong with the man? All he'd raved on about for the whole time she'd lived with him was getting this interview, and now he was spurning his golden opportunity?

"Actually, Ellie, I'm run ragged with the work I'm doing on the fire victims. The stories are going international, and I'm up to my ears getting the articles ready for the Chicago presses. Your section, what we discussed yesterday, will be the final segment."

"Hold it! You'd actually give up the chance to break this sensational piece yourself—allow another to get the inside scoop?" She crossed her fingers after bringing out the big guns.

"We-l-l, when you put it that way, how can I refuse?"

Was that chagrin she heard in his voice?

"There's a rather lovely restaurant, the Rhapsody, not far from your hotel. I thought we could meet there tomorrow, say at seven, for drinks and dinner, in a relaxed atmosphere, so to speak."

"I could come to your office. No problem. It would be much better." He spoke very quickly, the words shooting across the lines like projectiles from a Gatling gun.

"Troy! I hardly ever get a chance to go out for an evening, to dress up for a change. You'd be doing me a great favour by escorting me."

A rather long hesitation followed. "Well, since you put it that way, how can I refuse?"

Exactly! "I'll look forward to it. Ta-ra."

His distant manner worried her, because she knew it went against his nature. But her persistence had worn him down. He would be hers for the evening. She hung up the phone and wiped her perspiring hands over her jean-clad knees. Now, she needed to find the perfect dress.

And let her bosoms do the rest.

Chapter Thirty-Three

While Troy walked Buddy before his dinner date with Ellie, he plotted the casual approach he would use later. She'd talked him into the coming date against his better judgement. He wished now that he hadn't succumbed to the insecurity he'd heard in her voice. A woman with her looks? What the hell was that all about?

A man approached him. "Mr. Brennan, can I possibly have a minute of your time?" The fellow looked familiar.

"What can I do for you?" Troy's pleasant attitude stemmed from his childhood lessons of the golden rule— treat others the way you'd like to be treated.

"My name's Philip Butcher, Mr. Brennan." His hand extended to Troy with the obvious intention of starting the conversation on a good note.

Troy shook the hand and then stepped back, his arms crossed as he waited.

"I'm a reporter with the *Manchester News*. I'd like to ask you a few questions about the fire at the Kingsly Boarding House, and how you saved Mary Conway from being burnt to death. It was a pretty heroic act—"

"I'm sorry. I don't want to talk about it. I—"

"Mr. Brennan, most folks would have waited until the firemen arrived rather than take a chance on being injured themselves. People want to know what made you risk your own life to save an old woman, and furthermore a stranger."

"I don't care what people want to know. It's my business, and I'm not sharing."

Who the hell cares what others want to know, he thought before he realized the irony. He could never explain the reasons for doing what he did. First of all, who would believe he had a sixteen-year-old angel lurking inside him, encouraging him to take the plunge and be a hero? And secondly, all his life he'd gotten into these kinds of situations where he'd jump in first and worry about the consequences later. Why would he share any part of this information? He'd look like an idiot who couldn't mind his own business.

"Mr. Brennan, I don't want to hound you, but I'd really appreciate a quote and some idea of what transpired during the rescue. If you don't want to get too personal in the interview, that's fine, but like I said, people are interested in what you were thinking and how it felt to be in a burning building."

People are interested. They have a right to know. How many times had he used those same words? Now he found himself on the other end of this particular spectrum. It was his turn to feel the discomfort and anger at having his affairs investigated. At having a perfect stranger approach him and take for granted his private feelings should be an open book.

He bent to pick up the whining pup that sensed his master's ire. Cradling the furry mutt close, he faced the other man. He shook his head once, twice, and then sighed. But he still didn't speak.

"Look, sir, it's my job to ask you questions. We've gotten an interview with Ed and Mary. Therefore, we'll run the story anyway, but it seems only proper to get your input before doing so. In my experience, fear makes most people react in a specific manner, like calling for someone else to help them rather than take a risk themselves. You didn't do that. You acted on your own."

"I didn't act alone…" Troy stopped. *This guy is good.*

Softness descended over the other fellow's homely face, a face that again struck a chord somewhere in Troy's memory. "You had help from above, sir?"

"You could say that." Troy had to smile at the look of wonderment on the other man's face. *He probably thinks I'm loony-tunes*, popped into Troy's head. But the man surprised him.

"Wait'll my son Archie reads this story. He keeps on about a man who turned out to be his angel, over a week ago. Seems the bloke saved him and a stray dog Archie was trying to protect from a bunch of hooligans. He told me how big the Yank was, and that he wore a leather…" A sudden light of recognition and gratitude flooded his face. "It were you! You saved my boy."

"And ended up with the dog." Troy's large hand gently soothed the animal, giving lie to the tetchy tone in his voice. "Your Archie took off the minute he'd passed me the animal. Said his mom was *algeric*." Troy's grin took the sting from his words. "I'm still stuck with the bloody mutt."

Shared laughter broke through the barriers. Philip Butcher sheepishly began. "Mr. Brennan—"

"Call me Troy."

"Troy, then. My wife *is* allergic; Archie got it right. We can't own a pet. The lad knows this to be true, because there's a cat lives next to us and periodically sneaks into our garden. My wife has a terrible reaction, gets sicker than a dog—no pun intended. Otherwise, we'd likely end up with a whole kennel if Archie had his way. I could try and find a home for the doggy, if it's a real bother."

"Actually, I think I have found a good home, but thanks for the offer. Philip, about the story, I did what I had to do. If you had seen the agony on the old man's face when he begged for help to save his wife, no doubt you would have done exactly the same. Please, write the article, but I'd rather not say anymore."

"Thank you, Troy. I will write it, and as hard as I find it not to elaborate, I will respect your wishes. Oh, and I'll tell me boy I've had a chat with you."

"Thanks for understanding. Tell Archie not to worry. His little buddy will be well looked after."

Chapter Thirty-Four

Holy Cow! She looked gorgeous! Trouble with a capital *Oh-oh!* stared him in the face.

He'd been waiting at the bar and watching the entrance, on his second bottle of courage when a stunning lady arrived. Casually, he'd glanced her way, and then swivelled back toward the counter, not recognizing her. However, unable to resist looking at any beautiful woman, he'd double-checked in the mirror and realized his mistake. The doll in the low-cut, slinky black dress was his date for the next few hours.

It was going to be a long night.

His thoughts rioted while sweat accumulated in his hands. His collar shrank one size. *This is one mean joke!* Hesitant to turn and collect her, he didn't move. She'd done something different with her hair. The rioting red-gold curls were piled on top of her head and secured with black ribbons. At various places wavy strands had been allowed freedom to frame her face.

Her beauty transformed from lovely to dramatic. Luminous amber eyes, the very ones that held him mesmerized the day before scanned the place. Many people waved her way to acknowledge the town's star. Troy's overpowering instinct screamed *Run—Fast.*

A pep talk seemed necessary. Get a grip, Troy. That gorgeous creature is your date. Act the man, not a scared chump, and while you're at it, get the story you've been after all along. He squared his shoulders, cleared his throat, and approached her cautiously.

The smile she flashed in greeting all but took him to his knees. *Oh, shit! He was in big trouble.* Her hand gracefully lifted towards him. He gripped hard, pumping it like he would another man's. Then he dropped it quickly, just barely stopping himself from shaking off the sparks resulting afterward.

His eyes fixated on the wickedly enticing neckline of her dress. He felt positive the garment had been seeded and cultivated right on her body. How else could she have gotten into it? Her breasts beckoned—soft luscious globes of pure sweetness. "Miss Ward. Pleased to see you."

Aware of where his eyes lingered, and that his particularly dim-witted choice of words had brought a wicked smile to her lips, his composure crumbled. He blushed and felt sixteen again. *What a schmuck!*

"Call me Ellie, Troy. You did at our last meeting. I feel as if I've known you for a very long time, so let's not be formal."

"I wouldn't presume, Miss Ward. After all, you're famous and I'm, uh, just me. It's best we keep focused. The maître d' promised us a table by the fountain as soon as he knew you were my guest. I believe it's this way."

He waved his arm in the direction of the ornate marble statue decorating a huge birdbath in the middle of the spacious room. Water jetted to the centre of the bowl from three or four different directions. Hidden lights shone on the sprinkles and in the dim setting turned them into sprays of effervescent diamonds.

Before he could say another word, the restaurant owner himself approached Ellie to fawn. He guided her to their table, pulled out her chair, and blathered on about how she graced his premises.

Troy grinned and watched her frustration heighten. He had to give it to the classy lady; she didn't let on how uncomfortable this over-the-top treatment made her feel.

"Henry, thank you. My friend Mr. Brennan and I have looked forward to eating your wonderful food and enjoying your restaurant's discreet ambience. Troy, this is Henry Scott, an old school chum and a wonderful restaurateur."

The two men shook hands, and Troy's antennae picked up on the other man's attraction to Ellie. Pulling out his own seat, he turned to her, stunned by the hunger he happened to catch in her glance before she lowered her head to the large leather menu.

God, he hoped food sparked that craving. As a man of the world, he knew better.

He waited until they were alone and asked, "Can you recommend anything?"

She didn't answer.

Her soft skin glowed from the fountain's special effects. The illumination filtered a miasma of flickering light that mesmerized, enhancing the white skin of her graceful neck and shoulders, and especially the ivory valley between her pronounced breasts.

His fingers worked at the collar of his shirt, and he sent up a silent prayer of thanks for deciding against wearing a tie. His dress shirt and leather jacket constricted him enough without the discomfort of even more tightness. He removed the jacket, hung it on the chair, and, without thinking, began rolling his shirtsleeves up.

Enough time had passed since he'd asked his question, and he cleared his throat.

Catching his hint, she looked at him and spoke, her low voice husky and, for some strange reason, oddly familiar.

"Everything here is good." She put the menu down and dazzled him with the full effect of her avid gaze, her eyes a soft green weaving throughout dreamy brown. Her smile, inviting his response, captured, beguiled—enchanted.

"I'm glad you agreed to come with me tonight. After rushing to finish my last book, get it edited and to the publishers for deadline, I haven't had many chances to relax. When we're in the final phase of publication, my life gets pretty crazy. Also, I've been doing some plotting for my next novel, but so far the ending eludes me. For the first time in my life, I'm blocked." The twinkle in her eye, and her wry grin let him know it didn't concern her terribly.

"Dr. Troy's diagnosis is meltdown from overwork. It's happened to me once or twice in my career, so I get it. No one in our business goes unscathed, but professionals always work their way through, and you are an expert in your genre. How many best-sellers have you written so far?"

"I knew you'd make me feel better. You have a wonderful way with words." Not wanting to sound like a braggart, she ignored the last part of his question. Instead, she reached across the expanse of white linen, moved the candle, and stroked his hand.

He jumped like a scalded cat, gave her hand one clumsy pat, and swiftly put both of his under the table where he could white-knuckle them.

He glanced up and saw the hurt flare in her previously flirty eyes. Ranging through his mind for a different subject, he finally spoke. "I understand you've spent many hours with the old folks lately. They're full of stories about how you've been coming to visit each of them, along with the contractor you've hired. It's a great plan, asking for their preferences before rebuilding."

"I'm astounded by these people. After losing everything they own, at their age, you'd think they'd be devastated, but it's just not so—not with most of them, anyway. They mourn their precious items and irreplaceable photographs somewhat, but their biggest sorrow is the heartache from missing their mates who passed on. It's like they were all one big happy family. And they're grieving for what matters most—not things, but friends."

"I noticed the same thing." Keen about her topic, his interest captivated, he forgot his discomfort and leaned forward. "The truth of the old saying 'Wisdom comes with age' stares me in the face every time I'm there for another interview. Their spiritual beliefs help the old folks accept their plight in such a brave way it dazzles me—humbles me, actually. They cope by joking and hugging, and with sincere grief. Stories of past glories are shared and honoured, never ignored. Snivelling has no place with these men and women, and I want to be just like them when I grow up."

She laughed. Her beauty intensified.

"I know exactly what you mean. I visited Mary and Edmund Conway a few days ago, and they're still full of your heroics. You saved Mary's life."

"I had help from an invisible source." His face softened. He felt the goofy grin plaster itself over his face.

Whenever he thought of Dani there was the same reaction. Love for her swelled from his heart, leapt into the creases around his eyes, and even his lips seemed to connect with the feeling.

****

Faced with his obvious adoration for her other self, Ellie couldn't act the tart any longer. Jealousy mushroomed and grew.

Her hand rubbed at the headache pounding in her forehead. Remorse burned all the way into her stomach, becoming a fiery, aching throb made worse by the sudden fatigue washing over her.

Weak and shaky, accepting failure, she grabbed her purse and moved, ready to stand. She craved solitude for her tears and a glass of wine for her pain. Never had she felt so weighted down.

So disheartened.

So lonely!

Harshness rang in her tone. "You were right. This was a bad idea. If you still want the interview, we can go to my office, and I'll give you the facts."

Startled, he quickly stood and went to pull out her chair. Efficiently, she made their excuses, extricated them from the grovelling owner and got them into her car parked in a stall for special guests.

The drive took only a few minutes. To her, the silence spoke volumes. Her aching heart, heavy with regret, seemed to fill up her whole chest. The pain, worse than anything else she'd ever known, would disgrace her any minute. Her eyes burned with unshed tears, while her damp hands grasped the wheel, clinging to its solidity.

She needed to get away from him before she collapsed like a puddle of remorse right in front of him or screamed like a fishwife because he didn't recognize her.

Knowing he'd be coming for her on Saturday didn't alleviate her misery at all—it only made things worse. Call her an idiot, whatever, but having him fall in love with the person she was today meant so very much to her, because the Dani he knew really didn't exist anymore. She'd grown and developed into the smart, loving mother and career woman sitting next to him.

Dani would have added the term self-confident, but since he'd returned to her life that attribute had flown out the window. She'd even started biting her nails again, a habit broken years ago. What the hell was wrong with her?

Where did the vibrant, successful author disappear to, the heartbreaker who, over the years, had easily handled the many men attempting to flirt? Troy needed to meet that female. Her problem was that being in the same space with him made her stupid tongue disconnect from her brain and her nerves unite into one big malfunction.

What if, after he saw her at the party, his disappointment showed? Or anger? How could she possibly deal with it? A headache crawled up from her tense shoulders and lodged itself smack-dab above her eyes.

Meanwhile, the cheeky devil sat next to her in the dark and whistled. While she suffered through such turmoil, he sat relaxed and made a—a racket. Arrgghh!

"Stop that!"

"Stop what?"

"Making those silly noises."

"You don't like whistling? It's usually an indication of happiness."

"Well, I'm not happy. Please!" She pulled into the drive, shut off the engine, and laid her face over her hands where they still clutched the wheel. "Please." This time the word was a whisper.

"Aw, sweetheart! I'm sorry. I'll stop teasing." His mesmerizing voice oozed regret. "It's a bad habit I have when I'm nervous." Darkness shrouded them, creating their own little world. The night breezes wafting through the open window carried scents of jasmine and honeysuckle, while the full moon shot rays of golden magic to enclose them.

Sweetheart! It was the last word he'd said to her ten years earlier, and it broke her. Tears gushed. She flung open the car door and ran for the shelter of her private space. The room where she'd shed a million tears, written a million words about their love, and spent the better part of the last ten years planning for when they'd meet again. Except nothing was happening according to her plans. He didn't recognize her, and she'd always imagined he would.

He followed her. "Ellie, I don't know what I've done, but if it's any consolation, honey, I'm sorry." He moved behind the chair she'd flung herself into, and she felt his big rough hand stroke her cheek.

Her breathing stopped as if a spell had been cast. She sat motionless. And waited. He stood behind her, continuing his gentle treatment as if sensing she needed to be touched.

Very slowly, she twisted her head and kissed his palm. He hesitated, and before he could withdraw she put up her hand, trapping his.

"Ellie, I need to tell you that I have a girl. I'm not free."

"I'm not a girl, Troy." She stood and faced him, only inches away. "I'm a woman." She moved closer, slowly—very slowly—and then she stopped, her breasts against the front of his body.

He wavered.

Only seconds separated their lips. Heat ravaged her and pooled in her lower area, where heavy pulsations screamed for her to do something about them. As a candle's flame can light another, her desire ignited his.

Her eyes begged.

His eyes smouldered.

He reached to cup her face. But instead of taking her lips, he laid his forehead against hers and groaned.

"My girl's name is Dani. I'm in love with her, and I don't want to want you."

"Oh, Troy, I'm—"

"No, don't say anything yet. Right now, I'm so close to making love to you that I'll go crazy if we stop. Let me touch you for a few more seconds." As he whispered, his hands continued to stroke and caress her lips, her cheeks—he smoothed her hair—an unconquerable task. Neck muscles gave way and her face fell forward into his big palms. He gently lifted her chin as if he couldn't stand for her to be turned away. Her eyes grew heavy and closed; sensations rioted as the desire in his look grew too much for her. Under his touch, her body moved like a cat arching to its owner's hand.

Another harsh groan—this time the sound of unmistakable pain. He thrust her away and strode to the window, hands clasping his lean hips while his head hung dejectedly.

"You are one beautiful woman, Ellie Ward. If my heart didn't already belong to another, we'd be in a bed right now making love every way I know how."

Unforeseen anger snuck up on her and blasted through her control. "Where is this paragon of virtue you're so in love with? Why isn't she here with you..." Huskiness plagued her voice, and forced her to stop spilling out her bizarre resentment. In one more second she would have told him his Dani wasn't with him because she no longer existed. She'd grown up.

"She's dealing with some family issues. There's a situation she's gotten into, and it needs to be resolved before we can be together."

"What kind of situation?" *Keep him talking so he won't leave.* The voice in her head refused to be ignored. Since she couldn't bear to be alone just yet, she asked. "How old is this person you keep referring to as a girl?"

"That's not important to how I feel."

"How old?"

"Seventeen." He answered, grumbling audibly.

"Seventeen? She's a child." The look on his face made her back off that issue. "What's so important to her that she left you alone?"

"Nothing to be concerned about. She's in a bit of trouble and—"

"Trouble? She's pregnant?" Did he truly mind? It wasn't a question she'd ever asked him. Her heartbeats quickened. To breathe became difficult over the barrier of fear that instantly attached itself to the swallowing apparatus in her throat. Her hands felt clammy as she gripped them together. She hoped the queasy feeling in her stomach wouldn't erupt and shame her.

"For heaven's sake! I'm not the father. Look! In the short time I knew her; she grew to be a part of me—more than I can ever explain. And trust me; her kid will be very lucky. Dani will make a wonderful mother. Even though I've never thought of being anyone's dad, with her child, it would be a privilege." He turned away as if his emotions were too private to share.

She couldn't help herself. She walked up behind him and wrapped her arms around his waist, clinging with everything in her.

He put his hands over hers, and let his body relax. "Knowing how much I love her, I can't understand what kind of magic web this is that you've spread over me. I do know that if I turned around at this moment, I couldn't stop myself from taking you in my arms."

"Then turn. Please!"

"No!"

"Even though it's what you want?"

"More than my next breath!" As if the words he'd uttered in a low growling voice had been replayed to him, he stiffened, broke away, and headed for the door.

"I've gotta go. I'll return tomorrow for the interview." The door slammed behind him.

If he'd looked back and seen the brilliant smile plastered over her face, he would have had questions. A lot of questions! He'd rejected her, hadn't he? Except for one very important thing.

He hadn't wanted to!

She attracted him, and that fact alone restored her joy, her equanimity, and the contentment she'd clung to for ten long years. She was getting to him.

Unused energy had her swaying around the room while her hands rubbed together. Her feet, seeming to have a mind of their own, soon began swinging her in dizzying circles.

She loved the fact that letting her go hadn't been easy for him, but he'd done it. He was a man of strong principles. If he thought it hard tonight—the double entendre made her giggle—he didn't know what she had in store for him tomorrow. Her arms lifted as she waltzed in and out of the moonbeams reflecting in the glass of the uncovered window.

Her silhouette stopped her. She stared at her image and slowly moved towards her chair, settling inside the safe haven where she'd spent so many lonely hours fanaticizing, building characters and making them fall in love. Pondering their two meetings, her previous giddiness faded.

She'd always visualized that Troy would instinctively recognize who she was at first glance. Some kind of a mysterious pull would occur the moment he set eyes on her, and he'd just know. Not once did she imagine a scenario where things didn't happen in that way. And the fact that he hadn't known she was Dani threw her off kilter, messed with all her plans.

Over the years many men had pursued her, tempted her, and tried to start a relationship. They hadn't stood a chance. She'd obsessed over Troy to the point where no other man could ever live up to him. His pedestal loomed so high that even she was afraid. On the other hand, in ten years of growing up in the modern world one thing stood out clearly: attraction counted—physical attraction. If there was no sexual pull, they didn't stand a chance.

She hugged herself and rubbed her hands up and down her arms. Thoughts played ping-pong in her head. Why was I so scared to gain some experience? I'm like a child when it comes to knowing what pleases a guy. How can I carry this seduction off when the only time I've ever carried on with a grown man was between the pages of my books?

A sigh sounded, deep and long. Maybe I should just tell him who I am? He wanted me tonight. Then words poured out from inside her before she could stop them. They sounded loud in the quiet, moonlit room. "Sure, he wanted you, but he loves Dani." Her voice broke on the last word.

So, why couldn't it be enough? That he loved the girl. What was driving this overpowering need for him to be attracted to the woman? The answer came to her in a flash.

After writing so many romance stories where the hero and heroine couldn't keep their hands off each other, she wanted the same for herself. A man to want her beyond all that was sensible and all that was ordinary. Why couldn't it be her turn to entice a man to where he'd be so crazy for her, he wouldn't be able to turn away? One thing was certain. Her bosoms had worked tonight. Maybe showing off a little more of her body would work some additional magic?

Planning, and counting the hours until she'd see him next, she pictured her weapons. A lovely halter-top, one that revealed more than she normally felt comfortable showing, came to mind. Shorts—the really short ones that showed off her curves—yes! And her hair left free so he could run his hands through, as he'd tried to do earlier. The curls would be soft from the rainwater she'd use, and fragrant from the perfumed shampoo that would heighten his ardour, and...

She couldn't wait for the night to pass. When he returned the next day, he wouldn't know what hit him. Then, after they made beautiful love, she'd tell him her secret.

Chapter Thirty-Five

Would the night never end? Guilt had kept him awake and pacing for hours. He'd almost cheated on the love of his life, and he would never, ever, have imagined himself as a slimy, cheating bastard.

His conscience hounded him, driving him to knuckle-grinding desperation. Turning the remorse off wasn't an option. Whenever he closed his eyes, the red-haired siren he'd craved and burned for earlier snuck into his thoughts. Naked, he lay on his bed and fretted, while the blanket, a victim of his restlessness, ended up pooled on the floor, a warm nest for a tired puppy.

There'd been no respite since he returned to his lonely room and a happy Buddy. The ramifications of recalled images of the earlier evening had him suffering like a horny teenager. He needed a woman, and the only one he wanted wasn't available until Saturday.

Lying bastard!

He left the bed to pace again, his brain searching for some form of sanity. Nothing seemed normal to him anymore. Magic benches, time travel, spirit invasions... For heaven's sake, he'd fallen in love with a seventeen-year-old pregnant girl he'd never laid eyes on but who had lived inside him long enough to sabotage his wits and steal his heart. Didn't sound very normal to him.

On the other hand, he'd just spent the evening with a gorgeous woman who made his eyes go crossed from desire and hunger and... Accusations and remorse followed. There was nothing supernatural about the way his body had reacted to the woman he'd held earlier. He'd wanted her like he'd never wanted another. His brain knew she wasn't the girl he loved, but his body couldn't have cared less.

God, he was so screwed up! Probably not a good verb to use right then. The picture it brought to mind didn't help with his goal to get some shuteye. He fell on the bed, snatched the pillow, folded it in half, and shoved it under his wild hair.

His mind whirled, snagged a "what if" and then switched to a "maybe." Despair had him questioning whether Dani had been real or only his imagination. During those magical days spent with her, could he have been in a state of enchantment, like a spell or a pseudo hallucination?

Not a chance!

He lay on his bed hour after hour, wringing out his guilt and feeling as low as a snake. When his stamina finally waned, he gave in to his dreams. Dreams that took him where he couldn't go awake—right back into the arms of the fascinating woman he'd torn himself away from earlier.

The smell of her permeated his subconscious. A sensuous, stimulating odour that drifted into his head and took hold. Lips ripe and wanting trailed over his face, and her soft hands first soothed the skin of his cheeks, then plunged through his hair, forcing his head closer. His power to refuse shattered. Like an addict whose drug has been withheld for too long, her kiss drained until his body shuddered and all but collapsed. He scooped her closer.

Dream Girl still wore the low-cut black dress he'd so admired. His lips travelled to her neck. He sucked and licked her skin, winding his way first up to her ears, under her chin, and then downward to the slopes of her breasts. His hands joined his mouth as he scraped the slinky material and her lacy bra—first down, then under, forcing enticing mounds to protrude until her nipples stared him in the face. Suckling, biting, he made love to one side and quickly shifted, not forgetting the other.

Her moans of approval heightened his pleasure, and his voice joined hers. They hummed together—electric sparks heating to burn temperature. Trembling limbs, both his and hers, forced him to slow down. Lack of breath made him stop.

He looked his fill—past the white skin, the secretive eyes, and into the heart of the precious fantasy woman he held so gently in his arms...

And he knew.

The knowing wasn't an explosion of wisdom, but a soft smile of acceptance. How could he have been fooled for even a millisecond? She was his feminine side, everything beautiful in his life, his very own Dani. No one but Dani could make his heart sing this way or twist his senses into loops of happiness.

His eyes opened. The dream drifted away. He was left with a memory—and a body so aroused that he endured carnal discomfort once again.

From the first moment in Ellie's company he'd felt a strange link existing between them. He'd been attracted to her more than to any other female he'd ever met. Obviously his physical side connected even when his common sense hadn't recognized her.

Her way of laughing about things had seemed familiar, and his instinctive understanding of why she found something humorous made being in her company so easy. Thinking back, he recognized that even the inflections of sadness in Ellie's voice were the exact replica of Dani's. When she'd discussed the old folks' future after the fire, he'd known exactly how she felt. He remembered quaint phrases she'd used at their last meeting and shook his head at his blindness.

The more he thought on it, the more it made sense. Only she wasn't seventeen. How much older was she? After the bank robbery, he remembered that he'd done a bit of research, and her bio had listed her as twenty-six. He calculated quickly. Holy hell! It meant that, for her, their days together must have happened some ten years ago.

Heck, even her daughter, Amy, looked the right age and fit into that picture perfectly. Seems Dani's intuition had been correct after all. She had been pregnant.

Fury surpassed sexual dissatisfaction. Why the hell hadn't she told him? He sat on the side of the bed, head in his hands. Why hadn't she approached him honestly, explained the truth about the time travel, about the difference of ten years? What possessed her to play games—to fool with him and his emotions? The only ideas that made any sense at all disturbed and saddened.

She mustn't trust him. If he'd done the deed with Ellie, she'd have had proof he was a womanizing jerk who couldn't wait even a week to claim his girl.

Anger simmered, boiled, and ran over at her treachery. The muscles in his arms tightened as fists formed and clenched. How could a man put his faith in a deceiver? How could she have done this to him after what they'd been through? The smile he wore wasn't pretty—diabolical would describe it more accurately. He'd repay her for her lies and secrecy.

What if I turn the tables on her? Payback might be wrong, but it'll be damn satisfying. After all, making love to Ellie would really be making love with a grown-up Dani. It wouldn't be cheating—not really; only she won't know I've figured out her secret.

His girl—no, his woman—needed to be taught a lesson about manipulating people. And he was just the man to teach her.

Chapter Thirty-Six

Dani looked into the mirror for the umpteenth time, checking to be sure her shorts weren't too short. That her halter-top fit exactly right, and that her crazy hair, which normally gave her conniptions, didn't ruin the image she wanted to portray.

With gardening gloves and her pretty shade hat ready as props, he'd think she'd been gardening when he arrived. In actual fact, her everyday gardening gear looked more like ragged jeans cut off at the knee, worn with an old T-shirt tatty from too many washes, and a squished and ancient sunhat that fit tightly enough to control her flyaway curls. Not the look she wanted for today. She had in mind something quite different.

Mouth-wateringly sexy, yes—but not easy.

Interested and willing. Good.

An equal—a woman of today who had the poise and pizzazz to choose whichever man she wanted.

If his resistance still couldn't be overcome, she'd have to accept it, but knowing that Dani the woman attracted him as much as Dani the girl would go a long way to putting her mind at ease.

The hands on the clock moved too slowly. Changing her mind about her outfit wasn't an option; she'd already tried on half her closet. She knew, having lived with him, not to expect him for at least a couple of hours. He used the mornings to write the work he'd gathered the day before. Therefore, she wouldn't be seeing him any time before lunch. What to do? She'd go crazy without something to occupy her. Forget starting her new book. She hadn't made any sense on paper since he'd arrived in Bury.

Updating the beautifully tooled leather scrapbook she had lovingly kept on his work and successes all these years pleasured her immensely, but she had nothing more to add. She'd already put in the latest fire-victim articles.

Amy, her wonderful, annoyingly brilliant child, couldn't be talked into playing hooky this morning, because the summer-school teacher had promised the class a spelling bee, with a surprise for the winner. Wanting to be a writer like her mother, Amy loved this class the best of all.

In need of something to do or someone to talk to, she decided on a quick visit to her uncle, to get his moral support for the plans she'd set in motion.

Using the devil doorknocker reminded her of the day, ten years earlier, when she'd come to this very house for help. She'd ended up embroiled in a preposterous adventure. On Saturday, her life would come full circle. Imagining Troy's face when he realized that Ellie and Dani was the same person brought a smile to her heart.

Mrs. Dorn opened the door and immediately the good woman's mouth dropped open and her smallish eyes protruded. She scanned Dani's outfit.

"Hel-lo, pet. Where're ya going? To a hooker convention?"

"Too much? Is it the makeup? Or the clothes? What?"

While Dani turned in a circle, she spotted her uncle coming in from the garden. "Uncle Robert, you're a man. We need your help."

"Thank you, my dear. I don't believe you've ever been so loquacious with your compliments. A man, indeed!" Reddened cheeks, tight lips, and a raised eyebrow revealed some discomfort while he scrutinized her attire.

Dani, putting his attitude down to his being an old fuddy-duddy, ignored the signs. She followed him into the garden with Mrs. Dorn bringing up the rear.

"I need your help with my pursuit of Troy, which by the way is madly complicated, but coming along splendidly. He's falling for me and…" Dani wiggled a jive step while singing the words of the popular Beatles tune, "I Feel Fine."

A strange movement to his left beckoned the doctor. He swung around to watch Mrs. Dorn's older version of the jive, her arms waving, ample hips gyrating, while her head bopped.

Caught unaware by their high jinks, his grin responded to her silliness before he could check it. Dani cut him off as he opened his mouth with the obvious intention of speaking.

"But…!" Her uplifted forefinger emphasized. She grimaced, then wiggled her head. "Something is bugging me, and I can't understand why. After all, everything is going according to plan."

"Dani, go and make yourself comfortable in the garden while Mrs. Dorn and I get the tea tray. Then we'll all visit and find out what's bothering you. Excuse us for a few moments. Come, Mrs. Dorn." Sweeping his astounded housekeeper from the room and down the hallway took some doing.

"Doctor, stop 'ere, give over. Are you coming down with something? In all the years I've worked with you, not once have you ever wanted to help me make the tea."

"I still don't, Mrs. Dorn. I only wanted to get you aside to be sure we were on the same track. In our thinking—so to speak." He made a comical face when he heard what he'd said. And the whispered words "God forbid" slipped out.

"What do you have in mind, Doctor?"

He cleared his throat. "Did we encourage my niece to play the trollop, to engage with her fellow in insignificant sex?"

"No…" First her head moved to the negative. She watched him for signs and, reading his expression, slowed to a stop, then started moving in the positive. "Did we?"

"Mrs. Dorn. Did we or did we not persuade her to act the floozy so she could determine if Ellie the woman attracted Troy Brennan as much as Dani did as a young girl?"

"That we did, and it looks like we did a fine job, sir." This time her head did move up and down—a beatific smile lighting up her face.

"Oh, twaddle! What the hell were we thinking? The poor girl's in a pickle now, and it's entirely our fault. Come, Mrs. Dorn, no lollygagging. We need to get back to her and see if we can straighten out this mess."

Dr. Andrews, carrying the tray of cups, saucers, and condiments, was the first to brush aside the hanging fern leaves, step into the garden and see red hair splayed over the side of the rose-decked bench.

His fright at seeing the limp body, its seemingly lifeless arm hanging close to the ground, made him relax his hold on the tray, and everything slid toward the side. At the last moment, thankfully, catching the tiny grin on Dani's face stopped him from dropping the works and joining Mrs. Dorn in her screaming reaction.

Dani jumped up and ran to the shocked woman. "I'm so sorry, Mrs. Dorn. It was only a joke. I'm fine. Please forgive me. I'm really, truly sorry."

Mrs. Dorn fell back three steps, clutched her heart, and knocked over the flowerpot sitting in the centre of a table. The doctor wrested the teapot from her frozen fingers in an attempt to save some of the tea, although much of it had already poured out of the tilted spout. Dani guided her toward the bench, but with a look of horror the older woman jostled her aside and instead collapsed on one of the wicker garden chairs.

"Ya wee monster! You'll feel the back of me hand, ya will. Always knew a good tanning on your backside wouldn't come amiss. How dare you frighten a poor old woman like this? It'll be your fault if I lose a few years off me life for this bit of nonsense."

The grin couldn't be stopped. "I am sorry, Mrs. Dorn." Trying to straighten her face and look sincere took all Dani's acting ability. "Really!"

"After I've caught me breath, and me heart stops pounding, I'll be needing the loo right quick." With a dark look at the young girl, whose lips still quivered behind her fingers, the housekeeper heaved to her feet and stomped from the room.

"Uncle Robert, I'm sorry. I don't know what's gotten into me. I thought it would be a silly joke, and we'd all laugh about it. I never thought either one of you would get so upset."

"I've never seen you so witless, my dear. One minute you're questioning everything, and the next you're playing silly games."

His words produced the desired effect. Chastised, she sank onto the bench, and her complexion paled. "Oh, God! I am sorry."

"We reacted like we did because when you left us, ten years ago, those days were some of the most frightening and horrible ones we ever lived through."

"Yet for me, they were the best days of my life."

"Daniell, put yourself in our position. We had no knowledge of where you were, what had happened to you, or if were ever coming back. It was a nightmare. If not for Mrs. Dorn and Nurse Joye, I think I'd have gone mad."

When he called her by her full name, she knew he felt strongly and she needed to listen. Dani reached over and threw her arms around her uncle and best friend. She nuzzled into him like a child who knows a welcome is always there for her. "You're right, Uncle Robert. I'm an ungrateful, thoughtless, stupid little—"

"You've made your point, child. Let's move on. Forget the bad things, and let's dwell on the good." He patted her back, set her aside, and then reached towards the teapot.

"Speaking of good, how is Grace Joye, Uncle? I haven't seen her at all lately." Dani watched as her uncle's face underwent a complete metamorphosis, from a kind and loving uncle to a man in turmoil. "What's happened?"

"There's a secret matter that has been eating away at me for quite some time, dear. Nurse Joye is on an adventure, something similar to what you had. It's all I can tell you for now, but if anything would happen to me, I want you to be the first person to go into my personal files and deal with my research. I've given instructions to Mrs. Dorn, and she will abide by them. She'll keep all the paperwork safe for you to pass on to my colleague, John Norman."

"Mrs. Dorn won't abide by anything unless she gets her tea." Entering their retreat and making her way to the messy tray, Mrs. Dorn poured herself a cup, sniffed in the direction of the other two indignantly, and sat down on the chair she'd recently vacated.

Watching her uncle imitate zipping his lips, Dani caught on, nodded and changed the subject. "My dear Mrs. Dorn, Uncle Robert has reminded me how difficult things were for those of you left behind during the period I disappeared. And how insensitive it was of me to have played such a hideous prank." She moved over to kneel in front of her best supporter and gazed upwards beseechingly. "Please, don't be angry with me. I am truly sorry."

"Oh, get on with ya! I'm fine." A gnarled hand, smelling of bleach, a faint odour of gin wafting with it, reached to gently fondle the girl's cheek. "But—no more shenanigans. Now, how come you want our help?"

Dani resumed her seat next to her uncle, took his hand in hers, and closed her eyes for a minute. Two deep breaths and she lifted their locked hands and pounded them back down on her knee.

"Right! I'm happy, don't get me wrong. I invited Troy to have dinner with me last night, and after we returned home I inveigled him into an embrace. I sensed how extremely difficult it was for him to turn away from me, but he did. I understand this goes to prove he's a man to be trusted. The thing is, I didn't want him to leave. I wanted him to be so overcome with passion for me that he'd lose control and stop thinking at all, particularly about Dani."

Mrs. Dorn couldn't help her crowing. "Bosoms always work. I told ya so, now, didn't I?"

Dani's uncle winced, then turned to his housekeeper and answered, "Yes, my dear lady, we bow to your perceptiveness. Cleavages do seem to have their place in the natural scheme of things. All that aside, there still seems to be a problem." He turned back to Dani. "I don't understand why you're upset."

"Last night I planned to storm his boundaries, attract his pants off—literally, and it worked to a point. Today I want to turn up the heat, make it even harder for him to refuse a physical relationship. He wanted me. I know it. He tore himself from my arms, and I have no doubt about how difficult it was for him to do so."

"Dani, as the only man here, I must support him for his convictions. Why do you want to overcome those? And why are you questioning his attraction to you?"

"Because he left me for her! He's smitten with a seventeen-year-old who's got her claws dug into him, who in my heart I know is me, but in my mind she seems to be someone else—a completely different person. Can't you understand? I'm in competition with myself. I guess I need to know that he's as taken with me—the woman I am now—as he is with Dani." Her voice rose, the beseeching quality clear to both who listened. Releasing his hand, she aimed her finger towards her chest. "I need for him to love *me*."

"And you're basing all this anxiety on his physical responses, as if that's all that matters. What about his reactions to you as an individual, a lady, and a mother? It seems to me it should be as important as his sexual interest, or am I an old stick-in-the-mud psychologist who doesn't know what the hell he's talking about?"

Dani watched the crafty look he couldn't hide and knew what he'd said was important. She focussed. She revisited his words. And, as with a child who finally grasps a contrary mathematical problem, so came her awakening, her proverbial inner light bulb turned on.

She'd put sex at the root of her dilemma, because after ten years of celibacy she'd been so tied up with lustful cravings that her brain had all but turned to mush. Realization, once started, couldn't be stopped. Other important points came to mind. He'd never made love to Dani, and yet he'd loved her enough to spurn Ellie. Without a boastful thought in her head, she knew it hadn't been easy.

Last night, Troy's hard body and spontaneous reactions proved he wasn't immune to her charms—quite the opposite. Except the situation wasn't about the body's performance but the heart's elation. Peace stole over her, and for the very first time since this week began she knew which direction to go.

A huge weight dissipated inside her. All the upset muscle-clenching and nervy tingling that had been going on throughout her for the last few days miraculously slowed and let go, relinquishing their hold. Finally, she felt solid again.

Happiness flowed, but this time it wasn't attached to strings. She just felt light and carefree, looking forward to her coming reunion with Troy without any stipulations of behaviour, without any expectations. Just two adults learning to know each other, to like each other, and, with a little luck, to love each other.

She looked over at the two people watching her closely. She knew why she'd come to this discerning scholar today. The cunning old charmer had never let her down, and his sidekick, Mrs. Dorn, would agree with whoever seemed to need it the most. How lucky to have two such caring people in her life to support her, listen to her, and stand by her.

"Thank you, Uncle Robert. You're a genius." Kisses for each of the startled people left them both happy. While one still felt slightly bewildered, the other nodded knowingly and smiled. She might be his sister's birth daughter, but his endearing niece had always been the joy in his world.

Chapter Thirty-Seven

All morning Troy doggedly tried to focus on his work. His responsibilities came first; then he'd have the rest of the day to teach his naughty little friend a lesson she wouldn't soon forget: Don't tamper with a man's emotions—don't play him for a fool.

Resentment still fired all his nerve endings. It made his stomach violently reject any food and had his head pounding from the punishment he'd inflicted by staying awake most of the night.

Trying to understand what prompted her wicked thoughtlessness was time wasted. He stood up, wiggled his cramped hands, and stomped to the end of the room and back again. This time the sleepy puppy only watched from his nest on the soft green shirt. He whined softly. His little feet were still sore from their last march.

The questions still seethed. Why hadn't she approached him openly, honestly, to tell him the situation? What about the week she'd requested? He'd believed she wanted that time to strengthen her ties with her parents and organize her life so she could come to him unhampered. But that was when she was a pregnant seventeen-year-old.

His jumbled thoughts floated here and there like a tarnished autumn leaf riding air currents. Anger battled with sadness, but hurt won.

He couldn't see any way around it. She must have known about the time difference right from the beginning. In fact, when they were first together on the bench, and they'd both seen Ellie in the distance, had she understood the irony even then?

That said, how could this paranormal baloney even happen? Hadn't he had trouble accepting the truth despite her explanations? Maybe he needed to rethink everything.

Since he'd awakened to Dani and Ellie being the same woman, he'd been tagging her as a two-faced bitch—literally. But to give the devil her due, how could he expect a teenager to think straight at a time like that? He sure as hell hadn't.

She would have recognized her parents, though, and must have figured the little girl had to be hers. Maybe she didn't tell him at first because he would have wanted to interview her as Ellie, which obviously wouldn't have worked.

Okay, he'd accept that she didn't want to share with him at the beginning of their time together, but why hadn't she confessed about the ten-year gap before she left? She must have known, and she didn't tell him. That's what he couldn't get past.

Thoughts didn't revolve in his mind in any orderly fashion. They jumped around randomly. Neither coherence nor credibility seemed important.

His anger abated for a few seconds as reminiscences flooded. He dredged up recollections of how Dani cared for other people, and how she'd always wanted to put their needs first. How important it had been for her to help Archie, the little nipper who'd rescued Buddy. How she'd willingly put off her return home to answer the call to rescue the victims of the fire. And how she'd made Troy feel special, and loved, and happier than he'd ever been in his whole, lonely life.

He groaned, clutched his head in his hands, and fell back on the bed. A tiny pink tongue eased his pain somewhat as it snaked around his thumb and worked its way toward his palm. Soon a furry face followed, and then a wriggling body filled his hand to overflowing. As he picked up the jubilant little fuzzball and cuddled him, the troubled whine and adoring gaze made him smile.

"I guess it's time to take you to your new home, my friend. I bet there's a little girl who's going to be very happy tonight. Once I pay back both Miss Dani and Miss Ellie with a lesson they won't soon forget, I'll be on the plane heading to Chicago. I want no baggage and no regrets. I'll give them both what she tried to take last night, and I'll chalk the whole experience up to a lesson on the devil inside a woman…"

Buddy cut him off with a bark and a nip on his ear.

Troy held the dog away from him and looked into the gentle black eyes. "Cut that out! She deserves everything she's gonna get, and more. Then I'm going to make like a tree and leave." The small head turned to the side enquiringly. "Sorry, my sense of humour seems to have vanished."

A knock startled him into putting Buddy down on the bed and moving over to within a foot of the door before demanding, "Who's there?"

"It's Bunty, Troy. A package came for you, and it's marked urgent. I have it here."

His hand made short work of the hair falling over his forehead as he opened the door, but he needn't have bothered. No sooner had his fingers forged through the strands, everything returned to its earlier attractive messiness. He leaned one hip against the frame intentionally, a blatant message—do not disturb.

"Hi! Troy, it's your tickets from the travel agent. I can't believe you're really leaving us; we'll miss you so much. It's been rather special having a celebrity staying in our little inn." Bunty passed over a thick envelope, and when he reached to take it she wouldn't let go. "Troy, something isn't right. You haven't eaten all day, and your pacing can be heard all the way downstairs. If you need a shoulder—or any body part—I'd be happy to help." He couldn't keep from returning the teasing smile she threw his way.

"Bunty, my love, if you weren't such an incorrigible flirt, I'd wonder if you might be serious."

"You fancy someone else, otherwise I would be. Let me know if there's anything else we can do for you, and in case we don't see you again, be happy, lovie." When she kissed his cheek, her perfume surrounded him and rekindled his earlier rage against the female gender.

He closed the door roughly just as the downstairs phone drew her away. He engaged Buddy's leash, stashed the brown envelope and his morning's work into his briefcase, and lifted his newly purchased matching suitcase. It was time to even some scores.

If there is such a thing as a sixth sense, it must have been what stopped him to comb the room one last time. A green shirt lay crumpled on the bed where Buddy had been. The same one Dani had asked him to buy because she loved the colour. "Shit!" He hesitated. And in a symbolic gesture, he turned away.

As he stepped into the vestibule, Bunty stopped him. "Hold on, Troy, there's a call for you. It's long distance from Chicago."

He passed her the leash and put his baggage down by the counter, then made his way to the big black wall phone. With his face turned towards the wall, he spoke into the receiver and greeted his new boss, Chief Editor Tom O'Grady.

"Hey, Boyo, glad I caught you. I see, from the message I have here, you're intending to be home tomorrow."

"You got the final piece I phoned in on the fire victims yesterday?"

"Yep, it's right in front of me. Great work, Brennan! Glad those poor folks got themselves a happy ending. We're looking forward to seeing you, but I figured since you're in the same town as Ellie Ward you might like to take a bit longer and go after that—"

"No can do!"

"Wait a minute. You mean I'm not talking to Troy Brennan, the hotshot reporter who always gets his story, no matter who, no matter where, no matter how?"

"No matter *what* you say, it ain't gonna happen. She's shut tight on the issue and won't open up for anyone."

"Use the old Troy charm—she'll open for you."

"Nope!"

"You disappoint me, my man. I would have put money on you."

"I know what you're trying on here, Chief, and it won't work."

"Hey, gimme a break. I'm just doing my job. What can you call a man for doing his job—go ahead, spell it out."

"A-S-S-H-O-L-E."

A gruff snicker broke the silence after five long seconds. "You got balls. I gotta hand it to ya, Brennan."

"As long as you don't hand *them* to me, we'll be fine. See you tomorrow, Boss."

The bell over the door tinkled and caught Troy's attention as he dropped the receiver into place. He scanned the room looking for Bunty, but she'd made off with Buddy to the back garden. A scholarly-looking middle-aged man stood there wearing a strange expression, as if he knew Troy. Only Troy had never seen the fellow before in his life.

Rudeness never sat well with him, so he smiled pleasantly and said, "Can I help you, sir? Bunty, the proprietor, is in the back right now, but she should return shortly."

"Thank you, you're very kind. I believe I'm to meet a friend here, but it seems I must be early." The scrutiny from keen eyes staring over the rims of lowered glasses made Troy feel a bit disconcerted until the other man smiled and held out his hand. "Hello, I'm Robert Andrews."

"Pleased to meet you. I'm Troy Brennan." The handshake that followed was firm from both sides. Troy knew when he was being closely examined, but for some strange reason this man's gentle manner didn't unnerve him.

"You're the young reporter who wrote the wonderful stories in the paper about some very good friends of mine. A tragedy, what happened to the old Kingsly Home, and to the seniors who lived there."

"Yes, there were lives lost and hearts broken. But the townspeople are coming together to take care of their own. Especially Ellie Ward, who has bought The Gardens and is organizing renovations so it can be donated as their new Care Home. Do you know of it?"

The other man nodded. "A rather splendid idea, if you ask me. It's exactly what they need."

"In the end it'll be bigger and far better than the old rickety place they had before."

The genial fellow watched carefully as Troy spoke about the issue close to his heart. Whatever he said or did seemed to please the other man, who answered with a smile. "Strange how every once in a while, in certain situations, good deeds are born from tragedies. It's one of those unexplained mysteries, I suppose."

"Or else it's people striving to find a bright side—"

"Or being motivated to think positive."

The two men stopped and started to chuckle. Troy felt better somehow for having had this interlude with an intelligent man who saw things in the same way.

Buddy, followed by Bunty, made his usual ecstatic appearance and broke the spell. *Time to go!* Troy hugged

Bunty quickly, picked up his suitcases, and reached for the dog's leash. As he passed the other two, now in conversation, he noticed the older fellow answered his goodbye smile and nod with a worried frown while staring at his luggage.

Now why in the world would his impending departure bother the bloke?

Chapter Thirty-Eight

Troy knocked at the outside door of Ellie Ward's office. No answer. He walked around to the back of the house, where he thought he'd be able to see into her room, but the sheer white drapes at the picture window were closed. He peeked in through the glass high on her door and didn't see any movement. A small green-glass lamp shed its light over her desk, diffusing an eerie-mystic glow. A large expensive-looking book lay half on, half off the flat surface, as if tossed there and the culprit hadn't taken the time to check and see where it landed.

Ellie most likely had stepped out for a moment, so Troy placed his belongings against the outside wall, a little behind a large rhododendron bush. Then he released Buddy from his leash so the four-legged ball of energy could go explore in the huge garden. The eager puppy, ears flapping, white patches evident in the soft brown fur, took off to give chase to a butterfly. The image lightened the tall man's spirit. He stood, hands on hips, and watched—storing memories.

Then he tried the door handle and, when it opened, stepped inside the dim room, leaving the entry ajar. Wandering around and touching her things soothed him and eased the uncomfortable spikes of hostility still gnawing steadily in his stomach. He sat down in her chair. It fit him well. Her typewriter, the best available, instilled envy in his heart and had his fingers rising to the keys to try it on for size.

After a few moments, his hand reached towards the beautifully tooled leather binder on the edge of the table. Opening the flap, he eased back into the chair, and his eyebrows rose while his heartbeats hammered away inside his chest. Hand shaking, he started to turn the lovingly prepared pages of a schoolgirl's idolatry of himself. There were hearts embellishing all the columns, the tops and bottoms of each page, and many of the side margins.

Sections of newspaper clippings had been carefully glued onto each page; his photographs decorated with ribbons, gold or silver edging, many done in the shape of a heart. All the best stories of his earlier career were there, along with handwritten blurbs in a variety of pen colours, telling her personal views of his chronicles.

Footsteps approaching hadn't caught his attention, but her joyful greeting with Buddy did the trick. He jumped so fast he accidentally flipped the scrapbook to the floor and was caught red-handed, snatching it up, when she stepped into the room.

"Snooping?" She stood just inside the door with the sun's rays as her backdrop. Her hair had been left to fall naturally, soft and lovely, to frame her shoulders.

"Gardening?" His eyes explored the outfit she hadn't had time to change. God, she was one beautiful, hard-hearted doll. The short shorts had him gulping repeatedly, trying to dislodge the lumps of now-what-the-hell-am-I-going-to-do lodged in his throat. And her top, what there was of it, created a sublime setting for the same breasts that had kept him awake half the night.

Ignoring his comment, she stepped forward and grappled her possession from his loose grip, putting it behind her back like a child confronted by a questioning adult.

"You're probably wondering why I have this, ah, this old scrapbook—"

"As a matter of fact…"

"Yes, well, I—I started it many years ago when I was young-ger. Very young—little more than a child."

"A child?"

"Yes, very young, still in scho—"

He squinted, and then interrupted. "I can see that." Using his hands, he drew a heart in the air in front of him.

Blushing became her. "Did you…" Her voice, shaky and high, had to be cleared before she finished the sentence in as nonchalant a manner as her acting ability could stretch to. "Look through the whole book?"

"Nope, didn't have long enough. Only saw the first couple of pages." Lying came easy to him. Anger overrode guilt.

She swallowed and the redness in her cheeks lightened. Her fluttering eyelashes slowed. She threw out as fake a laugh as he'd ever heard. "It was a school project from years ago. I remembered it after you left last night and decided to dust it off and show it to you. But on second thought, it's a bit embarrassing to admit what a daft, dim-witted teenager I was. Therefore, it's probably best to put it back in the dark bowels of the shelf where I found it." By the time she finished this announcement, she'd already dashed across the room, thrown the book into the far reaches of a cupboard, and slammed the door.

Reaching next to the cupboard to grasp a tall cylinder placed there, she abruptly changed the subject. "Here are the recent plans for The Gardens. They delivered them this morning, and I know you wanted to see them, to be able to finish the piece you're doing about the fire." She spread them on top of the others already lying flat on a side table. A handful of ordinary garden rocks held the pages firmly in place and worked well in keeping them open.

"These are the second set?" Curious, he moved over to stand next to her, where he could lean down and survey the blueprints. His shoulder brushed against hers. Beguiling perfume attacked his senses, and made his head spin, reminding him of his intentions. Purposely, he leaned a little more into her.

"Yes," she replied, an edge to her voice not normally heard. She stepped back. "From the beginning, I've insisted the building be made to resemble a home for any age rather than a nursing residence for the elderly. I asked that all the servicing and medical areas be put on the lower floor, separate from the second and third levels where the apartments for the healthier old dears are to be located to take advantage of the view. This way they needn't be constantly reminded of their senior status and of the fact they live in a medical facility."

"I knew you weren't just a pretty face. What a great idea."

"I can't take credit for it. One of the older gentlemen, who just happens to be a retired architect, gave me the suggestion. I loved it as soon as he brought it up. He also recommended a lot of the grounds be developed as gardens with pavilions, where the residents can visit with each other, take walks, even plant things if they so wish. He had so many good ideas. I'm only glad I insisted they have input so their wants and needs will be taken into consideration."

The mutinous look on her face told Troy there was more to the story. "And?" he prompted.

"I wasn't taken seriously. I will be now, because as of yesterday there's a different contractor looking after the project. Seems Edmund and Mary Conway's grandson is one of the builders who worked on the original structure years back. He was more than happy to take on the job. Since he has a vested interest and, shall we say, an 'in' with the residents, I feel pretty secure that our wishes will be adhered to in the future."

"For such a sprite, you sure are loaded with attitude."

"I had a very good instructor, years ago, who taught me that I needed to go after what I wanted and not let anyone or anything stand in my way. So, yes, I can be a bit stubborn when it matters."

"And this matters."

"Of course! This is something I've been planning for many years."

"Pardon me? How could you know years ago that this would happen?" His voice rose as he questioned her, scoffing. *Caught! Would she admit who she was now?*

"I meant I've waited for years to be able to help someone in need. The world's been good to me, Troy, and I've wanted to repay the debt, but only in a way I knew would really matter." She stood in front of him, like a child would in front of the headmaster. Explanations poured out of her lying mouth. She stared up at him with the eyes of an angel—wide, appealing, and wholly deceitful.

He sighed. She still didn't trust him. Damned if he knew why. The simmering torment resumed in his gut while his cheek muscles tightened. He clenched his teeth, biting down on the harsh words on the verge of spilling out.

She'd caught him in her trance once again. For a short time, he'd felt pride in his little inner-mate, but the brazen woman standing in front of him wasn't her. She was phoney, a sham—a manipulative fake. Time to give the siren what she'd wanted last night. Afterward, he'd hit the road. He had a plane to catch.

Unable to stop himself, he drilled her with eyes half-closed until she dropped her gaze to her clasped hands.

"I need to change," she muttered.

"I think not. You look perfect for what I had in mind." Huskiness invaded his voice as it lowered several octaves, coming close to a whisper, matching the intentions he made clear in his body language as he leaned into her personal space.

Her smell, heady as any he'd known in his many years of bachelorhood, enticed him, had his male hormones leaping for joy. She was ripe, and he was picking.

"No, it's not what you think. Really, these are my—my gardening clothes. I'll go change," she babbled, and made to leave the room. But he snaked his hand towards her, moving quickly, reflexes honed from years of reporting on dangerous assignments in places where staying alive could depend on the difference between a slow reaction and a quick response.

****

Her hand was trapped. The tease lifted it to his mouth. Her breath caught, audible in the silent room. The devil licked the centre of her palm with the tip of his tongue until she swayed closer, and her heavy eyelids fluttered and lowered. She moaned and let his lips do what they wanted while the nerve endings in her palm celebrated. Her brain's signals seemed to be jumbled, as if an overseas switchboard operator had plugged in all the many lines incorrectly. Nothing made any sense.

His head bowed over the hand held captive while the fingers of her other hand itched to stroke and feel his soft gold-tinted, auburn waves—and so they did. The texture of his thick hair compelled her to sift through, not once but over and over. She made love to the strands like a mother does with her child—gently, blissfully touching him. Finally!

Long seconds passed before she realized he wasn't stirring. Her hand cupped his cheek. His lips didn't move. Silence reigned. Then she heard him sigh—an uneven harsh sound.

She found it hard to believe the fantasies she'd conjured for ten endless, unfulfilled years could soon become reality. Her hero, the one she'd imagined while writing all her romance books, the man she'd fallen in love with as a woman-child, was here in the flesh, kissing her body, wanting her.

The male image she'd mentally reproduced over and over while writing, creating scenes and plotting, was a person any woman would lust for—a real man. One whose strong arms she'd savoured for a short time last night and had hungered for since.

This time, by God, the devil wouldn't leave her crying, aching, with her flesh craving. She couldn't stand it. Every cell in her body cried out for passion. For loving and completion. One word reverberated over and over in her mind, and her lips took up the mantra.

"Please. Oh, Troy, please!"

****

Like a key switching on the ignition, her pleas stimulated his earlier intentions. Why the hell was he stopping? He needed to teach her a lesson about playing with a man's illusions. How dare she not tell him about the time difference, about the fact that she'd let him build all his dreams around a young girl who would need him to teach her the ways to love a man?

Instead, he faced a grown woman, a sophisticate, a writer of sex scenes and—in his mind—a total disenchantment.

He felt robbed of the years he'd imagined living with his young lover, years where he could adore her, spoil her and watch her grow both in body and spirit. Not only that, he'd lost out on Amy's baby years. The hours he'd spent lately, his imagination filled with pictures of him playing with his daughter or son, teaching and loving, had disintegrated like a curl of cigarette smoke in the wind.

The strength to walk away from her seduction yesterday was possible only because he hadn't known Dani and Elli were the same person. He knew better now, and he'd make her pay for the hell she'd put him through. The pot of anger Troy had fed and stirred earlier boiled over again.

Uppermost of all the thoughts ricocheting in his overtired mind lurked revenge. After all, she looked like a tart. Therefore, he had every right to take what she'd been offering, what she was offering at this very moment, wavering toward him, trembling. She begged "please," and he'd be answering, "Sure—and thank you, ma'am."

Rage stirred, bubbled, and blocked out every coherent thought—poof, gone, overtaken by pure animal lust. He crushed her tiny frame in his arms, muscles hardening. There was no gentle coaxing. He was all male dominance. This female meant nothing to him. She was a separate being from his Dani. The grownup Ellie wasn't anyone he'd come to care for yet.

He attacked her throat, rubbing his face into its contours while his tongue and lips feasted. Nips of passion jolted her, as he devoured her skin.

She squeaked. No other word for it. He yarded her into his arms, and she squeaked. A noise that a young girl would make, absolutely, but not the mature, chic woman of the world he'd imagined Ellie Ward to be.

The sound made him feel as if he'd been doused with ice water. He slowed his attack while his memory flipped to the evening before, when she'd sweetly offered her body— but she'd never demanded. She'd followed his every move, but not once did she initiate, come on strong or try to set the pace.

No longer comfortable with his he-man actions, he pulled back. Unaccustomed anger cooled as quickly as it had built; the initial sparks he'd fanned had been ego-driven. He knew it, and he also knew it wasn't his normal style.

She must have sensed his withdrawal, because she went into action. Wrapping herself around him as best she could, she pushed her trembling frame against his hardness. Soft arms encircled his neck while bare legs rubbed against his, bringing their bodies closer. It took Troy a little time for her behaviour to register. This was no femme fatale but an inexperienced bundle of shaking, moaning ingénue.

Her kisses were unschooled, mostly closed mouth and hidden tongue until he co-operated, and then she followed his lead just as she had before. Her unpractised embrace of enthusiasm touched him. But pain had ridden him for too many hours, and totally letting it go, or justifying her betrayal, wasn't an option.

****

His sweet ministrations to her neck awakened all the nerve ends in her inflamed body and left her weak and giddy at the same time. Every one of her five senses kicked into high gear from his loving.

It likely helped that she'd reminisced about Troy and dreamed about his kisses for ten years. Ripe for this moment, her emotions overrode inhibitions. Her insides felt like a pool of hot, wet mush. She lifted her head to plead, if need be.

The slumberous, smoking intent shining in his beautiful sultry eyes lasered at her and twisted her desire up so many notches that she knew if he left her now she'd go completely bonkers and turn into a cross-eyed, slathering fool.

He towered over her, his muscular chest blocking out her surroundings. Captured in a hypnotic state, she stared. Their gazes searched until he broke the spell and looked down towards her mouth. He raised his eyes to hers once more, imploring, daring—waiting.

She couldn't speak. There wasn't a bit of saliva left in the desert regions of her mouth. She couldn't even swallow. All she could do was hope that her heart wouldn't blow up and kill her before the release her body screamed for came to pass. Feeling helpless, she tried to signal him by pleading silently. *Help me! I'm untutored. All I can do is show you how I feel...*

From my eyes to yours,
From my heart to yours,
From my soul to you.

Eternity passed, and then he responded, his messages sweet, everything a woman in love wanted to see—and then a light went out inside him, and he growled.

Harshness had no place between them, but there could be no other word to describe the sounds emerging from between his clenched lips. Those same angry lips descended and attacked.

The onslaught of feelings when his mouth touched hers buckled her knees. If he hadn't wrapped his arms around her just then and plastered her body against the length of his own, she'd have fallen in a puddle of loose skin, because the muscles were gone—disintegrated.

"You want me. I know you do. And I want you. So, why not pleasure each other?" His husky voice brought uneasiness.

Whatever possessed her to remember a betrayal was involved, she'd never understand. If any actual thinking went on at all, it was her telling herself to shut the hell up. Too late! Words popped out before she could choke them back. The green-eyed devil rode her hard.

"What about your girl?"

"Forget about her. I want you."

He couldn't have said anything more apt to bury her unsettling doubts and snuff out the jealousy. Limp and befuddled, she followed where he led.

His lips forged trails over her face, while his hands cupped the back of her head and moved it to fit his purpose. Completely in control, he played her as a musician would lovingly play his instrument.

Having him take over suited her because she had no idea what to do besides offer herself to whatever he had in mind and go along for the ride.

Moving backwards, he leaned on the desk and held her tightly to him. Then, taking advantage of her acquiescence, he made love to every inch of her face and throat. He took his time and left no spot free from his licks and kisses.

He suckled her lips, pulling at the bottom one until he held it captive in his mouth. He released it and blew upon the wetness. She smiled. It tickled. Then he moved to kiss his way upwards to her eyes, stopping religiously at every curve. His hands cupped her skull with loving fingers as he sifted through the long strands of soft shiny curls.

Sounds issued from between those pliant, skilful weapons he used so effectively. Moans and growls that destroyed any remaining brain cells in her head. She felt his day's beard graze her neck as he worked his way along her throat to her ears. His breath blew shivers all over her body; her skin goose-bumped as if cold air attacked.

His nuzzling near her chin prompted her to lift and give him full access to anywhere he wanted to travel, and she prayed that his direction would soon be downward.

Her breasts puckered, painfully, craving his mouth. In fact her whole body flamed and writhed, shuddering for attention. When her cries of passion finally caught his attention, he shushed her all the while he descended, pleasuring her neck and the mounds on her chest, swollen and sensitized.

"Yes, please, Troy. Let me take my blouse off."

"No! Not yet, I'll do it—" Finally his hands moved to her shoulders and down her arms. His warm palms left a trail of fire in their wake.

When she sobbed in frustration, he took pity on her. He lowered the thin shoulder straps of the eyelet top ever so slowly. His mouth, moving all the while, bathed the mounds of skin until they were damp from his ministrations. Without any warning, his tongue snaked inside and licked the nipple.

She lost it. An overpowering, intense orgasm plundered through her body, and she rode it against his outthrust knee. Whimpering, her head rolled backward, exposing her lovely neck. If it weren't for his hard arms surrounding her, she would have fallen. Her legs gave way.

He gathered her to him, supporting her weight while his tongue never stopped its magic, and her sensations kept coming, wave upon wave.

Wetness pooled and saturated, preparing for his coming invasion. By the time she'd regained some semblance of thought, her blouse was lying on the chair behind her, and so was her lacy white strapless bra.

Her rubbery arms lifted to encircle his neck and she thrust her breasts upwards, aiming herself to his mouth and his needs. She'd never felt so alive, and every second she breathed him in, touched his body, and heard his male responses she surely existed in heaven.

"Don't ever stop. I love…"

"How I make you feel. I know. And baby, wait, I've only just begun."

So saying, Troy reached behind him and, in one fell swoop, cleared an area on the top of the desk. Lifting her easily, he turned to gently place her on the hard surface in front of him, on her back and completely in his power.

He slowly took off his shirt, one she'd never seen before. She took pleasure in the fact that he'd chosen to buy her favourite green. Off it went, on the floor. Then he loosened his belt and unzipped himself. Hesitating, he saw her eyes following and growing wider.

She looked upwards and caught the grin she'd memorized for ten long, lonely years, and she relaxed, sat up and reached for him. He moved between her open legs, ran his hands up her back, around to the front and over both breasts at the same time. He spent long seconds on each, kissing and loving them, and she watched him, all the while feeling wantonly sexy for the first time in her life.

In every story she'd ever written she'd described her heroines in the throes of passion, and she realized she'd come nowhere near the reality. How could a person who'd never gone through such gratification describe sensations of pleasure so strong, so sharp, that a brain could short-circuit from being overwhelmed?

There weren't enough adjectives to portray how beautiful a strong male body looked when aroused. Hard, while still smooth and soft to the touch. Sculptured muscles toned and formed to a specific build. When he stepped back and looked his fill, so did she. His face, passion etched on every feature, illustrated to a woman unquestionably that everything he wanted sat right in front of him.

****

The adoration that lit her features all but did him in. Intense amber flecked with green glowed with an inner radiance and showered him with sultry desire. Every movement of her wriggling body, every touch from her trailing fingers, every sigh, every whimper told him she wanted him inside her. He looked at her form and saw the daintiness, the tiny body of a small female, and something inside him loosened.

Her quivering skin, in the light of the small green desk lamp, glistened from her earlier climax, and her mop of reddish-gold hair swirled out from her head in every direction, a curiously touching sight.

She was the very image he'd carried in his heart of Dani. The night before, when they'd been together, he'd seen her dressed in all her finery, looking like a cosmopolitan woman of the world. He'd gotten an impression of chic that he now understood wasn't real.

Before he could follow these thoughts, she fooled him again by wrapping her legs around his hips and rubbing her bare chest against his. The touch of her small, hard nipples teasing him made his breathing quicken once again, and his male parts let him know they needed some attention. The kiss that followed all but unmanned him. Her enticing, womanly scent went straight to his head and put his thinking cells out of commission. He shifted to responses driven by pure adrenalin.

"Please, Troy. Please, love."

"Sweetheart, you don't have to beg. Just hang on."

She swooned. He took it as a sign that she was willing, and he was certainly able. There'd be no stopping him now.

He reached for the zipper on her shorts and, lifting her in his arms, he lowered them and her panties to her ankles, where she helped by kicking them off her feet. As quick as a flash, she had her legs open to him, and she leaned back, balancing on her elbows, smiling up at him as he undressed and moved forward into place.

For an instant, he wondered at himself, making love to her on a desk, for heaven's sake, but stopping now seemed beyond him—and beyond her, if her behaviour signalled anything. He watched as she licked her lips, trying to control her breathing. She squirmed, as hot for him as he was for her. Her head looked too heavy to hold upright, her long locks sweeping the desktop as she rolled her neck from side to side, her eyes beseeching.

He pulled her forward into his arms. Kissing her, he let his fingers slide down to her breasts where he spent some time cupping and gently squeezing, making sure his thumbs brushed back and forth, celebrating her nipples.

She grabbed his head and forced it downward, showing him where she most wanted his attention. His mouth, glad to obey, worked its magic once again as his tongue tasted her tight little buds while he sucked gently. Restive, his hands glided down her sides and over her hips to his goal—her thighs and sweet derrière.

Lying back, she readied herself. His fingers soon bore down on her wetness, and he engaged in manipulating her—stretching her, all the while soaking up her whimpers as his mouth once again attacked hers.

In no time she moaned, tightening around his fingers. He took this as a sign and, placing himself just right, he began to push into her soaking entryway. She stiffened for a few seconds, and then relaxed. Careful of his weight, his hips drove forward, gaining admission with every thrust. Strong female legs encircled, imprisoning him in a place he never wanted to leave. He slid in and out, again and again, circling and wiggling, faster and harder.

"Baby, oh, yes! Baby!" She was tight, virgin tight. It added to his gratification, and after the first plunge it seemed to add to hers, also. As he moved, so did she. Their groans synchronized, a symphony of sex. Just when the pleasure rose to the level of being unbearable, her inner muscles flexed, clenched and drained him. Wrapped together, they both reached the pinnacle in a crescendo of passion.

The pulsations went on far longer than he'd ever experienced before, and she throbbed along with him for what seemed like forever. They both moaned their completion.

Weak, he rested his face near hers. He felt both her hands slide over his hair and then his back, caressing. He could stay right here for the rest of his life. It felt that good. The softness of her body—everything a man could ever hope for—cuddled all around him, encasing him in utter contentment.

That is, until a child's voice could be heard in the distance, joyously calling, "Buddy, come here. Buddy!"

When she flipped him backward to the floor, his ass took the worst of the fall. She landed on top of him, all knees and elbows digging into places not made to take the brunt of such sharp appendages, especially in his condition.

"Oof! Ow!"

"Quick—get dressed. Amy's outside, and if she comes in, our goose is cooked."

What happened to the sexy vamp from just minutes ago?

"I can't find my shirt." He swivelled around on all fours, feeling like a fool. "Got it!"

Meanwhile, quick as only a mother could be at a time like this, she slithered into her undergarments and then stretched for her shorts and halter-top.

"Your pants, put on your pants." Her voice, husky and demanding, brooked no argument.

"Mummy, are you there? Come see who's visiting." A pounding on the door had both culprits visibly jumping and breathing a sigh of relief as they heard the puppy barking, moving away from the house, and Amy's laughter following.

From one minute deep in the throes of passion to the next in spasms of giggles, Dani pointed at her lover. His shirt buttons were done up, but not one in the proper hole.

He stood sheepishly in front of her, rubbing his elbow, his jeans on, but undone.

"You dump a poor guy on his arse and then laugh about it? What kind of a monster are you?"

"I'm a mother. Sorry, but it's my only excuse." Still smiling, she moved towards him and rebuttoned his shirt.

His hands worked their way first through his hair and then towards his collar to make sure it sat properly. Without intending to, or knowing he would, he reached for her hair and gathered the soft mess in his hands. Trying in a very manlike way to bring some semblance of order to the curls, he patted them and wove them over her shoulders.

Dani stood in front of him like a child. She couldn't have moved if her life depended on it. With his warm breath filtering over her, heaven couldn't be better. It was the moment she'd waited for, the moment to tell him her secret. No more holding back, no more games. It was time.

Chapter Thirty-Nine

Mummy, please come and play with us." Another thumping at the door from small, determined hands broke the spell. Both adults moved at once.

Too late! Her confession would have to wait for now. But not for long. She'd tell him as soon as she fixed herself.

"Troy, do you mind going and talking to her while I straighten myself a bit more?" She pushed against his chest, loving the idea that she could touch him. He was real, physically here, not in her imagination where he'd lurked for ten years.

The fact that she could assume he would do as she'd asked pleased her no end. She could almost imagine they were back together as they had been in the past, linked inside—one.

"Sure!" His hands lingered for a moment and then dropped from her body slowly. He leaned over and kissed her forehead, then nuzzled her hair as if her scent attracted him.

He turned to go to the door, opened it and looked back at her watching him move. He winked, and her heart's pump worked double-time. The pulse in her throat throbbed in unison. Romantics and poets wrote the truth. Love wasn't just an emotion—the physical reaction truly seemed as real. The door closed behind him. She breathed deeply, and then counted.

"One, two, three…"

Going to her bedroom through the passageway leading into the rest of the house, she stopped in front of the full-length mirror. The pronounced red abrasions on her cheeks and neck prompted her to take a few minutes to change and fix her makeup. Her hair, the bane of her life, looked horrible. Even after Troy's gentle tweaking she still looked like Medusa—corkscrew curls sticking out everywhere.

Stripping off her clothes, she blatantly stood naked in front of the mirror, trying to see herself the way he'd seen her. The vision that greeted her wasn't very encouraging. Her breasts were equal to filling a man's hands, but her nipples appeared like pebbles instead of stones. In fact, her whole body looked diminutive—puny almost. Everything was attached where it should be, and in proportion, but...

Oh, God!" Sudden realization of the possible aftermath from what they'd done stunned her. She could be pregnant! After all, she'd only "done it" one other time in her unexciting life, and Amy was the result. Her hands cradled the small protuberance of her tummy, and she smiled contentedly. Wouldn't that be a corker?

****

"Buddy is a wonderful little dog, Mr. Brennan. He comes when I call him, and he sits and listens when I talk." Seeing she had Troy's full attention, Amy continued. "His head twists sideways while he stares at me, as if he understands everything I tell him. Watch!"

Her finger pointed to the attentive mutt as she said, "You are the best dog in the world, Buddy, aren't you?"

In answer, the animal's alert face flipped to the right, his ears attempted to stand up, and he barked sharply.

Both Troy and Amy watched and laughed.

"He's as smart as they come, princess. Every time we've been anywhere near this neighbourhood, during our walks, he's pulled on his leash, trying to drag me back here to see you."

"Does he really?"

"Cross my heart." Troy followed through with the action.

"Cool!" She took his hand and yarded on it to bring him down to her height. Like her mother's, her stature was pint-sized.

He hunkered down in front of her, and she stared at him straight on. "My mum likes you a lot."

"She does?" He grinned, devilishly.

She returned his smile with a bit of the devil in her own grin visible.

"Uh-huh! She has a book just of you, with pictures and write-ups. I've seen it."

"You have?"

"Yep! She hides it, but one day I found it on the desk, and I peeked. Then I waited for you to come and find her. I'm so glad you finally did."

"You are, are you?"

"Uh-huh! I knew you'd make her happy, but I never knew that you might bring me the one thing I've wanted forever. The one thing I've begged for and never got."

"A puppy! Right?"

"Nope!' Blonde curls bounced as she shook from side to side. Her eyes narrowed, and then she stared at him strangely. "A daddy."

A bullet right in the middle of his forehead couldn't have blasted him more than those words. He'd be her father. This precious, beautiful little girl would call to her daddy, and he would be the one to answer. He looked directly at her while she watched him like a hawk.

Not too stupid, this child. She was waiting to see his reaction, and she hadn't long to wait. She'd seen the shock her words had produced.

Instinctively, she pulled back. The damage had begun. It showed in the slump of her shoulders and in the tears gathering in the corners of her eyes. Sadness appeared in the greeny-brown mirrors of a heart not yet protected by adult cynicism and caution.

"Sweetheart—" The yearning he'd seen scrawled across her face couldn't be confused with anything else. She swiped at the wetness and bit down on her bottom lip, then kept it trapped between her teeth. As though he were a magnetic force drawing her, she leaned towards him.

"You don't want a little girl?"

He gathered her into his arms, cradling her, rocking them both side to side. "Amy, I never thought I'd ever be lucky enough to have a little girl." He kissed her forehead. "And if you were that girl, nothing in the whole wide world—no, let's make it the whole entire universe—would make me happier. Nothing!"

****

"Amy, where's Troy—I mean, Mr. Brennan?" Reappearing after a short time, Dani found her daughter with a beatific look on her face as she hugged a wiggling pup trying to escape. His cries increased until small arms opened, allowing the agitated animal to run to the woman who reached down to lift and cradle him.

"He's gone."

Shock ripped through Dani's throat and emerged in her words. "He's what? Gone? Where has he gone?"

"He didn't say. He gave me Buddy. Then he took his suitcases from behind the bushes, and he waved, and said goodbye."

"Suitcases? Are you sure?"

"Yes."

"Did he say anything else?"

"Nope!" Amy, attention totally focused on the pink tongue licking at her reaching hands, didn't look into her mother's face, didn't see the disbelief or the tears.

Dani's chest tightened, and her hands, releasing the pup into her daughter's waiting arms, flew up to cover her mouth. Her mind screamed, but only one small word reverberated as it escaped.

"No-o!"

Chapter Forty

The next day, Troy arrived at the appropriate address a little earlier than the allotted time. He'd paced his room, then put in a few more miles around the vicarage garden. His final destination, scribbled on the paper he'd carried for a week, drew him. The large older home had a wall of trailing ivy and advertised a doctor's office on a small tasteful sign hanging from a wooden frame: Robert Andrews PsyD, Doctor of Psychology, Office at the Rear. The notice, spelled out in gold letters, was easy to read.

Where had he heard that name before? It sounded familiar. A good reporter retained that kind of information, but today things weren't working all that well. Troy scanned his memory bank. Nope, wouldn't come to him. Not surprising! On the little sleep he'd had the last few days, recalling his own name was something of an accomplishment.

The devil's face doorknocker spurred him on. *What the hell! So he arrived before anyone else. So what.* He lifted and banged the quaint appliance a couple of times and waited.

As soon as the man's face appeared, Troy remembered where he'd seen the fellow before. The door opened and a hand extended, along with a knowing smile. The dapper gentleman, dressed in a dark suit, white shirt, and red tie, wore the same spectacles as on the day he'd visited the inn.

"Couldn't wait, huh? I'm glad to see you again. Come in, please." Dr. Andrews' welcoming smile beckoned Troy across the threshold and into the large foyer. They shook hands again while eyeing each other closely.

A newel post, dark like mahogany, decorated the staircase leading upwards. An overgrown fern spilled from an antique wooden holder next to a full umbrella stand. An atmosphere of wealth and hominess was apparent.

"Hi, again. Guess you were checking up on me the other day?"

"Do you blame me?"

"When it comes to Dani and Amy's future, not at all."

"If it's any consolation, as soon as we shook hands I knew my fears to be unjustified."

"Oh?" Troy's baffled expression established interest. "I know you're a psychologist, and it's a requirement to be able to profile someone's personality, but how could you tell from so few words and a handshake?"

The doctor nonchalantly leaned back against the wall behind him. "Not the handshake, other than that you gripped firmly and made eye contact. And not the words, either, since we didn't speak at length—it was your whole manner. Before I came into the inn, I'd seen you in the window organizing your belongings as if you were in a hurry. You didn't know me at all, but you took the time to try and help me. You were kind. I liked you instantly. Whether you're good enough for my girls remains to be seen. I'll be watching closely."

"You're willing to give me the benefit of the doubt?"

"Actually, no. I just have a lot of faith in my niece. Dani has always been a wonderful judge of character, and she's told me that she learnt a lot of those skills from a very intimate friend of hers about ten years ago."

Troy melted. The pride he felt for his young roommate intensified. "Her pregnancy—did she suffer many cruel remarks from thoughtless fools?" This question had needled him and had to be asked.

"She did, yes. But she took every smirk and sneer and turned the hurt into a reason to show everyone what she was made of. Once her mother came around and supported Dani, the village backed off. Funny thing, though. At times I had the feeling Dani existed more in her head than in the world around her, at least for the first while. I'd say it became her greatest protection. Once Amy arrived, everything else slipped into place."

"Was Amy's dad ever in the picture?"

"Only until his death in a car accident when Amy still wore diapers. But then, that's a story for Dani to share."

"Ahem!" The first throat clearing hadn't registered, but the last blasted through the room, and put paid to further intimate conversation between the two men.

Dr. Andrews turned in the direction of the sound and, sighing resignedly, he extended his hand towards the stout woman in a flowery red dress as she hovered near the doorway of the large open parlour. "Mrs. Dorn, I'd like to introduce you to Dani's young man, Troy Brennan."

The woman swayed into the room, a born performer, and coquettishly placed her hand into the larger one waiting. Her whole demeanour entranced Troy as memories of Dani's stories about this woman flooded into his mind. Dani loved and trusted Mrs. Dorn, and her eccentricities.

His warmth engulfed her as he squeezed her fat little hand gently. "Hello, there. I've heard so much about you, Mrs. Dorn. Dani spoke of you with great affection." The smile he worked up just for her melted any resistance she might have felt towards him coming into their lives and disrupting the rhythm of their days.

"You're a bit of all right yerself, dearie." Her flirty smile had the doctor's eyes rolling. "Dani's talked about you so often. I'm that pleased to finally meet you."

The sound of a beeping horn caught everyone's attention. The doctor peeked out the ornamental window next to the door and recognized the vehicle being parked.

"It's Marion and Henry, Dani's mother and father. Did you want to meet them now, or wait for Dani to make the introductions?"

A firm look replaced the warm smile he'd held in place for Mrs. Dorn. Troy answered, "I'd like to meet her mother now. We might have some air clearing to do, and I'd prefer it finished before Dani and Amy arrive."

Approvingly the doctor nodded. "Good thinking." He moved to the door and waited to open it, while Mrs. Dorn patted the younger man's arm and winked conspiratorially.

"I'll wager she's met her match 'ere. Don't take no guff, me lad. Come find me in the kitchen when you've had enough, and I'll slip ya one of your favourite pints Dani brought over for you a few days back." Another pat and she bustled out of the room as if she couldn't get away fast enough.

Swinging the door wide, Dr. Andrews greeted the distinguished older couple with a hug and a handshake. Dani's mother stopped short upon spying Troy casually propped against the stairwell. His pleasant smile, polite but in no way toadying, was returned by Henry, who stepped forward and introduced himself.

"You must be Dani's American friend. I'm her father, Henry Howard, and this is my wife, Marion. It's a pleasure." His hand extended and gripped Troy's. Eyes the exact mix of greens and browns as his daughter's beamed.

"Troy Brennan," he replied, and added, "likewise." He straightened as he shook hands, letting the older man peruse and decide. In a very few seconds, he returned the satisfied smile offered to him from a contented father. An added squeeze and an extra shake sealed their unspoken acknowledgement.

He turned to find Dani's mother warily watching the performance in front of her. Her face, pale but staunch, showed no welcome whatsoever. Troy waited. *One, two, three...* She took her time studying him. He did the same. Tension built, but neither one looked away. An arm lifted, went around the woman's shoulders, and squeezed. Her brother lent his moral support without words. She smiled his way, and that was all it took.

Her face lit up in exactly the same way as her daughter's and granddaughter's. Troy was entranced, a goner. The special smile he'd used to enchant Amy and Dani was now employed to work the same magic with the mother.

"Mrs. Howard, I'm Dani's future. I hope we can be friends." He held out his hand, his charisma encasing her in his circle of warmth.

She slowly faced his way, her reluctance obvious. Her smile started to slide away but stopped before it completely disappeared. For an instant, portraying the uncertainty of a child, she bit her bottom lip. Then she placed her trembling fingers upon his. This was no handshake. She just held onto him, and that gorgeous smile again lit up her countenance.

"Hello, Troy. I should have recognized you the other day from a photograph Dani had of you in her office. She's been waiting for you a very long time." Her soft voice oozed over him like warm honey.

Sighs of relief echoed throughout the room.

Chapter Forty-One

The day she'd yearned for had finally arrived. It was her birthday. Dani got out of bed and, in her pink see-through baby-dolls, walked over to her mirror—and gasped.

Swollen eyes and an aching stomach were her reward for the crying jag she'd surrendered to the night before. Cold, trembling arms wrapped themselves around her upset tummy, where nerves played hell with her tense muscles. For ten long, hellish years she'd scratched days off calendars, planned and re-planned for this day. Now all she wanted to do was go back and hide in her bed.

A long sigh groaned through her without warning. She thought about everyone attending her party. They knew her well enough to notice her evident unhappiness. For their sakes, she needed to hide her sorrow, work on her appearance and pretend. After all, she was a grown woman, a world-famous author and mother to a wonderful little girl. Too bad she wasn't an actress.

Grabbing her hair and twisting it into a knot at her neck, she slowly trudged to the shower. As she passed her messy bed, where creamy rose-decorated sheets and quilts lay tangled, she stopped to peer at the enlarged photograph of Troy. Until recently, it had hung in her office. Taken in the jungles of Cambodia—war clearly evident in the background showing tanks and machine guns—Troy, the soldier, hunched down. She reached out and gently touched the face of the man she loved. It was her favourite of all the pictures she'd kept of him over the years. He'd grinned directly into the camera in much the way she remembered

him smiling at her years before in a clothing store mirror—
cheeky, eyes lit with humour.

Minutes later, water cascaded over her weary body.
She'd put her life on hold for the man she'd just lost. The
only way to combat her heartache was to have an itinerary
for her future. An agenda to get on with her life.

For as long as she could remember, everything she
chose revolved around Troy and her desperation to be with
him again. Trying to turn herself into a woman he'd be
proud of, she'd taken self-protection classes, kept up on
current affairs, read all the classics and poetry she knew he
favoured, even learned to cook the dishes he'd ordered
while they were together.

She'd wanted to be a person he would like as well as
love. Visualizing their life together, she knew how important
it was in a relationship to have similar interests, friendship,
and—God help her—trust. But during the endless hours of
the night she'd come to realize she had withheld the one
element he would consider most important. Her forehead
leaned on the glass, her head too heavy to hold upright.
Tears blended with the flowing water, but nothing could
dislodge the lump in her throat or the blinding pain
radiating from the back of her neck to the top of her head.

Why the hell hadn't she come right out and told him
who she was at the beginning instead of playing her silly-
bugger games? In retrospect, she knew his heart was huge;
he would have understood. Then they wouldn't have wasted
these last days. Instead, he'd left her and was now in
Chicago.

She'd blown it. Her relentless but juvenile need for him
to choose Ellie, the woman, over Dani, the girl he loved,
had started the problem. That and, even more important,
her stupid lack of self-confidence.

She studied her thought processes over the last few
days and realized her immaturity had taken over; her lack of

experience had marred her ability to think clearly. Hell, she could write this kind of conflict in a plot, but who in real life would believe anyone her age could be this dense?

Heart-sore and towel-clad, she lackadaisically moved around her room, dreading the irony of the next few hours. She relived those moments when he'd left her to go and visit with Amy—she'd been in heaven, happier than she'd ever felt in her life. Their lovemaking had been exciting, tender, and beautiful. Her breath caught as a jumble of reminiscences overruled her self-control. With her arms again wrapped around her middle, she lowered her weak body onto a chair and rocked.

Amy had said he brought his suitcase and left it outside the door. In her misery, she'd revisited that one incongruous point many times. He'd planned to leave town before he even saw her. Dani's shaky hand knuckled her eyes and then covered them completely. She wanted to shut off her thoughts, but the internal lever wouldn't move from rewind.

He must've decided that he'd betrayed Dani that night after we left the restaurant, because of his attraction to me, and for him that would be unforgivable. Then today, their lovemaking would have made his feelings of treachery even worse. No doubt there will be a letter awaiting me at the address I gave him. I have to face it. In his mind, his only honourable option would be to leave. The thought of his confusion and suffering made her tears start once again.

My fault.

Like a refrain from a song, those words popped into her head—again and again. Blasted hell! Why hadn't she confessed? Why carry things to such lengths?

Because she hadn't trusted. She'd wanted proof, and she'd gotten it. There was no longer any doubt about Ellie's allure. Her heart hurt so much.

My fault.

The towel fell to the floor as she stood, moved to her dresser, and slathered on body lotion. Then, naked, she walked to the wardrobe and pulled out the most beautiful dress she'd ever owned. It had taken her over a year to find the perfect one, because today was to have been the most important day in her life. Scrunched in her hands and cradled close to her heart, the turquoise chiffon material drifted and billowed in a shimmering pool of lavish beauty.

How was she to get through this day? Uncle Robert, Mrs. Dorn, even her parents, all had gone to so much trouble to make this year special. She couldn't stay home.

Not wanting to add the title of coward to that of fool, she squared her shoulders, slid into matching panties and bra, then the dress, and settled on the low seat to lean toward the mirror of her vanity table. She'd need all the creams, powders, and acting prowess she could amass today, just to appear to be someone she didn't hate.

****

A few hours later, Dani, head held high and tears choked back, walked with Amy to where torment lurked, waiting. The anguish of knowing this would be the worst instead of the best day of her life had to be lived through, and then it would be put behind her once and for all.

Amy, dressed to match her mother in a lovely white satin number trimmed in the same turquoise chiffon as Dani's outfit, skipped alongside. Her quaint shoes, dyed to match the sash, were flat-heeled, not high like her mother's, and were displayed with each running hop. Small fingers, wrapped around Dani's, tugged her forward while the child's nattering covered what would otherwise have been a conspicuous silence.

They sauntered along the cobblestone lane past rows of cottages barely visible behind abundant beech trees interspersed with birches.

Buddy, wearing a white bow Amy had attached to his collar, pranced in front of the two females, sensing how very handsome he looked in his finery.

"Mummy? Aren't you excited to see what your presents are? I made you something, but it isn't very big. I hope you like it. Do you want me to tell you what it is?"

Dani's sad thoughts lifted for the first time that day. "No, darling. Please let me be surprised. I have no doubt that, whatever it is, it will be my favourite gift of the day."

"No, it won't. I know what your best gift will be, but I can't say anything." To make sure, Amy plastered her hand over her mouth and looked adorable as she shook her head in a negative way. Lifting two fingers, she added, "You could torture me, and I still won't tell. I promised!"

"Then you mustn't say another word." Dani knew her daughter well, and her penchant for blurting out the very thing she tried to hide. She only hoped the girl retained this flaw as a teenager. It would make life as her mother a whole lot simpler.

Upon their arrival, Dani pasted a smile on her face, greeting each person with a hug, a kiss, and kind words. She played her part well as she wove through the room toward the kitchen and Mrs. Dorn's welcoming arms.

"Lass, you're a sight for me poor old eyes. It's lovely you look, but then, I never expected less." Chubby fingers wiped plump, wet cheeks and searched in the sleeve of her best dress for her perpetual hidden hanky. Her hair, dyed a deep unnatural brown, permed, and thinning to baldness in the front, was tightly curled in honour of the special occasion.

The door behind them opened and Uncle Robert's beaming face peeked around in a teasing way before he snuck in to get his cuddles as well. She'd missed him when they arrived. He'd been away from the front door, probably visiting with some of the many wandering guests.

"There you are." He lifted her two hands wide and looked his fill. "You're enchanting, little girl."

The first true smile in many hours lit her features. "How can you still call me that when today I'm twenty-seven years—"

"Years young." He hugged her to him. "To me, you'll always be my curly-haired, precious little niece, and more beautiful with every passing year."

She replied charmingly, "Thank you, kind sir. Your eyes, ever so perceptive, have remained true even in your dotage." A giggle escaped.

"And you, my dear, have remained a little horror."

Laughing, she hugged him with all her might, and stifled the escaped sob with a cough.

He stepped back and beamed. It was the only word to describe the happiness he couldn't hide. "It's finally here. The day we've been waiting for. Ten years! Are you excited?"

Her face fell, and the previously veiled sadness became apparent. "I don't know how to tell you—"

"Never mind. I'm so flustered, I'm not thinking straight. You mustn't tarry any longer with us old meddlers. You need to go into the garden for your best present." So saying, he led her towards the doorway and gave her a little push.

She stopped dead, turning towards him, wanting to explain, to save them from any embarrassment, but she was manhandled into the previous direction and gently nudged again. Still she froze in place and then again faced the two who meant the world to her. Before she could speak, the lovable housekeeper urged her on, prodding and waving with her hands.

"Go, lovie," Mrs. Dorn's arch look spoke volumes. "Don't keep him waiting."

They were only words, small silly words, so how could they produce such a change? But with those very few syllables Dani's world righted itself, twisting towards a future she'd envisioned for ten long and lonely years. Her heartbeat rose from normal to insanely hard-to-breathe in just a few seconds.

She flew to her favourite place in the house, only to come to a dead stop under the overhanging greenery. Troy sat waiting, looking slightly uncomfortable on the bench, his hands well away from the roses trailing behind.

Chapter Forty-Two

Y ou came?" Her words brought him out of his reverie. Her trembling lips and the tearful way she said the words brought him to her side in an instant. "Of course I came. I promised, didn't I?"

His hands cradled her face as he looked his fill. He saw joy, overshadowing recent distress, and knew they both had a lot of explaining to do before moving forward.

"Why didn't you tell me?" He didn't need to spell it out. They were still on the same wavelength, just as they were when merged.

She sighed and shook her head regretfully. "At first I didn't understand it myself. Remember when we were first together, and we saw the woman in the vicarage garden? I felt her mixed emotions, but I didn't know who she was. It scared me. Then my parents appeared, but much older. I recognized them. The child was a mystery."

"Amy."

"Yes. It took until we went to the house before I knew precisely who she was. Remember, I only thought I might be pregnant, but to a sixteen-year-old, there's always wiggle room, and I didn't know how old she was then. I still hadn't accepted that I was actually going to be a mother."

"Okay. I get that. When did you know about the time difference?"

"There was no exact moment. It just slowly seeped in. Once when you were reading the newspaper I saw the date, and all my suspicions were verified."

"And you didn't tell me what you'd discovered because…?"

"Because it wouldn't have been at all fair to you. Don't you see? Before I left you I knew there would be a ten-year wait for me, but only one week for you. If you knew I'd have to wait that long before we could be together, either you would have refused to even consider tying me to you for such a long time, or you'd have felt compelled to follow through. No matter what you thought once you met me today, you—"

He interrupted her, angry sparks lighting up his golden eyes. His hands tightened around her face and gave her a little shake. "You had no faith in my feelings for you."

"No!" The truth rang in her voice and showed in her expression. "No, that wasn't it at all. In fact, just the opposite! I didn't have faith in my ability to attract you as the person I am today. I had ten years to let stupid doubts creep in and to lose my youthful self-confidence. I knew I'd changed from the girl you fell in love with, and I couldn't be certain you'd care in the same way for the woman I've become."

His gaze noted the swelling around her eyes, veiled by creams and only noticeable because he was so close. He couldn't mistake the recent ravages of trauma written plainly over her features. This was not the same glowing woman he'd left in her office the day before.

Displeasure at his behaviour seeped in. Yesterday's punishment seemed childish in the light of today's honesty. Her words had driven a spike straight into his puffed-up indignation and labelled him exactly what he was: a stupid ass!

"Aw, sweetheart! What a mess! Okay, I understand why you didn't tell me while we were bonded together. However, this last week after we'd met again is another story. Especially after I'd begun making love to you." He shook his head. "I don't get it."

When understanding dawned, she stepped back from him and pushed at his hands as he tried again to gather her close.

"You knew it was me yesterday—that I was Dani. You knew! You jerk! Why didn't you tell me?"

"*Me*, tell *you*?! Listen, brat, it was your place to enlighten me. And I didn't know until the middle of that night when we'd gone to your place following the restaurant. After I'd pulled myself away from you—and, I might mention, suffered the pangs of hell—I had a dream about you." His face reddened and his eyelashes lowered for a few seconds, a good indication of the nature of the intriguing dream. "I woke up knowing what I should have always known, I suppose. Especially since I couldn't accept that I'd fallen for two different females in the space of one week. The first day I met you, I had such an overwhelming feeling to open my arms. It baffled me. Everything seemed skewed, out of whack."

She nodded. "Pretty much how I felt from the minute I walked into the vicarage gardens and saw you sitting there. I knew our time had finally come, and I was terrified. I realized I had to wait for the right moment to tell you the truth, but my obsession with having you be attracted to me as Ellie took precedence over any rational thinking."

The wary look in her eye told him she still didn't believe in her power of appeal, her desirability. She turned away; as if afraid he would see what she thought hidden. The vulnerability of a girl camouflaged in a woman's body.

Confidently slipping his fingers around her upper arm, he swung her around, the frothy fabric of her turquoise skirts swirling around both their legs. His hands lovingly encircled her tiny waist as he moved into her space.

"You love me that much that you'd be willing to wait ten long years and then still give me a choice?"

Looking up into his beloved face, she saw the amazement glinting from his beautiful soft eyes. "Of course! I love you. But I need for you to love me, Daniell Howard, and not because of a promise you made to a sixteen-year-old. And not because of your attraction to me as Ellie Ward, which was probably physical—my fault, because I worked at that."

"You sure did. I'm still not over how gorgeous you looked in that little, and I do mean little, black number you tortured me with. You have no idea what it did to me."

"Yes, well…" She cleared her throat, taking a few seconds to organize her thoughts. "You need to answer me one thing. I wondered about your attraction many times during those empty years. Mostly I questioned what a man like you saw in Dani."

"I saw her more clearly than anyone I'd ever met before. And her beautiful spirit made it easy to love her— you. I guess when two meld as one the way we did nothing is hidden. All the flaws are exposed. My Dani—oh, you were a gem without any imperfections. In fact, you challenged me to be accountable, made me want to be good enough for you. And I love challenges."

"I'm afraid you'll find I'm not that same girl. Will you mind?" She lifted her face to his, trying to read his features. What she saw blazing from his eyes stilled her questioning heart.

"Sweetheart, as much as I loved you as sixteen-year-old Dani…" He kissed her gently. "…you, Ellie, my little hussy, were still able to capture my attention and melt me like butter on a hot frying pan. As much as I fought my attraction, nothing I did stopped me from wanting you. I despised myself for my disloyalty, until I realized who you were. Then for a short while, I thought I despised you. That lasted as long as it took to see you again." He snapped his fingers. "It disappeared like that."

"So, when we made love, you knew."

"Yes."

"And you didn't let on."

"I was still angry."

"When did you stop being angry?"

"Much of it disappeared when I realized I was making love to a very untutored woman, and the rest faded after visiting with Amy in the garden. Your child has the same instinctive knowledge of human nature as you had at sixteen. She told me you'd had a crush on me for years. She set me straight by reminding me again of the difference in time, and of the ten years you stayed faithful."

"So, the suitcases meant nothing?"

"They did when I went there. Until I saw you looking so sexy I couldn't keep my hands off you. After I talked to Amy, I had to rush because the stores were closing, and I knew I needed to buy your birthday present. Didn't Amy tell you?"

"Not a thing, the little monster. She kept your secret, and that's a first for her." The tension in Dani's body slowly uncurled, lifting away, leaving her feeling lighter than she had for a week.

She stepped closer still and watched the play of emotions spill over his face. With eyelids lowered to half-mast, his smile, one-sided and sexier than hell, warned her of his intentions. Her heart tripled its beat. Warmth spread throughout her chest, down to her stomach, and pooled exactly where it was meant to go. The resulting wetness was erotic and welcome.

Angling his head to the right, his gesture questioned, just like she'd seen him do many times in the mirror when she'd teased him while he shaved. Her hands itched to touch, and there was nothing to stop her except her own timidity. She smiled invitingly, pleading.

Not being a fool, the man's next move was exactly what she'd planned. Taking her hands in each of his, he wrapped them around her back, trapping her in close, forcing her breasts forward.

His lips showed no mercy. Hungry, her sexual appetite only teased by her one encounter with him, she was more than accommodating. His kiss took her on a journey she wanted never to end. When he pulled away, she moaned. "More!"

"Soon, love. More than you know." He released her and stepped back.

She tried to follow, but he shook his head. By taking one of her arms in each hand, he carefully pushed her a few steps until she felt a barrier behind her legs. With gentle guidance he settled her next to him on the bench. Then, reaching into his leather jacket pocket, he retrieved a small, beautifully wrapped package and lifted it in front of her. His intense expression warned her that this moment ranked as special.

"Do you want me on my knees?" His tone conveyed playfulness, but an unspoken appeal flashed in his eyes.

She shifted closer to him on the bench. "I want us to always be on the same level."

He closed his eyes for a few seconds as if in prayer. When he opened them a hint of moisture appeared, illuminating the embers of love. "God, Dani, I love you so much. I'm crazy about your daughter, and I need to be a part of your lives, your future. Please say you'll marry me, come live with me, and make me happier than I probably have any right to expect."

His hand trembled, while the look on his face took on a seriousness she'd never seen before. Earnestness battled with his teasing personality and won.

"Oh, Troy, I love you, too. Today started out as the worst day of my life, and now it's the happiest." She took the proffered parcel and carefully undid the bow and the silver paper while he watched, entranced.

Nestled inside a royal blue velvet box sat a ring so breathtaking that tears gathered and her breath caught.

She put a hand up to her mouth, her fingers firm against her quivering lips to stop the sobs. He lifted her other hand as he took the ring from its slot to slide it home, a perfect fit.

Rustling caught her attention. She whispered in his ear as they hugged. "How long have they been eavesdropping?"

"The first time they snooped a few seconds—this time longer."

She turned in his arms and loved that they followed to enfold her, holding her close. They stood up together.

"Would you like to see my ring, Mrs. Dorn?"

"It isn't me; it's your Uncle Robert." The voice was heard but the person not yet seen.

Another voice joined the first. "Oh, there you are, Mrs. Dorn, I've been looking for you."

Shushing and pushing noises were heard, and then two sheepish eavesdroppers emerged.

"You have summat to show us? I've got baking in me oven, a birthday cake to bring out, and a little girl who's given me no peace wanting to come and find you."

The woman actually harrumphed as she stomped closer. Her handkerchief dabbed at the streams of tears visible as she got nearer.

Dani's arms opened, reaching for her uncle, who got the first hug before she turned to engulf the weepy woman.

"Don't be sad, Mrs. Dorn. This is the happiest day of my life. Troy and I are finally together. We're engaged." She proudly displayed the glittering diamonds on her left hand.

Mrs. Dorn sniffed loudly. "Well, and it's about bloody time."

Afterword

Thank you so much for reading *Together Again* the 4th book in *The Vicarage Bench Series*.

I loved writing this story and I hope you enjoyed reading it. If so, I would ask you for a favor. If you purchased this book at Amazon, please take a few minutes and leave an honest review. Authors enjoy hearing that readers like their stories, and hopefully, others will read your words and choose to buy the book because of your sentiments.

A word about the author:

Mimi Barbour lives on the beautiful East coast of Vancouver Island and writes her paranormal romances with tongue in cheek and a mad glint in her eye. Asked why she prefers paranormal, she answers, chuckling, "Because it's fun! Imagination can be a lot more interesting than what happens in real life, to so-called normal people. I love my characters, and my goal is to make readers love them also. To worry about what happens to them while the story unfolds. If I can steal my booklover's attention away from their everyday grind, absorb them into a fantasy love story and make them care about the ending, then I've done my job."

As for her own everyday life, she says, "My husband is supportive of my long hours, drags me from my office to feed me and plans occasional forays into the outside world. I have a son who makes me happy I was born a woman so I could be his mom, and a niece whose family adds to my full cup of happiness.

"Gardening lights my inner fires, and I need no urging to get out into the yard when the weather dictates. I do have many hobbies but alas—no time."

Contact Information:

My website: http://www.mimibarbour.com/

Or my blogspot: http://mimibarbour.blogspot.com

Or follow me on twitter: https://twitter.com/MimiBarbour

Or on Facebook: http://www.facebook.com/mimibarbour

My author page on Amazon: http://www.amazon.com/Mimi-Barbour/e/B0051EAN52